DEATHWALKER

R.A. JONES

AIRSHIP 27 PRODUCTIONS

Deathwalker
© 2012 R. A. Jones

Published by
Airship 27 Productions
www.airship27.com
www.airship27hangar.com

Cover illustration © 2012 Laura Givens
Interior illustrations © 2012 Michael Neno

Editor: Ron Fortier
Associate Editor: Ray Reithmeier
Production and design by Rob Davis

ISBN-13: 978-0615597522
ISBN-10: 0615597521

Printed in the United States of America

10 9 8 7 6 5 4 3 2 1

CHAPTER 1

The Cheyenne youth named High Bird awoke to discover he could not move.

He sat cross-legged on the ground. Ahead of him, the flat prairie rolled off blankly into the darkness of night. He found he could not raise his head without experiencing jolting pain, but he was able to roll his eyes upward. There was no moon to be seen in the sky, but he could make out the Hungry Road, the shining pathway of stars that led to the Land of the Dead.

He tried to move his head, and sharply sucked in air as a biting pain tore into the sides of his face. With his vision growing accustomed to the dark, he let his eyes drift down and saw at last the source of both his pain and his immobility.

His body was staked to the ground by eight sinewy strands of rawhide rope. One end of each rope was wrapped around wooden stakes driven into the baked, iron-hard soil. The other end was attached to sharp slivers of bone, which had been poked through folds of his skin. Two such slivers pierced each of his legs; others pierced his upper arms and chest.

The final two shards of bone pierced the soft flesh below each eye. The tightness of the rawhide bands attached to them pulled his lower lids painfully downward, preventing him from closing his eyes or turning his head from side to side.

(But if he could not close his eyes, he pondered, how could he have been asleep?)

Thin rivulets of blood flowed from each piercing, sliding across the bronze skin of his naked body. The slightest movement he made brought a new sharp pain as flesh was pulled nearly away from bone.

The ragged hiss of his own breath in his ears at first kept him from hearing the voice in the darkness. When it finally penetrated his haze of pain, he recognized it as singing, though he could not place the song. Even the language in which it was sung was foreign to him.

The boy tried to squint his eyes, attempting to penetrate the dark, only to gasp at a jolt of pain that the attempt to narrow his eyelids sent shooting through his skull. At last he was able to make out the figure of a man near the far horizon, walking slowly toward him.

As the figure came close enough to make out clearly, the boy softly mouthed a prayer to Maheo, the Creator. Though the creature approaching him wore the form of a man, it was clear he was no human being.

The buckskin clothing the creature wore was torn and tattered, hanging in shreds from a sickly thin frame. It had the face of a man six moons in the ground. The flesh was gray and stuck tight to the protruding bones of the cheeks. Its eyes looked as if they had no lids, for they bulged out grotesquely and stared at the boy without blinking.

The creature's greasy black hair hung in long, wispy strands that a sudden wind whipped about its face. Tiny, skittering critters could be seen burrowing into it. A familiar, sickly smell issued from the creature, an air of decay that told the boy with gut-wrenching certainty who this night horror must be.

Death.

The gaunt creature stopped while still several feet away from the Cheyenne. As those horribly bulging, bloodshot eyes continued to bore into him, the boy felt streams of fearful sweat trickle slowly down his forehead. The salty trickles burned his exposed eyeballs, nor could he blink the sweat away.

The night creature seemed almost to smile, his lips peeling back from blackened, cracked teeth with an awful sucking sound. He stepped forward, leaning down so his caricature of a face was on an even level with that of High Bird.

"You'll do."

The personification of Death spoke in a voice that was surprisingly soft, yet still it carried a hint of danger that danced up and down the Cheyenne's spine. The breath from the specter, smelling like meat gone bad in the sun, washed over the youth and made his stomach churn.

"You've come seeking your power," the specter said. "And you have found it."

The boy devoutly wished he could close his ears, shut out the words that were to come.

"You'll be like me," the ghostly apparition continued. "Your power will be the power to bring death to your enemies and the enemies of your people. Wherever you walk, blood will stain the ground, for you will not be able to stop killing. Even those who love you will fear you, and you will know no peace in this life."

"No!" the boy gasped.

"No?"

"Where is the honor in what you describe?" High Bird said breathlessly. "Just to kill? Where is the courage in that? Courage, and the honor it brings, comes from counting coup, from touching your enemy at close range. You can kill from far away. Any coward with a bow can do that."

Death slowly dropped to his knees, the bony joints in his legs cracking like spring ice in a thawing river. Now he needn't bend to stare directly into the boy's fearful eyes. His thin shoulders bobbed up and down slightly, as though he was enjoying a dry and silent laugh. When next he opened his mouth, a buzzing insect flew out and flittered away. A rotten tooth popped from his upper jaw and fell to the ground.

"Ah, yes," he hissed, his putrid breath whistling out and causing scalding bile to rise up into High Bird's mouth.

"Honor. You speak of the old ways. The old times. Do you know the story of the old times, boy? Do you know the story of your people?"

"Of course I do."

"Tell me."

High Bird stared at his inquisitor, unsure if he really meant for the boy to relate the story of the Cheyenne.

"Tell me."

"We were fashioned from soft earth," the boy began. "Men and women alike, made by the hand of the Creator, Maheo, just as a man carves a bone into a whistle. When the Wise One who lives above blew his breath into their mouths, they came to life."

"And where was this?" Death prompted.

"Beneath the earth," the boy replied, "in a great cave, like the one in which the god Wihio lives. But after a time, the people were led to the light, and came to live above the ground."

High Bird paused, searching his memories for all the details of the story he had heard many times in his young life.

"For a time," he continued, "Maheo lived on the earth with his children. When he taught them all they needed to know about living, then he left and returned to his home in the sky. From there he watches over us.

"Because he watches, he knows that life on the earth is hard, that we all face many troubles in our lives. But we know that when we die, everyone, whether good or bad, will follow the Hanging Road to the Place of the Dead, and live with Maheo forever."

Death chuckled with a sound like burning kindling. "You've been taught well. Who gave you the knowledge of the old ways?"

"My father."

"As it should be. And what have you learned from your mother?"

There was a pause before the boy answered. "Nothing. When I was just a child, she went on before us."

"That, too, is a lesson, if you know what to take from it."

A sudden cough wracked Death's chest, and dust flew from his mouth and nostrils.

Tiny grains of dirt and filth stung High Bird's exposed eyes. The pain caused him to inhale reflexively, sucking dust into his lungs. This set off his own spasm of coughing, which in turn caused the rawhide bonds holding him to the earth to tug sharply on the bone slivers skewering his flesh. Red lights of pain flashed behind his burning eyes, but he made no outcry.

Death reared back slightly, then swung forward so his face was mere inches away from the boy's. The skin of the creature's cheeks creaked and cracked as his lips curled back in an ugly parody of a smile. The stench of his dead flesh washed over High Bird, who again choked back his own vomit.

"But when Maheo left for his high, holy loft, all was not right with the people, was it, boy?"

"No," High Bird gasped, "for he left behind no laws. And without law, men fell into thievery and murder and all manner of evil."

"Yes," Death hissed. "Good times."

"For who?" the puzzled boy asked.

"For me." Death extended a gnarled, bony finger and tapped the boy lightly on the tip of his nose. "But something changed all that, didn't it?"

"Some *one* changed it," High Bird asserted. "The hero we call *Sweet Medicine*. He came from the mists, and he gave us laws, and taught us the value of honor, of respect.

"And what else?"

"He created the Soldier Societies: the Dogs, the Foxes, the Elks and the Bulls."

"So he did." Death swung his head from side to side as if making sure there was no one else around to hear his words. He leaned even closer to the boy, and spoke his next words in a conspiratorial tone.

"And some day, boy, you too will join the Dog Soldiers. Some day…you will lead them."

Forgetting for a moment that he was literally staring death in the face, High Bird smiled at this pronouncement. But even this movement brought pricks of pain to his cheeks.

"But Sweet Medicine was not a god," Death continued, "and in due time even he passed on. But before he did, he left the people with one final prophecy, one final warning of their future. Do you know of this, too?"

"We all know it," High Bird replied grimly.

"Tell it to me!" Death commanded.

The boy recoiled slightly, then moaned as the rawhide thongs tugged painfully at his tender skin. He straightened back up, willed his breathing to return to normal, and forced himself to look Death squarely in the eyes.

"He told us of a time to come," High Bird began. "A time when all the world as we know it will change. A time when dark forces will descend upon us."

"What are these dark forces?"

"Sweet Medicine…did not say."

"What will happen when they come?"

High Bird ran a dry tongue over even drier lips, trying to remember all that had been told him.

"When they come," he said at last, "we must not fall under the spell of the dark magic they will possess, but stay on the path shown us by Maheo and Sweet Medicine. We must do all in our power to stop them, for they will be like the locusts who ride in on the wind and eat everything but the sun."

Death squatted back on his haunches as High Bird stopped speaking. The ghastly apparition made a slight clucking sound with his purple tongue, and another rotted tooth fell free from his lower jaw. Again he smiled, with the same creaking of dried flesh.

He then leaned forward and to one side. The desiccated flesh of his face slithered along High Bird's cheek, making his skin crawl. His rancid tongue flicked out as he whispered in High Bird's ear.

"From this day on, wherever you walk, I will walk beside you. You will kill, and kill, and kill again. All this will be in the service of your people. You will teach them to be killers of men as well.

"And they will call you *Deathwalker*."

Death pulled back slightly, so that his lidless eyes were locked into the fearful gaze of the boy, who could not have turned away even if he had not been staked to the ground.

"You will be loved and hated…sometimes by the same person.

"You will sire no children…but will be a loved father.

"From one end of your world to the other, at all four points of the wind, you will be challenged by men and beasts…and by those that are neither.

"You will see what no man should ever see, do what no man has ever done.

"You will earn your name a thousand times over. Neither fire nor water will ever be able to wash the blood from your hands.

"And on the day when the foretold dark forces die…you too shall die."

Death drew back even farther from the boy, whose chest heaved with the realization that he had not been breathing for several minutes.

"You did not ask for the horrible gift I give you, boy," Death intoned, almost with a sigh of sorrow. "But you will use it for all your days. You will be almost as feared as I. This is good."

Death nodded his head slowly several times.

"I will have you for my child," the apparition said, and the words seemed to boom and echo as from the walls of a steep canyon. The sound of thunder rumbled along the edges of the night sky.

Then Death slowly stretched one hand out toward the boy who had been High Bird.

"And this will seal our pact."

The Cheyenne youth spasmed in pain as the skeletal hand pressed palm down against the bare flesh of his chest. It was as if a hot brand was being pushed through skin and muscle in an effort to burn out his heart. His ears were assailed with a sizzling, crackling sound, and he grew nauseous at the smell of his own skin being cooked like buffalo tongue.

But he did not scream. Tears slid from the distended edges of his eyelids, and he bit through his lower lip in a bloody rush. But he did not scream.

Then the pain eased slightly as the spectral hand was removed. High Bird shivered uncontrollably as thin wisps of smoke continued to trail upward and swirl around his face. His head slumped down, and he could see the print of Death's hand, red and inflamed, burned into his chest.

"You can be like no other human being," Death said, rising slowly to his feet and stepping back away from the boy. "You will be among them, but always apart from them. To attain your vision, to achieve your true power to the fullest, you must rise above the bounds of earth and flesh."

With that, Death made a grand upward gesture with one hand. In response, the Cheyenne youth began to rise slowly upward off the ground, only to be brought up painfully short by the rawhide strands that still restrained him to the ground.

Death motioned again, and the boy's body strained to burst free of the constricting ropes. High Bird again bit down on his lip as jolts of fresh pain raced through him. His body pulled harder against its restraints. His skin bowed outward, and red lights flashed ever brighter behind his eyes.

Then, in one great ripping rush, the bone slivers piercing his skin were violently torn from his body, in spouting bloody sprays that gushed as dark as the night sky. With this, the agony became more than he or any man born of woman could bear. Deathwalker's head flew back, his mouth dropped open, and at last he screamed like a wolf caught in the jagged teeth of a hunter's trap.

CHAPTER 2

Deathwalker screamed again, not nearly so loudly, as he bolted upright from the thick robes on which he slept.

He sat in the near darkness, panting heavily. Beads of sweat stood out on his forehead, even though the air was cool. He swiped at the perspiration with a downward motion of his hand.

The hand continued down until it came to rest over his heart. He could feel it pumping hard and fast. He could also feel the scars on his chest.

There were two of them, one over each breast, still ragged and white, though they were now more than ten summers old. They were both a badge of honor and a reminder of his initiation into the Dog Soldier warrior society when he was but sixteen summers old.

For three days then he had performed the sacred ritual of the Sun Dance, staring into the face of the light of day and singing the prayer to Maheo to give him his vision. Before beginning the dance, his chest had been pierced with slivers of bone. From each of these slivers, rawhide ropes were attached to a pole that stood nearly three ponies high; it was in seemingly endless circles around this pole that he had danced.

Other cuts had been made, in his arms and legs; other bone slivers pushed through bleeding flesh. From each of these slivers hung more rawhide straps, and from each strap was suspended the bleached white skull of a bull buffalo.

The pain of the heavy skulls tugging at his flesh was still vivid in his mind. The pain, the dancing, the lack of sleep, the praying, all had served to open his heart to Maheo so he might deliver the Cheyenne's vision.

The vision of death. The vision that still haunted his dreams.

It was the vision that gave him both his power and his name: *Deathwalker*. But it was more than just a vision.

Even in the gloom of his lodge, he could faintly make out the outline of a hand, seemingly burned into the middle of his chest. No one among the people had ever seen such a physical manifestation of a vision quest, not even the oldest and wisest.

He started slightly as a cool, gentle hand slid over his shoulder from behind. He turned his head to look into the large, soft eyes of Crow Woman.

Though she shared his lodge with him, Crow Woman was but a slave. Having taken her in a raid against his people's hated enemy, the Crow, he would not allow her to use or be called by her true name, not even by himself. So it was that she was simply called *Absaroka*: Crow Woman.

Most tribes, if pushed to it, would admit that the Cheyenne were the bravest peoples who walked the earth. But the Crow, who had been enemies since the two tribes first met, declared that the Cheyenne were not brave at all, but merely crazy. He had no doubt that Crow Woman held the same opinion.

A hauntingly lovely young woman of no more than seventeen summers, she had been taken by him nearly two summers before. He had come to her village to steal horses, but she was the only prize he had taken. He wondered sometimes if he should have left her and taken the horses instead.

"Is something wrong, Walker?" she whispered.

Her mouth was near his ear, the warm air of her breath sliding down his neck. He twisted his head farther around, able to see her face clearly even in the semi-darkness of the tipi. High on the swell of her left cheek could be seen a small tattoo, representing the sun.

Crow Woman's habit was to rub her skin almost daily with a perfume of sweet grass and sweet pine. She consequently always smelled at least faintly of this, to the man's unspoken pleasure. Slave or not, she would have been prized anywhere for her beauty.

As her dark eyes continued to stare into his, her hand slid off his shoulder and down the sinewy length of his arm. She pressed closer against him and he felt the swell of her full breasts. Her hand left his arm and drifted sensuously along the hard muscles of his flat stomach before moving lower. He closed his eyes, inhaling deeply again of her perfume.

But then he jerked upright.

"Go back to sleep," he barked gruffly, shrugging off her hand.

Recoiling as if he had slapped her, Crow Woman scrambled back to her own bed, burrowing under the buffalo robe that served as her blanket, shivering slightly.

When she was in her place, he leaned back against the willow backrest of his bed, which lay against the back wall of his tipi. Across from him, he could see the first faint fingers of morning's light beginning to filter in around the edges of the skin flap covering the lodge's doorway.

Part of him wanted to sink back into the softness of his bed, feeling its willow reeds and bull rushes beneath the buffalo robe that covered them. But he knew it would be pointless. Since the days of his vision, he had seldom been able to sleep for more than a few hours each night.

Wrapping his thin deerskin blanket around his nakedness like a cape, he rolled from the bed onto the rye grass-covered floor. His lodge was not as large as a man of his pony wealth and position might normally own, but such things were of no importance to him.

It was big enough for his beds, sturdy enough to keep out the wind and elements. There was nothing more he needed or wanted.

Stepping down from the low earthen ledge on which the beds lay, the warrior quietly padded to the center of the tipi. He noted that the fire had died out, and he dropped to his knees, glancing back to see that Crow Woman was still shivering slightly. He sprinkled a handful of rotten bark onto the hearth and picked up his two fire sticks.

The flatter of the two sticks, a piece of cottonwood, he lay amidst the bark fragments. The second stick, a straight shoot of grease wood, he held upright between the palms of his hands.

He twirled the greasewood rapidly, until tiny tendrils of smoke began to rise. Blowing softly, he fanned the growing flame. Chips of dried buffalo dung were placed around the flames as fuel, and soon a full fire was illuminating the tipi.

Rising to his feet, he pushed through the flap of his lodge. Outside, he paused to suck in air. The crisp breezes of September ("Tomoishi" in his tongue: cool moon) drove the sweat from his brow.

As was his wont, he turned to run a hand up the outside wall of his tipi, tracing his fingertips along the pictures he had painted on the skin. Unlike the tipis of other men, his did not bear visual witness to personal deeds of valor nor bear images of vanquished foes. Rather, the paintings he had executed were memorials to the dead who had been his friends, his family, his loved ones. He who walked with death had great respect for its all-encompassing power.

A soft whinny caused him to turn, even as an equine head playfully butted him. It was Tall Dog, the black stallion that was his favorite war pony. Like most men, Walker always kept a pony picketed outside his lodge at night, as precaution against danger or attack.

He stroked Tall Dog under the chin with one hand, while using the other to scratch the spot behind its left ear that he knew was a favorite.

"I hope you had a better night than I did, brother," he said. "I'm sure you'll have a better day."

He freed Tall Dog from the confines of the picket rope, then gave him a slap on the rump. The dark stallion needed no more prodding than this to trot away from the shadow of the lodge, cantering off to join the rest of the tribe's herd that could be heard where they milled together not far from the circle of tipis.

Walker took a moment to look around him. As always, the lodges of the village were laid out in a near circle. The east end was left open to welcome the sun's arrival.

Near the south border of the village, he saw two very special lodges. Inside the easternmost of the two were kept the *Mahuts*, the four sacred arrows. In the western lodge resided the *Issiwun*, the sacred buffalo hat. Painted on the outer walls of both lodges were numerous double crosses, depictions of dragonflies.

To the east, the sun was rising more fully over the crest of a range of small hills as Walker made his way out of the village. He followed the path that Tall Dog had taken, and it led him to the main herd of ponies owned by the villagers.

He walked softly into the ponies' midst, talking to them, occasionally stopping to stroke one he recognized as being his own. It was well known among the people that his herd could be even larger if he wanted; if he did not give so many away to others he felt needed them more than he did.

To the people, this marked him as a generous man. To him, it only made sense; a man only needs so many ponies. His father had always taught him that a man should be measured by what he gave, not by what he kept. Like most of what his father said, Walker had taken this to heart.

As he stepped clear of the herd, he paused in mid-stride, tensing expectantly as he caught a flash of movement from the corner of his right eye. Then he relaxed, his oaken muscles uncoiling as he heard a familiar soft, girlish giggle come from behind him.

"Have you come to visit me, *Buffalo Boy*?" he asked, not bothering to turn around. "Or to steal a pony?"

"Hmmph! Why would I steal a pony?" came the reply from behind him. "I can run as fast as any old horse!"

Smiling, the Cheyenne warrior turned around. Facing him was a small creature who looked almost like a typical little boy, but not quite. His face was round and sweet in appearance, framed by thick, wiry black hair that grew halfway down his back.

Protruding from the thick ringlets were two small *horns*, growing from his temples.

His belly bulged slightly over the top of his breechcloth, and his willowy legs ended not in feet but in dark, cloven hooves.

His name was Buffalo Boy, and he was Walker's spirit guide. He could be seen and heard only by the warrior, and had appeared to him many times since the day of the vision quest.

He was a playful sort, though sometimes given to outbursts of petulant anger. On more than one occasion his counsel had proven invaluable; sometimes, though, not so much. Mostly, he just liked to visit.

"You've been having bad dreams again, haven't you?" he asked.

Walker shrugged.

"They come and they go."

"They'll never go," Buffalo Boy declared flatly. He bent and plucked a blade of tall grass from the ground. As was his habit, he stuck one end into the corner of his mouth and began to suck on it.

Not far away, two other men of the tribe stood together, watching as guards over the pony herd. One of them smiled and shook his head as he watched Deathwalker, seemingly gesturing and talking to no one.

"Walker is talking to the wind again," he commented. Like almost all in the village, he used the shortened form of the man's name. All held too much respect (and fear) of the warrior to use his full name loosely. For his part, Walker pretended not to notice the effect he had on others.

"Yes," said the second watchman, "but we'd best leave him alone – because sometimes it speaks back to him."

Meanwhile, Buffalo Boy had turned his back on Walker, seemingly losing interest in the man as his attention was diverted by the flight of a sparrow swooping low over the pony herd. The diminutive spirit guide galloped off in pursuit of the bird, laughing merrily. He leaped into the air as if to grab the sparrow, and his form vanished like a puff of smoke. Walker smiled again, not sure if the guide Maheo had sent him was meant to be a blessing or a curse.

He continued his trek, until he reached the banks of the small creek that ran down from the nearby hills. Dropping his blanket, he stepped into the water. Given the time of day, the time of year, it was almost icy cold. Extremes of temperature had little effect on him, though, and he walked calmly into its embrace until the water came to his waist.

As with most men and boys of the people, bathing was part of his daily ritual. It was well known that water would wash away sickness as well as grime, and was necessary to maintain good health. Summer or winter, he welcomed this morning ablution.

Even when he was amply clean, he did not leave the creek. Instead, he closed his eyes and dropped down below the surface, coming to rest on the creek's rocky bottom.

He stayed thus for several moments, listening to the muffled roar of the water as it rushed around and past him. Then came his favorite part of this ritual.

He opened his eyes, looking all around him. As always, the slightly distorted sights and sounds created the illusion that he had been transported to another world, a calm and placid place far different from the one in which he spent most of his life.

Of course, he knew, it was a different world. One filled with beauty, yes, but also terror. A place where monsters dwelled. Different, but the same as the world above the water in many ways. But he enjoyed the differences.

If an observer did not know him, they might fear he had drowned, so long did he remain in this watery world. Even a fish, they said, could not hold its breath as long as Walker could.

But eventually even he had need of air. When the tightness in his chest began to pain him, he thrust back up to the surface, gasping and filling his lungs to capacity.

Climbing up the low bank of the creek, he again wrapped himself in his blanket and returned to the village.

As he approached it, he could see and hear more signs that the encampment was coming to life. A small band of boys, whooping joyfully, each totally naked, trotted past him, barely noticing the man as they made their way down to the creek to bathe.

Other boys, slightly older, were gathering up the horses that had been picketed around the village, leading them out to join the rest of the herd even as it was being slowly driven in nearer to the village.

Walker stopped as he saw one particular boy break away from the others and come trotting his way. The boy looked slightly concerned as he drew near.

"Tall Dog is gone, Walker!" he exclaimed.

The boy's name was Three Willow, an orphan of ten summers. It was normal for him to take Walker's picket horse out to the main herd each morning. In return for this and other small services, Walker often gave food and gifts to the couple who had taken the child into their lodge as their own.

"It's all right, Three Willow," Walker explained. "He was eager to get back to the herd this morning, so I sent him on his way."

He could see that the boy was disappointed; he considered this to be his job, his way of showing that he was a useful member of the tribe.

"There is one thing," Walker continued. "It seemed to me that old Dog was a bit out of sorts today. I'd be willing to bet two arrowheads that he's feeling neglected and thinks he needs to be rubbed down good and hard."

"I could do that!" the boy practically shouted.

"And you wouldn't mind?"

"No!"

"Then get to it."

Walker smiled as he watched the boy eagerly race off to find Tall Dog. Then he shook his head slightly. It was a funny thing, he thought, how children seemed to like him. "Worship" might better describe Three Willow's feelings for him. It was only the adults who were afraid of the Dog Soldier.

"Maybe the little ones are just too young to know better," he muttered under his breath.

Some of the wives were also walking down to the creek, carrying empty water skins. They had already emptied them of any water remaining in them from the night before. To the Cheyenne, this was considered to be dead water; they wished to drink only fresh, living water.

The women were laughing and chatting with each other, save for one. Bringing up the rear, several paces behind the others, he could see Crow Woman carrying her empty skin. She walked with her head down, knowing the other women had still not accepted her even after these many moons with the tribe and that they would have nothing to say to her. Walker frowned.

Not many young adults were up and about yet. Having stayed up till very late, talking and playing games, they were still asleep. Walker often joined them in these pursuits, but even then he was usually unable to sleep beyond the rising of the sun.

In the shade cast by one tipi, he saw four old men sitting together, sharing a smoke. A youth of maybe twelve summers approached and spoke to them. The man holding the pipe could be seen shaking his head and waving the boy away with the hand grasping the pipe. Walker nodded. He expected the boy had asked to join them in a smoke, and had been justly sent on his way. It was well known that too much smoking could cut down on a man's wind, so it was rightly saved for special ceremonies and for indulgence by the elderly.

As his stride carried him at length into the circle of tipis, Walker could hear a voice calling out loudly. The voice was that of Strong Jaw, who was the village's *old crier*. It was the crier's job to spread any news around the camp that he thought would be of general interest.

The crier rode in a circuit around the village, starting at the open end of the circle, then riding to the south, west and north. Always staying close to the tipis, he would call out the news items of the day.

Strong Jaw was so called because of his tough teeth, most of which he still had despite his advanced age of well over forty summers. It was rumored that the horse he rode on his circuit was equally ancient.

Walker liked the crier, and knew that his information was always reliable. Being one who liked to keep up with what was current in the happenings of the village, he stopped to listen.

He learned that a new Cheyenne had arrived in the night, a baby boy born to Red Elk and his wife Slow Calf. Since they already had two daughters, both parents were especially joyful of this new arrival.

The doctor called Eyes Dance Wildly had performed a successful medical procedure in the women's menstrual lodge. Dog Runner's wife had been suffering from an overly long menses, and the doctor, who specialized in such ailments, had magically extracted from her abdomen an elk's tooth, doubtless the cause of her malady. A dose of hiseeyo tea had relieved her of any lingering pain.

Dog Runner had paid the doctor two horses for releasing her from her displeasure and restoring her to her wifely form, and felt the price paid was well worth it.

Strong Jaw was not one to inject opinion into his recitation of the news, else he would have added that the other women in the menstrual lodge felt likewise.

There was sad news as well. At a dance held for members of the Fox Soldiers Society the night before, a woman named Twice Cut Arm was thrown out of the dance by the drum (which is to say, divorced) by her husband, Sleeps Long.

Apparently, he had come to believe that she was in some way responsible for the deaths of her first two husbands. It was for this that she was now named, for she had twice cut herself in mourning for the passing of a mate.

Sleeps Long had decided that he no longer wished to risk becoming her *third* dead husband!

As Strong Jaw began to repeat his recitation of all that was new in the village, Walker smiled and shook his head.

Then he spun on his heels. It felt as if someone had tapped him lightly on his back. He expected to see Buffalo Boy standing there, come back to annoy him. But there was no one in sight, nor any sound that did not belong. His sharp eyes peered off into the distance, but all seemed normal.

He shrugged and headed back to his lodge. He felt the sudden desire to go hunting before breakfast.

CHAPTER 3

The old woman called Morning Sky sat on her haunches near her cooking fire, preparing a meager breakfast. She took a portion of pulverized acorns from a bag, pouring it into a bowl of buffalo fat. She had a few wild turnips she planned to add to this mush.

Meat for their meals had become rather scarce since her husband Bull had been laid up with broken ribs sustained when a skittish pony had kicked him.

No one in a Cheyenne village was ever allowed to go completely hungry, and a few meager offerings of meat, plants and berries had come her way, allowing her to stretch what food she already had laid up in storage.

It was common knowledge in the village that more would have been given if not for the fact that old Bull was a stern, harsh-speaking fellow who possessed few true friends. No one would speak this truth to the faithful and long-suffering Morning Sky, of course. Even had she known it to be true, she would have denied it.

Times were tough, she told both herself and her husband. If the people had more, they would give more.

A long shadow suddenly fell over Morning Sky, surprising her because she had heard no sound of approaching footsteps. She looked up and gasped, falling back onto her rump.

Such was the effect the Deathwalker sometimes had on others.

The woman shielded her eyes with one hand and eyed the tall, unspeaking warrior. The Cheyenne were known throughout the Plains for their long hair, and Walker was no exception. He chose to wear his shiny locks unbraided, and the wind lifted and tossed them slightly. At the moment, his scalp was also unadorned, save for two eagle feathers in the back, each tilted slightly down and to one side. He usually felt no need for further ostentation.

Morning Sky's gaze dropped and lingered for a moment on the strange handprint marking his taut chest. She knew they spoke truly who said that Walker was the only man to be touched by Death yet still live. She also knew that he seldom bothered to cover the mark with a shirt, even in the winter.

Her eyes were then drawn slightly upward. Just above the handprint lay a protective necklet Walker often wore around his throat. It was made from a string of twisted buffalo hair, and from it dangled a flat oval stone upon which he had painted the skeletal face of Death. The sight of it made her shudder slightly.

This morning, he wore fringed leggings that rose from his ankles nearly to his crotch. They were held in place by deerskin strings tied to the belt around his waist.

In addition, he now wore the usual breechcloth. Some men felt that they would risk losing their manhood if ever they removed the cloth, though Walker himself did not subscribe to this belief.

On his feet were deerskin moccasins, strengthened with parfleche soles and decorated with porcupine quills.

A panther skin quiver of arrows rode on his left hip, and he carried a bow in his left hand. Only now did Morning Sky notice that in his right hand he grasped some dead rabbits.

"Are you all right, mother?" he said at last, addressing her respectfully.

"I'm fine, Walker," she said, smiling back at him as she slowly rose up onto her knees, leaning back so her bottom rested against her feet. "You just surprised me, that's all."

"I didn't mean to."

"Don't worry about it," she replied, waving one hand dismissively. "If my ears weren't so old, I'd have heard you coming."

They both decided to pretend this was true. Walker jerked his head slightly in the direction of her tipi.

"How is he?"

"Cranky," she snorted. "Which means he's nearly back to normal."

Walker grunted and nodded, but said nothing more. He simply stared down at his feet.

"Is there something you wanted, Walker?" the old woman prompted.

"Yes," he said quickly, now that she had opened the way. "I, uh, I've done a bad thing, mother, and I was hoping you could help me make it right."

"What bad thing have you done?" she asked skeptically.

"I had a craving for rabbit this morning," he explained. "So I went out

"Are you all right, mother?"

hunting." He raised his right hand, displaying three dead rabbits that he held by the ears.

"But I let my belly do the hunting instead of my brain, and I killed more than I needed."

"Ahh. You're right," said Morning Sky with mock seriousness, already knowing the path Walker was trying not to walk in a straight line. "That is a bad thing to do."

"It is. I spoke to the spirits of the rabbits and told them I was sorry. I think they forgive me."

"Rabbits are good that way," she agreed, trying not to smile.

"Still," he continued, "I think it would offend them if I let their meat go to waste."

"You don't want to do that," said the old woman.

"No. I don't." He took two of the rabbits into his left hand and extended them toward Morning Sky. "That's why I was hoping you would help me by taking some of them off my hands. You'd be doing me a favor."

The woman was truly touched. She knew it would insult and embarrass the young warrior for her to acknowledge this as the obvious act of charity that it was. Just as she knew that Walker had already been their main benefactor all along, even though he sought to keep it secret from Bull by coming by after dark and leaving packets of food outside the doorway of their lodge.

"You're a good boy," she said simply, "and I wouldn't want you to be haunted by rabbit spirits. So I'll help you with your problem." She reached out and took the rabbits from his outstretched hand.

"Thank you, mother."

"You're welcome, Walker."

His stoic face did not show how glad he was that the woman had fallen for his tale. For while it was true that Bull's grouchy manners rubbed most people the wrong way, Walker had always respected and even liked the older man.

When a boy on the verge of manhood set out to find his vision, he first sought to find such a man as this as his mentor, one who was familiar with the spirits and their ways. A teacher who would guide and instruct the boy in the proper rituals that would be pleasing to the spirits who would open his eyes to his personal vision.

Walker had chosen Bull to serve this role for him, and Bull had accepted him without question, the first and only such pupil he had ever agreed to guide.

It was Bull who had taken Walker up to Bear Butte, that holy place where Sweet Medicine had first given the sacred arrows to the Cheyenne people. And Bull had stayed beside him through every hour of the bloody ordeal that led at last to the vision of the one who walked with Death. Stories of that day had spread among the people, though Bull swore he had told no one. With each telling, the details had grown and expanded, till only Walker himself knew for sure what had transpired.

Though he would never express it in words, Walker also adored Bull's loving wife. When Walker's real mother had died of the raging fever when he was but a boy of six summers, Morning Sky more than any other had stepped in to help with his raising, becoming like a second mother to him.

"I have something else for you, mother," he now said, fishing a small object from the pouch attached to his belt and pressing it into her free hand.

She smiled broadly as she saw that it was a piece of elder tree sap candy. Walker knew it was a favorite of hers, and Crow Woman had prepared it at his request.

"Those rabbits were lucky to have their lives taken by such a good man," she said, wrapping her hand around the candy and pressing it to her bosom.

"I'd better go," said Walker, not knowing what else to say. "I probably need to kick that lazy slave woman of mine, so she'll fix me some breakfast."

"Thank you for the candy, son."

Walker said nothing more, merely turning and walking away.

"Hey!"

The gruff voice calling out to him caused Walker to stop and turn back the way he had come. When he did, he saw Bull standing in the doorway of his lodge, scowling at him. His right arm was pressed against his torso, which was wrapped tightly to hold the broken ribs in place.

"Don't think I need you to bring me meat, boy," Bull snarled. "Even old and injured I can hunt just as well as you."

"Even better than me, I suspect," Walker cheerfully agreed, smiling disarmingly. "You're so *ugly*, all you'd have to do is look at the poor rabbits and they would die!"

Walker laughed and skipped away, dodging the small stone Bull had picked up and thrown at him. The old warrior groaned as the throwing motion sent a twinge of pain through his injured rib cage, then retreated back into his tipi.

Morning Sky, who was already beginning to skin one of the rabbits, said nothing. She merely chuckled and shook her head, amused by the games that men play with each other.

And then she frowned as she looked at Walker striding away. He could be so much like other men; she knew this better than anyone. But she also knew that if you looked beyond his eyes you would see a great darkness, and know that he was as much a part of it as it was a part of him. Truly, where he walked, death followed.

And Maheo help any who stood in his way.

It was hard to love such a man, but sometimes hard not to. His way was hard and rocky, and she didn't envy him. Exhaling a low sigh, she returned to skinning the rabbit.

When Walker drew near to his own lodge, he saw that Crow Woman, too, was busy preparing a morning meal for the two of them. He paused to look at her.

The beauty of her face and form was stunning. It was small wonder that the mere sight of her had driven all thoughts of stealing ponies from his mind when first he laid eyes on her that fateful night.

She was clothed now in a dress of soft, smoked elk skin. Ornate designs made of porcupine quills and elk's teeth ran down one side of it. She wore fringed leggings under the dress, painted yellow and tied on under her moccasins and above her knees.

Walker knew that underneath her clothing, at night or when he left her alone, she also wore the *Nihpihist* – the protective rope. This rope was worn around a woman's waist, then passed between the legs and wound around the thighs almost to the knees, and served as a measure to protect a woman's virtue, which was highly valued among the Cheyenne.

Crow Woman, being both unwed and a foreign slave, wore it for her own protection, but also as a means to send the unspoken message to Walker that she would allow no man but him to touch her.

Her long, shimmering hair was parted in the middle, then pulled back like a pony's tail and tied with a fringed roll of deerskin. The skin laid bare by the part in her hair was painted red.

Nor was that all that was painted. Crow Woman's dress was cut in such a way that her left arm was left exposed, and Walker could she that she had painted several sideways red stripes down its length.

Walker frowned. Such stripes were meant to signify how many coups a woman's husband had counted. That Crow Woman would choose to do this angered Walker's sister no end, as she liked to remind him, because the Crow was his slave and not his wife.

It annoyed Walker simply because he never bothered to keep count of his coups, did not even possess a coup stick. Unlike his brother warriors, he did not bother to merely strike his enemies – he killed them, or else left them alone. Still, like it or not, the killings also counted as coup, as did the horses he still stole from time to time.

He never spoke of such things, but Crow Woman often learned of his deeds from the wives of other men, or by eavesdropping as the men gossiped amongst themselves, and she thought it only fitting to commemorate them on her flesh.

On more than one occasion, Walker had threatened to beat her if she did not discontinue this practice, but she chose to ignore him.

He now licked his lips as the smell of her cooking reached him. She was using a ladle carved from buffalo horn to stir the rich concoction that was bubbling inside a kettle made from the paunch of a bull.

From the smell he could tell she was preparing a buffalo meat stew, seasoned with the wild onions the Cheyenne called skunk testes.

Looking up to see him, Crow Woman ladled some of the bubbling stew into a bowl made from the polished carapace of a turtle. Smiling, she held it out to him, but he did not take it.

"That dish would go better with some choke cherries," he said.

"We don't have any," she replied.

"Then go get some," he ordered. "You know I like them in the morning."

She nodded obediently. Setting down the bowl of stew, she grabbed a small, empty basket and headed out at a rapid walk toward the nearby creek, to the spot where the berries grew thickest.

"A *real* wife would have done that without being told," said a harsh voice from behind Walker.

Walker grimaced as he turned to face his older sister Snow Dancer. The scowl on her face was one he had seen many times of late. Standing beside Snow Dancer was her husband Long Stride, one of Walker's fellow Dog Soldiers. As was often the case, Long Stride was absently chewing on a piece of spruce gum.

The look he cast at Walker spoke plainly: "You have my sympathy, brother – but don't expect my help!"

"It's sinful," Dancer lectured her brother, pointing toward the departing slave woman. "It's sinful and wicked and shameful."

"Good morning, sister," Walker said playfully, reaching out to hug her. As he did, he glanced up at the tall Long Stride and winked. He then tried to hide his smile as Dancer roughly pushed him away.

"Don't try to make nice to me, Bird," she scolded. Snow Dancer alone of all the people refused to call her brother by his adult name. To her, he would always be High Bird. What he was called as a man, what he had become as a man, she refused to acknowledge.

"Speaking of shameful," Walker said quickly, hoping to divert her attention, "isn't it still considered wrong for a grown sister to speak to her grown brother?"

Snow Dancer's mouth gaped for a moment, then snapped tight as she took a step toward him.

"Maybe so," she snarled, "but shouldn't a sister be allowed to help guide a brother who has no mother?"

"I'm just saying," he replied, throwing up his hands in mock supplication. In response, Dancer shook a finger in his face.

"And I'm just saying," she growled, "that any decent, respectable man of your age would have already taken a proper wife from among the people and started making babies."

She crossed her arms across her bosom and sniffed disdainfully. Doing so caused the mussel shell ring that dangled from her nose to bounce about. Walker bit into his lower lip to keep from laughing. His harried brother-in-law did the same, rolling his eyes skyward.

"Instead," Dancer continued, undeterred, "you choose to sleep with a slave, and a Crow at that. For all you know, she may have been sleeping with horses before you stole her. Everyone knows those savages are little better than animals themselves." She jerked her head in the direction Crow Woman had gone.

"Now, granted," she said, "as a general rule, a Crow woman isn't quite as slutty as an Arapaho. Still, she's not fit for any Cheyenne man, especially one like you."

At that moment, a brief respite came by, in the form of a small group of laughing girls passing by, also on their way to gather berries. One of the girls in the cluster was Two Doves, Long Stride's young sister. She paused for just a heartbeat, swinging her head around to gaze adoringly, not at her brother, but at Walker.

When he rewarded her look with a flashing smile, she blushed with sudden color and lowered her head. Both she and her girlfriends, who had seen the exchange, giggled even more sharply as she trotted to catch back up with them.

"There you go," said Snow Dancer, not missing the girl's reaction to Walker. "Two Doves is a lovely girl. And she'd make a fine wife." She ignored the slightly pained expression that flitted across her husband's face as she said this. Walker didn't.

He laughed lightly. "Don't worry, brother. Your baby sister is safe from me." He shook his head at his own sister.

"And she is just a baby," he stated flatly. "She can't be more than, what, twelve summers old?"

"Nearly fifteen," Snow Dancer corrected.

"Really? Well, her age doesn't matter. She's like a little sister to me."

"Convince Lame Calf of that," Snow Dancer replied, indicating a stern-faced warrior who stood nearby, watching and trying to hear their every word.

Whereas Walker and Long Stride were members of the Hotamitaniu – the Dog Soldiers – Lame Calf belonged to the Fox Soldier Society. It was no great secret that he already had an eye on Two Doves as a potential wife. Less well known was the dislike he held for Walker and the envy he felt over the level of respect he commanded among the people.

"I'd sooner she married a buffalo than Lame Calf," Long Stride snorted.

"Oh, I don't know," Walker said. "After all, he's a good soldier, a good hunter."

"He's a horse's ass!" Long Stride interjected.

"Calm yourself, brother," Walker said, patting him on the back, "and walk with me while I wait for the rest of my breakfast."

"You wouldn't –" Snow Dancer began.

"He knows," Long Stride interrupted. "He wouldn't have to wait if he had a proper wife." He arched his eyebrows at her. "Like I do?"

"Oh. Oh!" Snow Dancer exclaimed, being reminded that she also had not yet prepared breakfast. She turned on her heels and trotted away.

"She means well," Long Stride said, as he and Walker began their stroll through the village.

"I know."

Most of the camp was fully awakened now, and going about its daily routine. The sound of splashing water told of boys swimming and playing in the creek. A circle of other boys cheered as two of their comrades engaged in one of the wrestling matches that Cheyenne males of all ages enjoyed, and for which skill they were renowned.

Two teams of girls were faced off in a lively game of Ohoknit, using curved sticks to slap around a ball made of deerskin stuffed with hair.

A half dozen men had decided to start the day with a little gambling, an activity also much loved by the Cheyenne. One of them laughed gleefully as the plum stones he rolled came up a winner.

Walker noticed another man standing near the gamers, not participating but looking on with envy. His name was Owl Eyes, and Walker suspected the other men had denied him a place in their game.

It was for his own good, since he often gambled neither wisely nor well. Proof of this had come in such a game of chance not two moons before, when he had foolishly lost his own wife to another man.

Moving in step together, without need of a word, Walker and Long Stride both altered their path so as to skirt around the women's menstrual lodge.

Walker then paused, smiling. Not far off, he could see his father, Listens To Elks. Respected for his wisdom, he was one of the four elected chiefs of the village. He was patiently listening as an old man spoke excitedly to him, gesturing wildly with both hands.

"Look at my poor father," Walker commented. "The day's barely begun and he's already been cornered by Bull Hump."

"Yeah," Long Stride replied. "I wonder what the old fart's complaining about now?"

"Careful, brother. Don't speak too disrespectfully. Some day you may be old as him and craving attention."

"No one's as old as Hump," Long Stride said. "He's so old, ravens were still white when he was born."

They continued their walk. Long Stride knew that Walker made a practice of this type of tour, as a way to keep up with the pulse of the village. He also knew his brother-in-law often paced the encampment in the hours of the night when most of its inhabitants had drifted off into the sleep that was often denied him.

In front of another lodge, they saw several young men who had finally rolled out of bed and were now engaging in a bit of personal grooming. Hairs were being plucked from eyebrows, lips and cheeks, while the hair on their heads was being combed and braided.

Walker knew that most of them would then dress in their finest clothing and begin riding slowly about the village, so that people – especially female people – might see and admire them. This too was a common practice, but yet another one in which Walker had not engaged even when he was younger.

Walker swiveled his head. He could see Crow Woman making her way back from the creek, her basket of choke cherries held under one arm. Three other women were headed in the opposite direction, and she stepped aside to let them pass. None so much as looked at her. He turned away from the sight, and Long Stride touched his arm.

"You know how unkind women can be, brother," Long Stride said. "But they'll come to accept her in time."

Walker shrugged.

"It doesn't matter to me if they do or not."

"I think it does."

Walker opened his mouth to respond, but was mercifully spared by the sound of a small commotion rising from the southern end of the village. Walker dipped three fingers into his belt pouch, pulled out a few of the sunflower seeds he favored, and popped them into his mouth. Then, motioning for Long Stride to follow, he set out to see what was happening.

They joined a small group of other onlookers in time to see several of the young men of the village come galloping toward them. The boys were whooping exuberantly as they drove a dozen ponies before them.

Most of the youths swerved their mounts, driving the riderless horses in the direction of the tribe's pony herd. The leader of their little band continued on into the village proper, leaping off his horse before it even slid to a full stop.

Walker recognized the boy who now stood before them, laughing and breathing hard with unabashed excitement. His name was Bowstring, a headstrong and impetuous boy who had not yet been inducted into any of the soldier societies, and who had caused trouble for others with his antics on more than one occasion.

"Yeee-haaa!" Bowstring yelped, throwing his head back. "Listen, people, to what we've done!" he shouted, motioning for all to come closer.

"We found a Pawnee village, not forty miles from here," Bowstring began. "And we sneaked up on them in the night, so quiet that even a mouse couldn't have heard us." He made broad gestures as he spoke.

"Then we swooped down on their pony herd like Hoimaha's breath blows winter into our camp. The men who stood guard over the herd stood frozen in their tracks. I think some of them wet themselves!" The youth strutted before his rapt audience, lightly pounding his puffed out chest with one fist.

"I personally counted coup on two of them as we drove their herd away. They're probably hiding from their friends now, to cover their shame!"

Bowstring ended his narrative, standing proudly with hands on hips and smiling broadly. Then there was a stirring among the gathered people, and their ranks parted to let Walker pass through their midst. There was no smile of approval on his face. Beside him walked Long Stride, who saw a familiar veil of darkness descend upon his brother's face, shadows deepening about his eyes. It was a look Long Stride had seen many times before, and it always foretold danger.

"Hello, Walker," Bowstring greeted cheerfully; yet there was just the slightest quiver in his voice now. "It's a great thing we've done, don't you think?"

"Where did you say that Pawnee village was?" Walker asked, brushing aside the youth's question.

"About forty miles to the south," Bowstring repeated. "On the Rope River. Why?"

Walker ignored him, turning to look at Long Stride, whose face mirrored his own grim expression.

"You know what this means," Walker said flatly.

"Yes."

"Listen to me," Walker called out loudly to all those assembled, turning away from Bowstring to address them. "I'm speaking to you as leader of the Dog Soldier Society." With this pronouncement, all grew silent.

"Pack up your lodges. Now," Walker ordered. "Move quickly. We've got to be gone from this place as soon as possible." The gathered crowd began to murmur anxiously to each other.

Walker's sister Snow Dancer had come up to see what was happening, and was clearly puzzled and bothered by his words. She began to walk toward her brother.

"Here now," she barked. "What do you mean by –"

"Shut up, woman!" Long Stride growled, grabbing her by the arms and spinning her around to face him. "Just do what your brother says."

She started to speak back to him, but the dark look on her husband's face made the words freeze in her throat. She backed away from him slowly.

"I said *now!*" Walker shouted. He then spun on his heels and stalked to where the young Bowstring stood dumbfounded.

"And you," Walker hissed, the menace in his voice causing Bowstring to suck in his breath and hold it.

"If any harm comes to my family because of what you've done…I'll kill you."

CHAPTER 4

The Pawnee *iruska* (that is, shaman) named Stands Alone sat cross-legged in the middle of a small clearing. His head was bowed as he sought to commune with the spirits whose power he was about to invoke.

If any had dared to gaze upon him when he raised his head, they would have seen an ugly man whose twisted features reflected the black emotions that dwelt in his heart. Two white stripes ran down the length of that face, passing over eyes that had rolled so far back into their sockets that only the whites were visible.

A mouth brimming with gnarled, stained teeth opened, and a sound issued forth that could not rightly be called a song. It was more of a howl, like that of the wind that cuts through flesh and muscle to the very bone.

Sitting in the lower branches of the trees surrounding the clearing was a small number of Pawnee warriors he had brought with him from his village. As one, they cringed at the not quite human sounds that issued from him. Several averted their eyes, unwilling or unable to even look upon him as he practiced his dark arts.

The mystical powers he wielded had proven to be a blessing to their tribe on more than one occasion, but in truth they feared him almost as much as did their enemies. Feared, and hated. But also needed, or so he had convinced them.

Stands Alone's upper body began to swivel around in a circular motion. He threw his head back, and the howling screeches spewing from his throat grew even louder in intensity.

One of the warriors waiting in the trees nudged the man nearest him and motioned for him to look down. Below them they saw a large gray wolf, creeping forward through the forest. Its gait was awkward, almost clumsy, as if it was trying to run away but couldn't.

Its lips curled back over lance-like fangs, a deep growl bubbling up from within. Then the lips dropped back into place, and the growl faded into a pained whimper. Its shaggy head drooped between its shoulders as it surrendered to the piercing wail that had summoned it to this place.

Looking now more docile than any camp dog, it slowly padded forward toward the clearing ahead. As the warriors watched in amazement, more wolves began to appear below them. Each went through the same fruitless dance of resistance, and each eventually surrendered to the mesmerizing summons of the shaman.

Soon, a full two dozen wolves had emerged from the forest, coming to stand roughly in a circle around Stands Alone. Their yellow eyes had gone blank as they fell fully under his spell.

The shaman's mouth snapped shut, cutting off the haunting wail. Even so, the wolves around him stood still as stone. The hint of a crooked smile tugged at the corners of his mouth, and he motioned with both hands to the waiting warriors.

Hesitantly, they dropped down from their perches in the trees. Each carried a long lance, tipped with chipped stone heads. Holding the lances out before them, they slowly crept up behind the ensorcelled wolves, who showed no signs of being aware of the approach of hated men. The warriors stopped within paces of the pack, fearful and unsure of what to do next.

"Strike!" shouted Stands Alone.

The men jumped at the barked command, but the wolves remained motionless. The men looked back and forth at each other, none willing to be the first to obey the command. But one finally stepped forward, deciding the wolf could do him no more harm than could the shaman if his ire was raised by disobedience.

The warrior raised his lance above his head, then drove it home with all the strength he could muster. The head of the lance pierced one of the wolves behind and below its left shoulder.

The sharpened stone of its tip tore through both lung and heart, tearing out through the wolf's other side in a great bloody gush. Only then, too late, did the feral beast seem to be ripped from the spell that had held him in its grip. Its head twisted and a loud scream of pain bellowed out, ending in a bubbling gurgle as his throat filled with blood and he fell lifelessly to the ground.

The other warriors jumped back a pace, fearing that the howl might awaken the other wolves into a killing rage. But not a one of the animals moved, not so much as the flick of an ear.

Emboldened now, another warrior raised his spear and leaped forward, yelling loudly as he, too, plunged his weapon into the side of one of the remaining wolves.

The killing became general now, as all the warriors sprang forward upon the wolves. Lances rose again and again. The ground was slick with feral blood. And the warriors did not stop their butchery until every one of the wolves lay dead at their feet.

Chests rising and falling from their exertions, the Pawnees looked down triumphantly upon their handiwork, then lifted their gaze to look upon their shaman, who had sat unmoving throughout the slaughter. Sprays and splatters of wolf blood speckled both his clothing and his skin. Droplets of gore sparkled against the waxen skin of his face.

When the warriors' breathing returned to normal, silence fell upon the clearing. But not total silence. One of the Pawnees curled his lip back in horror and disgust as he realized the shaman was chuckling lightly, as if amused by the bloody killing. Which indeed he was.

None of the warriors knew why they had killed the wolves. They had been ordered to do so, and they had obeyed.

But Stands Alone knew. Just as he knew this was but the first step in working the magics yet to come.

Behind his disturbing laugh and dead eyes, where none could see, rage burned in him like the sun. The Cheyenne had insulted him, insulted his power and prestige, by sneaking into the village under his protection and stealing ponies from under his very nose. They had made him lose face before his tribe. And he meant to make them pay for what they had done.

Pay in blood and tears.

CHAPTER 5

Back in the Cheyenne village, the work of dismantling the camp was proceeding quickly and efficiently. Already, some of the lodge poles were coming down. They would be used next to make the travois that would be tied onto the backs of horses and used to transport the tipi skins and all their goods.

Walker sought out his sister who, with the assistance of three younger women, was just taking down the last of her own lodge poles. She turned in the direction of her brother just as he came to a halt a short distance behind her, and she smiled at him. He looked first at her belongings scattered about, then back at her.

"I expect some of you women will go to help Crow Woman pack up my home and belongings when you're finished here."

Snow Dancer's brow furrowed in anger, and she opened her mouth to spit out a retort. But instead she swallowed it, having seen the look in her brother's eyes. This had not been a request, but a command. She nodded curtly and returned to her work.

Walker merely turned and walked away. He had expected nothing less than her compliance, just as he had known the tribe would heed his order to break camp. People usually obeyed the orders of the soldier societies, especially those of the Dog Soldiers. Punishment was severe if they did not.

The soldier societies served as both police and military force for the tribe. Many considered the Dogs to be the best and bravest of all. They were looked up to with respect, and often insisted that the tribe follow their wishes, an authority Walker was known to have never abused. It was because of his integrity that there was seldom the slightest hesitation in obeying his orders.

Walker stopped again, seeing a group of four men headed his way. His father Listens To Elks led the way, but the other three – Cut Calf, Blue Raven and Loves Horses – were his equals. All four had been elected by the people to serve as a chief for the span of ten summers, and each had been chosen on the basis of their hard-earned merit.

The chiefs of a tribe were expected to fulfill two main duties during their time in office. Their first duty was to see to it that widows and orphans were properly cared for. The second was to act as peacemakers, and to mediate disputes among the people. Walker knew that all four of them were good at these jobs.

In matters that dealt with war or the defense of the village, however, all were expected to obey the man who was chief among the elite Dog Soldiers. In elections held amongst their members the previous summer, Walker had been the unanimous choice of the other Dogs to assume that post.

The other three tribal chiefs stopped a few feet away from Walker, still well within earshot. Listens To Elks strode closer, his face reflecting the seriousness of his office.

"I'm not one to question your orders, son," he began, taking a position in front of Walker.

"Of course you are," Walker replied, the merest trace of a smile tugging at the corners of his mouth. Listens To Elks chuckled lightly, turning to look back at his fellow chiefs, who smiled knowingly.

"You're right. I am. I was just hoping you would tell us why you think we need to move. This is a good place we've found here."

"It'll soon be a good place to die," Walker said.

"The only good place to die is in a woman's arms," Listens To Elks rejoined. "And the only good time is when you're too old to fulfill your duties as a man."

"And how old is that?" his son asked, smiling at his father.

"When I get that old – I'll let you know."

Both men fell silent then, watching the women loading up the tribe's few belongings.

"We're all in danger, father," Walker said at last.

"I assumed as much. And from your actions, the urgency behind your orders, it must be great danger."

"It is."

"So, tell me what it is. So I can tell the others. I've found it makes the people feel much better when they believe we chiefs know what's going on."

"I knew about the Pawnee village the boys raided," Walker began, by way of explanation. "It's been there for some time."

"I'm surprised you didn't raid it yourself, then," Listens To Elks interjected. "I know you have no love for the Pawnee."

Walker grunted. "No. But I have plenty to fear from that particular village."

"I could tell. Why is that?"

"Because they are Stands Alone's band."

Listens To Elks gasped and cursed softly under his breath.

"Is that who I think it is?" he asked.

"If you think it's a mad shaman who's as powerful as he is vindictive, yes."

"And you think he'll attack us?"

"I'm sure of it," Walker stated flatly. "Revenge is like food and water to him. Bowstring's raiding party shamed him by robbing those who are under his protection.

"He's got to save face. And knowing him, he won't be satisfied until the bones of every man, woman and child in our village lie bleaching in the sun."

"And you don't think we can stand up against him?" his father asked.

"Some of us are going to find out."

Listens To Elks flinched slightly, knowing full well what his son must be planning.

"But in case we can't," Walker continued, "I want the rest of you as far away from here as possible. If you're gone when he comes, maybe he'll settle for just a little blood."

"As you say," his father said softly. He reached out and gave Walker's arm a brief squeeze. "Be as safe as you are strong, son. We'll wait for you where Otter Creek comes down from Smoky Hill and hits the prairie."

"That's a good spot, father. I'll join you there as soon as I can. Within no more than three days, Maheo willing."

"Maheo willing," the father repeated, then turned without another word and rejoined the other chiefs.

Before another two hours had passed, the village was on the move. On an outcropping of rock overlooking the path they would follow, Walker sat astride Tall Dog, watching over them.

Many men, when riding, made use of a saddle made of elkhorn tree wood covered in rawhide, with wooden stirrups attached. Walker preferred to use a simple pad saddle. The pad was made from a long strip of buffalo hide that was folded over, stuffed with dried grass, and sewn up. Such a pad, girthed about the horse's chest, was long enough to come down to the rider's knees on either side, and wide enough to provide a comfortable seat for the rider. A rope tied around the pony's nose served as a bridle. From experience, Walker knew that the lightest tug on it, the merest pressure of a knee into the side, was all he needed to let Tall Dog know his wishes.

For now, all the tribe would travel together. When an appropriate place was reached, Walker planned to fall back with a select few and fight a holding battle against whatever force might be coming behind them.

Walker swiveled his head as he heard the skittering of loose rocks. He relaxed as he saw it was only Crow Woman. She stepped gingerly, trying to maintain her balance, which was made precarious by a large bundle she carried in the crook of one arm. She stumbled once under its weight, but allowed herself neither to fall nor to drop the precious bundle.

"What do you want?" Walker asked gruffly, looking away from her. "Why aren't you with the other women?"

"They don't want me," she said softly, through gritted teeth.

"Then go with the children."

"I could stay with you," she ventured hesitantly. She ducked her head as he turned flashing eyes on her.

"You'd only get in the way, woman. Why are you here?"

"I brought your war bundle," she replied.

Kneeling, she unfolded the blanket covering the bundle she had carried up to him, making sure not to come in direct contact with any of the weapons contained therein.

"You could have gotten a boy to bring this up to me," he said.

"I could have."

He fixed her with a dark stare that could have cracked rock, then let out a long, low sigh.

"Join the others," he said. "You can ride with my sister."

"If I try to do that, she'll hit me with a stick."

"Then hit her back!" he barked with exasperation. "Go on – get! I've got work to do!"

As she turned obediently, he leaned over and swatted her on one cheek of her rump to help speed her along. She staggered away, rubbing the spot he'd struck as if it pained her, but he spied the wisp of a smile on her lips. He sighed again, shaking his head.

Swinging one leg over Tall Dog's back, Walker dropped lightly to the ground and knelt to inspect the bundle of weapons his woman had left behind.

First he picked up the war club that warriors often called a "skull cracker." Its head consisted of a smooth oval rock lashed to a long, springy wooden handle. A rawhide loop near the base of the handle was meant to be worn around the wrist. He slipped the club into the right side of his breechcloth belt. On his left hip he already wore a long sheathed knife.

Next he examined his bow. It was little more than three feet long, but the layers of mountain sheep horn of which it was constructed made it strong as a tree. He plucked lightly at its buffalo bull sinew bowstring, testing its tautness.

The quiver that held his arrows was sewn from the skin of a panther he had slain; the animal's tail was still attached to it. It held a dozen arrows made of red willow, each over two feet long. The shaft of each was painted with his personal mark. Buzzard feathers were used for the fletching, as they would not grow soggy if splashed with blood or water. Each rounded point was made of sharpened stone.

All Cheyenne men were considered to be good bowmen, and their arrows the best that could be crafted by human hands. Walker was even more exceptional than most, capable of hitting a moving target at over five hundred paces. When prepared for war, as he was now, he would braid three or four spare arrowheads into his hair, in case he should need them.

He hefted his war lance in both hands, thrusting it through the air to assure himself of its balance. Its heavy wooden shaft was as long as Long Stride was tall, its leaf-shaped head as large as a child's open hand.

Planting it head down in the ground for the moment, he next picked up his shield. Most young men refused to carry a shield into battle, but Walker believed in using all the tools of war available to him, nor would any think the less of him for this.

The shield was made from a circular piece of dried and toughened buffalo bull hide, taken from the neck. This was covered with deerskin, with a layer of buffalo hair stuffed between the two.

A man's shield held special power for him, and was not to be touched by another. On its outer side, Walker had painted the image of a human skull, and he had adorned its outer edges with eagle feathers.

Lastly, he slipped a slender leather band over his head and around his neck. Attached to it was a small whistle, such as was worn by every Dog Soldier when he went into battle. Walker's war whistle had been carved by his own hands from the wing bones of a sandhill crane, a bird known for its strong protective powers. In the midst of a struggle, he would blow it to encourage his brother soldiers to fight on bravely, and to show that he

"A man's shield held special power..."

would not yield in the face of their enemy.

Hefting his lance, Walker leaped back astride Tall Dog's back. He looked back the way they had come, wondering what would surely be following in their footsteps. He then swung the pony's head, tapped it lightly in the ribs with his heels and set out after the rest of his tribe.

The people's exodus went smoothly, and by the time the sun was dipping low in the west, they had neared the top of a range of low mountains they called the Bear Teeth. The pass widened and flattened out at the top, and here Walker called a halt. As most of the band rested from the exertions of the climb, Walker asked the four chiefs and most of the warriors to join him in council.

By now, word of the threat from which they were retreating had spread through the band like fire through dry grass. All had heard stories of the mad shaman Stands Alone, and none doubted the veracity of the tales. They would not have shown their backs to any normal danger, but they knew this was a man who consorted with demons, and much to be feared.

"When the women and children are rested," Walker began, "the people will move out." He motioned for one of the Dogs, a trusted lieutenant named River Hawk, to step forward.

"As always, Hawk," he instructed, "the Dog Soldiers will serve as the rear guard. I leave you in charge of them."

"As you say, brother," River Hawk assented. "But what will you do?" He knew the answer to his question, but had to speak it anyway.

"I'll stay here," Walker answered, "in case we're being followed."

"You won't stay alone." This was not a question.

"No. If one person could stop what's likely to be on our tails, I'd just leave a grandmother here." Walker smiled grimly, then walked over to where his Dog Soldiers were assembled.

"Long Stride," he said to his brother-in-law. "You'll be by my side."

"Always, brother," Long Stride replied without hesitation.

Walker had already given much thought as to whom best could defend the pass with him, and he called out their names in quick succession.

First came Two Horse, a lithe, stealthy sort of warrior. He was one of the best men you could have along with you on a pony-stealing raid, or any other kind of venture.

Then he called on Cloud Toucher, an enormous man who stood a full head and a half taller than even Long Stride. Cloud Toucher was half Cheyenne and half Lakota, as was the next soldier selected: Blue Feather, a quiet soul who seldom spoke, but who was deadly in close combat with either knife or war club.

Then came Bear Killer. As his name implied, he had a fondness for bear steaks, and always wore a necklace of many bear claws. Rain Dance, who seldom stayed inside his lodge even during a storm, was next. Rounding out the chosen band was Daydreamer, a little man prone to visions but a deadly fighter nonetheless.

"Make your hearts strong, brothers," Walker commanded. "I don't know what we'll be facing, but it won't be good."

As the seven soldiers turned away to make preparations, another warrior shouldered his way through the gathering and rushed to Walker. His name was Crazy Dog. He had fallen from a tree as a boy, landing on his head. Maheo had shown mercy and spared his life, but had taken a piece of his mind in payment.

"I'll stay too, Walker!" Crazy Dog said excitedly, grabbing the war chief by both arms. "I'll stand by your side and take on whatever comes at us! You'll see!"

Walker stared down into the eyes of the wild man; they danced with madness. Crazy Dog smiled broadly, a thin trickle of spit rolling out of one corner of his mouth. Walker smiled back at him; everyone knew Maheo had special love for those whose minds had known his awful touch. Walker tousled the eager warrior's matted hair.

"Of course you will, Crazy Dog," he said. "Get your weapons."

"Will we fight to count coup," the crazed warrior asked, "or to kill?"

"What do you think, brother?" Walker replied.

Crazy Dog's eyes widened further and a smile gashed his face. He then yelped gleefully and took off running.

"Let me stay, too," another voice called out loudly.

Walker frowned as he turned to see young Bowstring standing defiantly off to one side.

"Go away, boy," he growled. "You're the reason we're in this mess."

"Then I should be allowed to help get us out of it," Bowstring shot back.

Walker glared at the youth, then swiveled his head to look at his father, silently seeking the older man's wisdom. Listens To Elks nodded almost imperceptibly.

"All right," said Walker. "You'll stay. And you'll fight. And if you even think of running away, I'll cut you down like so much kindling."

As his fellow warriors began to check their weapons, Walker walked with his father back to where the rest of the village was preparing to resume their journey.

"When you get to the bottom of the mountain," Walker instructed his father, "it should be no more than two days' travel to the bend of Otter Creek. It should be safe for you there, no matter what happens here."

"Good luck, son," Listens To Elks said, gripping Walker by the right forearm. "I know you'll make us proud by fighting well – and by dying well if you have to."

Walker stood alone for some time, watching the caravan make its way slowly down the sloping side of the mountain. Then he turned to rejoin the comrades who would fight alongside him.

Already, they had begun to apply war paint to their faces and bodies. Cloud Toucher had applied a single, wide, jagged stripe of white paint diagonally across his face, in a manner that resembled a lightning bolt.

Two Horse had circled one eye in red, then applied a white stripe that ran from the bottom of the circle to the edge of his jaw. Blue Feather dipped two fingers into white paint and dotted his face. Bear Killer's mark was simply a handprint on the right side of his face.

Daydreamer had already applied three red stripes to his forehead and was now singing a war song. The song spoke of the bravery of the Dog Soldiers, and of how they would leave their enemies dead on the field of battle. Rain Dance, sporting a wide red stripe from the middle of his lower lip to his jaw, sang his own song of how they would battle with bare hands if need be. He and all the others had also put on the various charms and amulets they believed would keep them safe from harm.

Walker nodded approvingly. All Cheyenne men were warriors and were taught from birth that no pleasure equaled the thrill of battle. Such was their bravery that they were known to risk their lives in ways no other warriors would even contemplate.

"It's ready, brother," Long Stride said. He was standing beside a small fire he had built on the ground. His eyes seemed to gleam out of the wide black stripe he had painted horizontally across the middle of his face.

He stepped aside as Walker approached the fire. With his back to the other soldiers, he squatted down before it.

"What's he doing?" Bowstring asked no one in particular.

"He's about to put on his war face," Long Stride answered.

From the medicine pouch worn on his belt, Walker extracted a small quantity of special, powdered herbs. It was a mixture of a rare and unusual mushrooms blended with blood root and man sage.

Walker began to sing. His was a song of death, which conquers all, and from which none escape.

As the last note of the song trailed away, Walker dropped the powdered herbs into the fire. On contact, greenish-gray smoke began to billow upward.

With his right hand, he grasped the amulet upon which was painted the face of death, which he still wore around his neck. The stone had been found clutched in the same hand when he had awakened from his vision those many years past. How it got there, and who had emblazoned it with the deathly face, even he could not say.

He leaned forward slightly and, cupping the rising smoke in his left hand, he caused it to swirl about his head, as if bathing in it. A familiar and not unpleasant aroma swam up his nostrils. In the instant, the eye of his mind was filled with visions of all those he had sent to the Place of the Dead.

As if driven by a sudden gust of wind, the smoke swirled upward and dissipated, even as the small fire that birthed it was doused to nothing more than faintly glowing embers.

Walker remained squatting for several heartbeats, then pushed himself erect and turned to face his men.

Young Bowstring, who had been watching him the most intently, jerked with surprise and fear, gasping softly. He was clearly taken aback by the appearance of the war chief. He had never been this close to Walker when he prepared for war.

Walker had applied no paint to his face, yet its entire upper half was now colored a ghostly white, save for dark circles around his eyes. In appearance, it looked as if a human skull had glued itself against his face from his hairline to his lower cheeks.

The sight of this horrible living death's head caused tiny droplets of sweat to break out on Bowstring's forehead. It both repulsed and yet fascinated the youth.

"He...he doesn't look human," Bowstring muttered under his breath.

"I'm not sure he is," said Daydreamer.

CHAPTER 6

The light of day was beginning to fade as the ten warriors stood together in the mountain pass, keeping watch over the back trail. To their backs, the rest of the tribe was long out of sight.

In anticipation of the battle he was sure would come soon, Walker bent down and plucked a long blade of grass from the ground. He wet one end of it with his tongue, then touched that end to the inside of the medicine pouch on his belt.

He then spit on each hand, made several ceremonial gestures in the air, and stuck the spear of grass in his hair, as a charm to protect him in combat. The other soldiers did likewise.

"Look!" exclaimed Two Horse, pointing down and back in the direction from which they had come.

They all grew silent and hunkered down, straining to pierce the gathering veil of twilight. As first, Bowstring saw nothing, and relaxed. Then a slight movement caught his eye, in a stand of trees not far from the base of the slope. Moments later, a lone man emerged from their cover, riding on horseback.

"Stands Alone," Walker whispered. He had never laid eyes on the shaman, but was certain it could be no other.

They could now see that the Pawnee holy man held the lead reins of four other horses that trailed behind him. Each of these horses pulled a travois behind it, and each travois was loaded down with what appeared to be a pile of bloody furs.

But of course it was not furs at all. Rather, each travois bowed beneath the weight of lifeless carcasses – the wolves that had been killed at Stands Alone's command.

"What's he planning to do?" asked Cloud Toucher.

"It'll be bad," said Crazy Dog, giggling like a girl. "It'll be bad!"

"Even a rat speaks wisely sometimes," Long Stride agreed.

Stands Alone brought his mount to a halt a short distance from the base of the peak, and he slid to the ground. He moved forward on foot a few paces, then stopped to gaze up at the pass where the Dog Soldiers lay in wait.

Walker felt the hairs on the back of his neck stand on end. He had no doubt the shaman knew exactly where they were, though they were all pressed low to the ground or behind boulders.

Even in the fading light, he could likewise clearly see Stands Alone. The shaman was short and gaunt, all arms and legs. His hair was flecked with snow and stood out from his head in all directions. Various objects, surely containing strong magic, were braided into his hair: bits of bone, teeth, feathers, even what to Walker's straining eyes appeared to be a man's finger. The ceremonial shirt he wore hung nearly to his bony knees. Mystical signs were painted all over it.

Showing his disdain for the Dog Soldiers by turning his back to them, Stands Alone raised both hands high as he went to stand over the travois bearing the slain wolves. In his right hand he held a tortoise shell rattle, from which dangled turkey feathers. He began to shake it rhythmically and to sing.

"Why are we just standing here?" Bowstring whispered harshly. "Let's go down there and kill him!"

"Stay where you are!" Walker snapped. "It's best to stay far away from shamans when they're casting spells."

"Better still not to steal their ponies and make them lose face," Cloud Toucher growled. Crazy Dog snickered at this, and Bowstring hung his head.

"Besides," Walker continued, "for all we know he's got twenty warriors down there with him, hiding in the trees, waiting to pounce on us if we go down there. That might even be what he's doing now, trying to lure us down. Best to stay here, on high ground that's easy to defend."

On the plain below, Stands Alone continued his chanting, his voice rising and falling in intricate vocal patterns. The shaman then gripped his rattle with both hands and began to shake it ever more violently. In the rocky pass above, Rain Dance – who often bragged his eyes were like those of an eagle – let out a loud gasp.

"They're moving!" he exclaimed.

"What?" Bear Killer asked.

"The wolves on the travois...they're starting to move!"

All the Dog Soldiers stared intently down the slope, save for Crazy Dog. He covered his face with his hands and began to rock back and forth, mumbling something unintelligible.

It was as Rain Dance said. The furry mounds atop the four travois were beginning to twitch, as if something buried beneath them had awakened and was attempting to burrow its way free.

Stands Alone's eyes grew bright with the fire of power gone mad, his voice becoming as loud as a howling wind. At his chanted command, the lifeless bodies of the wolves began to rise up. Their eyes opened, gleaming blood red in the gloom, their lips curled back from fangs that now began to grow even longer than they had been in life.

Nor did the beasts stop when they had risen to all fours. Like camp dogs begging for scraps, they arose onto their hind legs. In the camp above, the Cheyenne warriors could hear a horrible sound, as of bones and tendons snapping.

The legs of the wolves began to change shape. Stands Alone raised both hands as if to likewise raise the wolves until they were standing fully upright, like awful, twisted parodies of men. The bones of their front legs twisted and contorted to become more like arms, and long fingers with lance-like claws sprang from their paws.

"Maheo save us!" Blue Feather gasped softly.

"I don't think he can, brother," Two Horse replied.

Now fully resurrected to a distorted mockery of life, the wolf men stood clustered together around Stands Alone. One of the creatures snapped at the shaman. The man waved his rattle at the beast and it staggered backwards several feet, yelping in pain.

Stands Alone then walked toward the beasts, and they let him pass untouched. He once again took up the lead reins of the horses he had used to transport the wolves, then nimbly swung himself up onto the back of the pony he had been riding. He tilted his head upward.

"Hear me, Cut-Arm People," he called out to the Cheyenne, invoking an image of their practice of cutting off the left finger, hand or arms of fallen enemies. His reptilian voice easily carried up the darkening slope.

"I am Stands Alone, of the Pawnee. It would be better to have the earth swallow you whole than to have me for an enemy."

Before he could say more, Walker yelled down at him.

"The Place of the Dead is filled with men who called us enemy."

"Brave words," sneered the shaman. "Who speaks them?"

Walker stood and stepped forward. Standing at the point where the path began to slope downward, he made sure the Pawnee could see him.

"I am called Deathwalker!" he shouted in a voice that rolled down the valley. The shaman involuntarily sucked in his breath, clenching and unclenching his bony fists.

"Your name means nothing to me," he cried at last.

"Then you're a fool," Walker retorted, "or a liar. My name is known well among the Pawnee, and feared." He struck his chest with one fist.

"I am Deathwalker, leader of the Dog Soldiers, of the tribe of Listens To Elks...and I am like the sun. If you can kill me, you will have done a great thing."

"Then I will do a great thing today, Cheyenne," the shaman practically shrieked. Then his voice grew lower, but still clearly heard.

"Let everyone know that you brought this upon yourselves."

Young Bowstring wilted as more than one of his comrades turned to fix him with baleful stares.

"But Stands Alone is not without mercy," the shaman continued. "The rest of your village will be spared. Only you on the mountain will be die." His cracked lips peeled back in a sickening grin.

"But you will die such horrible deaths that no man will ever again even think of bringing shame to the tribe of Stands Alone!"

Walker glanced around him. There was no mistaking the expressions on the faces of his comrades. It was not so much fear as it was resignation. Seeing this, he lifted his bow up over his head.

"You're out of arrow range, old man!" Walker shouted. "Come a little closer, and then tell us how fearsome you are!"

The other Dog Soldiers laughed loudly. The mocking smile on Stands Alone's lips froze in place for the barest moment before twisting into a snarl. He shook his rattle fiercely, and all the wolf men in his thrall turned great hairy heads to look at him.

He spoke not a word. His left arm slowly rose up and out, his open hand seeming to stretch out toward the top of the mountain. He then snapped his hand closed in a tight fist, and twisted it. Low rumblings deep in the throats of the wolf men told him they understood their mission.

"If you're still able to make jokes in the morning, Cheyenne," he called out, "then come to see me."

Stands Alone then reined his pony around and started back in the direction of his village. The wolf men stood silently watching his back until he and his small string of horses disappeared into the sheltering arms of the forest.

When the last sound of their hooves was lost to the darkness, the wolf men swiveled in unison, their crimson eyes glaring upward at the Dog Soldiers. Mournful wails slithered from their throats.

"Get ready," Walker commanded. "They're going to attack."

CHAPTER 7

A great gnashing of teeth could be heard from the pack of wolf men. One snapped his jaws savagely at another's hindquarters. Then, with no further warning, they set out at a run up the slope, covering several foot spans with each blurring stride.

"Use your bows first," Walker said. "We don't want them to get close enough to lay their hands on us."

The Dog Soldiers formed two ranks at Walker's direction. Five of them knelt on the ground, the other four stood behind them, with Walker to one side. Arrows were notched, but bowstrings were not drawn back. That would be done only as the inhuman pack drew closer.

Walker placed his whistle to his lips and blew. Bowstring jumped at the sudden and unexpected sound, then looked about as several of the other Dog Soldiers likewise filled the air with shrill whistles. When Walker stopped, they all gave out with a loud war cry.

Onward the wolf men rushed. Not accustomed to running upright, they would at times drop to all fours. The growls issuing from their throats seemed to come from no beast of nature, but rather from the deepest pits of the demon world.

In the fading light, the preternatural red of their eyes seemed to glow ever more brightly. As the space between them and the band of Cheyenne began to close rapidly, Bowstring raised his bow, drawing back the string.

"Not yet," Walker seemed to whisper in his ear. The youth relaxed the tension on the bowstring slightly, but felt that it had already grown slick with the perspiration from his hand. His eyes grew nearly as wide as those of the beasts rushing toward him.

There was a roaring in his ears, but not so loud that it could drown the howling screeches coming from the charging wolf men. All of the beasts were upright again as they neared their targets. Clawed hands were

47

stretched out, eager to rip and tear.

"Soon," said Walker calmly, staring intently at the slavering beasts as they ran and leapt ever closer.

"Soon."

As they drew within maximum range, Walker realized he was not breathing. He emptied his lungs through his mouth and drew in fresh air.

"Now!" he shouted.

In unison, the five kneeling warriors released their arrows. Five whistling blurs of death sped through the air. In the hands of an expert, a Cheyenne bow packed enough power to drive an arrow clear through the body of an adult buffalo. One shaft did just that now, striking a wolf man squarely in the chest. The barbed head of the arrow tore out of the animal's back, bringing bloody gouts of flesh with it.

The stricken wolf man howled hideously and collapsed to the ground. One of his comrades, who had been running behind him, jumped over his twitching body. In mid-leap, an arrow fired by Walker struck him in the throat. The force nearly tore his head off and flipped his body backwards, sending it tumbling down the slope.

Their Pawnee creator had apparently also imbued these unholy beasts with rudimentary intelligence, for they now began to zigzag back and forth as they made their way up the slope, causing most of the flashing arrows to miss their mark.

But not all. The Dog Soldier named Blue Feather, who had been known to bring down two birds with a single arrow, now took the leg out from under a wolf man with one of his shafts, breaking the creature's ankle.

Another shot struck a second beast in the abdomen. Clutching at the burning pain in its belly, the wolf man pulled up short, rearing up and back and bellowing to the sky. His cries choked off in a death rattle as Long Stride and Crazy Dog each put an arrow into his heaving chest.

Still more of the wolf men fell until at last, no more than forty paces from the summit of the mountain, the pack broke off its attack. Turning, they loped back down the slope.

As one of them passed near a fallen pack brother, he skidded to a halt. Roaring savagely, he buried his muzzle into the gaping stomach wound that had felled the beast, and began to feed.

A second wolf man leaped at him, and blood sprayed as both tumbled away from the corpse. While they clawed and snapped at each other, a third wolf man swooped in and grabbed the partially mutilated corpse in his massive jaws, dragging it down the mountainside.

His two pack mates broke off their fighting and pursued him. Others coming behind them also snatched up fallen bodies and dragged them into the darkness.

"They mean to eat their own," Bowstring gulped in disgust as he watched them disappear from sight.

"Wolf meat's good meat," Crazy Dog cackled.

"What do you expect, boy?" said Long Stride. "Unholy creatures commit unholy acts."

"Is it over, then?" Bowstring asked, turning his eyes to Walker. "Have we beaten them?"

"Not hardly," Walker snorted. "They'll be back."

He looked around, his eyes narrowing as he saw that, like himself, his brothers had used all their arrows in warding off the wolf men's first charge.

"Prepare yourselves," he said grimly. "Next time...the fighting will be hand-to-hand."

CHAPTER 8

Walker turned his back to his men, walked several paces away, then squatted on the ground. With his head hanging down on his chest, he closed his eyes and sought to empty his mind of all thoughts of what was to come.

"It doesn't look good for you, step-child."

Sighing wearily, Walker opened his eyes and raised his head. Buffalo Boy was hunkered down atop an outcropping of rock above him, lazily chewing on his omnipresent blade of grass.

"Well, you know what they say," Walker spoke stoically. "A soldier chief is chosen to be killed. I don't suppose you've actually come here to offer any help, have you?"

"Better," said the small spirit guide. "I've come to offer you hope."

"I already have hope."

"Oh." Buffalo Boy shrugged. "In that case, just remember this: with the right weapons, a sparrow can kill a wolf."

"What does that mean?" Walker growled.

"Walker?" a hesitant voice spoke from behind him. He looked over his shoulder to see Bowstring standing nearby, shuffling awkwardly from one foot to the other.

"I didn't mean to interrupt your prayers," the youth said respectfully.

"It's all right, Bowstring," Walker said, rising to his feet.

Without a word, Bowstring stepped forward and held out a water skin and a pouch containing pemmican. The leader of a war party was not allowed to ask for food or water; these must be offered to him by one of his soldiers.

Walker nodded in acknowledgment of the offering, and took it from Bowstring gratefully. He tipped the skin to his lips, gulping down the cool water. He then took a handful of the pemmican, that mixture of berries and pulverized buffalo meat and fat that was a staple diet for those without time to prepare a meal, and began to chew, savoring the taste. Only then did he notice the questioning look on Bowstring's face.

"Is there something you want?" he asked the boy.

"It's what I don't want that's bothering me, Walker."

"And what's that?" Bowstring seemed to visibly shrink before Walker's eyes before answering the question.

"I don't want to die."

"No sane man does, boy," Walker replied gruffly, "but no man can deny death when it comes for him." He placed a firm hand on Bowstring's shoulder.

"And only the stones stay on earth forever."

Walker's raised his eyes to look heavenward.

"If it comforts you, remember that all who die are equal in the eyes of Maheo, so long as they have not taken their own lives. There's no special reward for the good, no punishment for the evil, other than what they suffer in life. We all make the same journey, to the same place. No matter what happens here today, we'll all meet again in the Place of the Dead."

"You don't seem to be afraid of dying," Bowstring ventured.

"Don't be fooled, boy. Every man here has pissed himself during a fight at some time in his life. But I'm expected to die."

Bowstring knew that all men who held Walker's position of soldier chief were greatly respected, in part because others feared them. Walker was even more feared than most, yet also commanded much genuine respect and even affection among the people. As he studied the man now, Bowstring knew why.

"As for me," Walker continued, in a voice almost too low to hear, "I think I'm more afraid of killing."

"What do you mean?"

"Every man has a power, Bowstring. A gift from Maheo." Walker made a waving motion with his right hand toward their fellow warriors.

"Long Stride there, he's as good a tracker as you'll ever find. Bear Killer can't be beaten as a hunter." Walker gazed skyward as if peering at something that wasn't really there.

"You know what my power is?"

"What?"

"I kill."

Walker lowered his gaze until his eyes bore into Bowstring.

"I bring Death."

"That's what a warrior does," Bowstring replied, with a slight tremor in his voice. "You have to kill your enemies."

"That's true. But if you kill too well, too often, too long…death becomes more important to you than life. When that happens, you start to wonder if you kill only because you have to – or because you like it."

"Have you ever killed anyone who didn't deserve to die?"

"I never ask myself that question." Walker's eyes flared so fiercely that Bowstring felt fingers of fear close around his heart.

"And don't you ever ask me again, boy."

Bowstring said nothing. He merely stepped back slowly a pace or two, then turned around to go rejoin the other soldiers.

"Bowstring?" Walker said, making him stop in his tracks and turn.

"Yes?"

"Back in the camp, earlier today…I threatened to kill you."

"Forget it," the boy said dismissively.

"No," Walker replied. "You are my brother, like every other man in the village. A man does not kill his brother. Even to threaten him is unacceptable. Somehow, I'll make right the wrong I did you."

Bowstring smiled slightly. He knew that Walker spoke from the heart. To the Cheyenne, the murder of a tribesman was more than a crime. It was a sin that brought desecration down on the tribe's Sacred Arrows, and could be punished by as long as ten summers in exile.

"Just get as many of us back home as you can," he said.

"I will," Walker said. "But remember this: it is never shameful for a man to be killed in battle."

Bowstring nodded, then turned again and ambled over to where the others were gathered.

"Don't make promises you can't keep," Buffalo Boy said, having reappeared alongside Walker.

"I never do," the war chief replied.

CHAPTER 9

Even as Walker spoke, the rest of his tribe was spilling out onto the prairie floor on the other side of the mountain. They would take another brief rest here, but then continue on for a time in an effort to put as much space between them and the site of their previous encampment as possible. Listens To Elks reined in his pony, staring up at the heights they had just descended.

"Is something wrong, father?" Snow Dancer asked, pulling her pony up beside him.

"It's started," he said in a low voice. "Walker and the others are fighting for their lives. I can feel it."

"Can you also feel if he's still alive?"

The question came not from the chieftain's daughter but from the slave Crow Woman, who had now come up on his other side.

"Why do you care?" Snow Dancer spat, fixing Crow Woman with a baleful glare. "Do you think you might find yourself a better master if he dies?"

Crow Woman made no response, but simply lowered her head, twisted the reins of her pony and set out to rejoin the main party.

"There's something wrong with that woman," Snow Dancer hissed.

"There's something wrong with all women," her father declared, turning his pony away from the mountain.

"But it's the curse of men that we love you anyway."

"Are you saying you think Walker loves her?" his daughter pressed.

"That's none of my business," Listens To Elks replied. "Or yours."

CHAPTER 10

Back in the mountain pass, Long Stride approached Walker, talking to him in quiet tones.

"There's something wrong with Crazy Dog."

"Of course there is," Walker replied dryly. "He's crazy."

"I know that!" Long Stride exclaimed. "But he's acting even stranger than usual! See for yourself."

Crazy Dog sat cross-legged on the ground, rocking rhythmically back and forth. As he did so, he sang his Death Song, strange words that rose and fell like the wind.

He pulled his knife from its sheath, holding it aloft to point at the sky. The other Dog Soldiers stared in fascination as he then lowered the knife and began to draw it across the skin of his left arm, leaving deep furrows that spilled blood onto the dirt.

His eyes grew wide, though they seemed to see nothing. His rocking motion grew faster and more jerky, his song of death rose louder and louder. Next, he leaped to his feet. Arms akimbo, he threw back his head and screamed at the top of his lungs.

"It's all right," Daydreamer said soothingly, placing a hand on Crazy Dog's arm. "Be calm, brother."

Daydreamer sucked in his breath sharply as Crazy Dog turned his head to stare at him with eyes that burned like embers. He placed a hand to Daydreamer's chest and shoved, sending the slight warrior staggering back.

Crazy Dog pulled his spear from the ground, screamed again, and ran down the side of the mountain. Two Horse dived at his feet, trying to tackle him, but Crazy Dog hopped over his outstretched hands and raced away. Bear Killer and Blue Feather started to pursue him.

"Stay where you are!" Walker barked. His jaws clenched tightly as his soldiers turned to him.

"It's no good for all of us to die foolishly."

Moments later, the sounds of battle rose up to them from the darkness below. Crazy Dog's screams mingled with the snarls and yelps of the wolf men. Then there was only silence.

"Poor Crazy Dog," Long Stride said at last, breaking the quiet spell. "His heart was always braver than his head was wise."

"From the sound of it," said Cloud Toucher, "he took some of them with him. He died well."

"But he shouldn't have died at all," muttered Bowstring, so quietly that none but Walker could hear him.

Ever louder howling erupted from below, chilling each of the warriors to the bone.

"What's happening down there?" asked Blue Feather. "Is it possible that Crazy Dog is still alive, still fighting?"

"No," Walker said grimly. "Those are the sounds of the berserk. They're working themselves into a frenzy. They'll be attacking again any moment." He tightened his grip on his spear.

"They won't retreat again, brothers. It's kill or be killed time."

Walker examined the faces of the warriors gathered around him. Much as he tried to hide it, the fear in Bowstring's eyes was clear. The boy had been in battle before, but not often, and never against so unholy an enemy. His fear was to be expected.

But there were also traces of it in the eyes of some of the other Dog Soldiers as well. These men had faced death from human hands a score of times without flinching. But the howling pack down in the darkness below was as far from human as the hummingbird is from the bear.

They all needed to have some stone returned to their spines, and in the instant Walker made a bold and dangerous decision he hoped would help do so.

As they stared at him in silence, he reached to his waist and began to loosen a special item that was wrapped several times around it.

It was the *hotamtsit* – the dog rope.

In truth it was no rope at all, but rather a strip of buffalo hide as wide as his hand and nearly as long as two men were tall. The belt was decorated throughout its length with porcupine quills.

One end of the dog rope remained tied to his belt. He tied the loose end of it to a large wooden pin he carried in a pocket sewn to his quiver. Seeing what he was planning to do, Long Stride stepped forward and grabbed him by the arm.

"You don't need to do that, brother," he said to Walker, locking eyes with him.

"I think I do," Walker replied solemnly.

He dropped to one knee and, using his war club, pounded the wooden pin firmly into the ground.

Even the uninitiated Bowstring knew what this meant. When a Dog Soldier staked himself into position like this, he was pledging not to move from this spot unless he was victorious in battle...or he was dead. To pull the pin loose before one or the other outcome would be to admit to cowardice.

His face set, Long Stride reached for the dog rope circling his own waist, but Walker grabbed him firmly by the wrist.

"No, brother," he said. "This is my pledge alone. They'll find my body here, or they'll find my enemy's."

"Then it'll be your enemy's."

The words came not from one of the seasoned warriors, but from Bowstring. His lips were clamped in a tight line.

"You won't fight alone...and you won't die alone," he asserted.

"Hou! Hou!" the other soldiers yelped in agreement.

"Then take your spears in hand, brothers," Walker instructed, "and we'll give the monsters a fight they'll sing songs about forever."

As the others again yelped their approval, Long Stride stepped close, so only his brother-in-law could hear what he said.

"If your purpose was to strengthen their courage, brother, you succeeded."

"They already had plenty of courage," Walker replied. "They just needed to be reminded of it."

With one finger, Long Stride plucked lightly at the dog rope that held Walker in place.

"Well," he said, "next time, don't do it in such a stupid way."

Walker nodded curtly.

"Next time."

"Then take your spears in hand, brothers..."

CHAPTER 11

They came like wraiths from the other side, these creatures that were neither fully men nor beasts. Their howls of excitation leaped out before them, while they were still hidden from sight by the now full darkness of the night, and their claws raked across the stony pathway in hideous squeals.

The Dog Soldiers again formed two ranks in the path of the oncoming wolf men. Each warrior rammed the butt of his spear shaft into whatever purchase the hard ground provided, with the heads pointed straight ahead at the advancing foe.

"Hold fast!" Walker yelled.

Even as the words left his mouth, the first of the snarling beasts rushed upon them. Arms flexed in agonizing tension as the wolf men impaled themselves with such force that the spears bowed nearly in half.

Blood and fetid wolf breath sprayed the men's faces. The warriors screamed nearly as loudly as the dying beasts. With loud snaps, the spears broke under the assault.

As a dying wolf man fell to one side, carrying half the length of his broken spear with it, Walker lowered his hands down the remaining length of the shaft. Another beast leaped at him over the body of its fallen brother.

Walker thrust upward. The jagged end of the broken spear shaft penetrated the wolf man's lower jaw. Flailing claws raked the Cheyenne's upper arm, but he ignored the searing pain, throwing his weight harder against the shaft. It now tore completely through the wolf man's mouth, penetrating the roof and plunging into its feral brain.

As it fell backwards in its death throes, Walker released the spear shaft and reached for his war club. A familiar red curtain descended over his eyes, and all the world took on the color of blood. He stepped forward to meet the onrushing beasts.

He swung his club in a compact arc, smiling tightly at the crunching sound he heard as its blunt edge ripped away the lower jaw of one of the wolf men. The creature's knees buckled as he began to choke on his own blood and bone.

Walker surprised a second wolf man by leaping directly at him. Moving quickly inside the sweep of the beast's claws, the Cheyenne tackled the monster, falling heavily atop him. The wolf man's face seemed to fold in upon itself as Walker's club struck him square between the eyes.

As Walker rose to his feet, a scream, this one human, pulled his head to one side.

He saw Blue Feather, eyes wide with fear and pain, staring down at a gaping wound that had been torn in his belly. He had dropped his weapon and was using both hands in a vain effort to keep his innards from spilling out on the ground.

The mortally wounded Dog Soldier seemed not to notice when one of the wolf men leaped on his back, sinking distended fangs into the warrior's throat. A great spout of blood sprayed out and Blue Feather collapsed, dead.

Bear Killer raced up behind the wolf man who had slain Blue Feather. He grabbed the back of the beast's furry head and pulled it back sharply. Reaching around with his right hand, he dragged the blade of his knife across the wolf man's throat, neatly slitting it from ear to ear.

Raking claws tore bloody gouges in the big man's back as he was himself attacked from behind. Spinning with a speed that belied his size, Bear Killer grabbed the wolf man by its throat and its crotch.

Lifting the beast man high off the ground, Bear Killer slammed him down on a low boulder, snapping his back in multiple places.

As he straightened, Bear Killer jerked, and blood began to fill his mouth. Looking down in shock, he saw a bloody paw that had thrust through his back and out his belly. The world grew darker, and he pitched forward, lifeless.

To his dismay, Walker saw that Cloud Toucher's height had made him a target for three of the wolf men, who were trying to drag him down by sheer weight of numbers. He was able to push one of them away and bring his war club down upon the crown of its head. With the third blow, its skull caved in like a sparrow's egg in the jaws of a snake.

But this merely gave the other two wolf men time to sink their claws and fangs more deeply into Cloud Toucher's flesh. Even as one sank its yellowed teeth into the side of his throat, the other used its claws to tear a great bloody gouge out of the soldier's side.

Though it was too late to save Cloud Toucher, stealthy Two Horse avenged his death. He rushed up behind the two wolf men with a knife held firmly in each hand. He drove both blades into their backs, then heaved upward with all his might, tearing through the beasts' innards.

As they fell forward, Two Horse released the embedded knives and reached for the war club dangling from his belt. Before he could pull it free, though, another wolf man bowled him over. Before the man could catch his breath, the beast grabbed him by his ankles and swung him completely off the ground. Two Horse's head smashed against a boulder; death came instantly.

Walker winced as he saw this, and as he saw the beast remain bent over the fallen warrior. Its snout had just plunged into the gray matter oozing from the gaping hole in the man's skull, intent on devouring it, when Long Stride charged him from one side.

With a backhand swing, Long Stride cracked his war hammer against the beast's slavering jaws. It turned on him, but he brought the club back across the other side of its head.

The wolf man staggered backward as Long Stride continued to pelt him with blow after blow to his shaggy head. With its next step back, the beast's left foot came down on nothing but air.

It wavered on the edge of the precipice, its long arms flailing about in a losing effort to regains its balance. A final blow from Long Stride's club sent it hurtling down to the rocks far below.

As Long Stride turned away from the cliff, another wolf man pounced upon him, sinking teeth into the man's shoulder and dragging him to the ground.

Without thought, Walker sprang forward to go to the aid of his brother-in-law, forgetting the rope that tethered him to the ground. It snapped taut as he reached the end of its length, pulling him up short and causing his feet to skid from under him, slamming him to the ground.

He rolled to the side and came back up on his knees barely in time to react to one of the wolf men swinging a heavy paw at his head. He ducked beneath the raking claws, already glistening with another man's blood.

Missing its target, the wolf man was carried past Walker by the momentum of its swing. As it spun past him, Walker slapped his war club against the back of the beast's ankle, severing a tendon.

Left without that leg's support, the monster sank to its knees. Walker swung his war club again, this time aiming for the base of the beast's skull. Its neck broke and, its head tilted to an odd angle, it pitched face first in the dust.

Walker leaped to his feet, seeking out the wounded Long Stride. What his eyes fell upon instead was the sight of Rain Dance and Daydreamer, standing back to back as they fought off more of the wolf men.

Both men were covered in blood, their own and that of the dead wolf men who lay at their feet. The warriors continued to flail away with arms grown weak and weary, and more beasts fell to the ground.

Then the thin Daydreamer's loss of blood drained him of the last of his fading strength. He slumped to his knees, and may not even have felt the killing blow that tore away one side of his face.

His killer stepped on his body and sprang onto Rain Dance's back even as another wolf man rushed the soldier from the front. The Cheyenne's body bowed backwards as the first wolf man's clawed hands wrapped around his neck and pulled. The beast in front swung upward, ripping the man from belly to sternum.

Walker, thankfully, had no time to watch what happened next. He turned at a movement out one corner of his eye, to see a wolf man leaping toward him.

He took the brunt of the attack on his shield, heaving the beast to one side. He rolled with the momentum, swinging his war club. The sharpened side of its head bit deep into the beast's skull, causing it to split nearly in two.

So deeply did the stone bite, however, that the club became lodged in the bony skull. Walker straddled the fallen wolf man, bracing one knee against its hairy chest for leverage as he sought to pull the blade free.

A great mass struck him then, throwing him onto his back. Gasping for breath, he looked up to see a wolf man astride him, roaring in animal rage. Struggling vainly to throw off the beast, Walker saw its clawed right hand rise in preparation for the killing blow.

CHAPTER 12

Hot spittle from the beast's gaping maw splashed down onto Walker's face and into one eye with scalding intensity. His vision swam, but he could still see the bloody paw that was about to rip the life away from him.

Then a strange, gurgling sound issued from the wolf man's throat. Its mouth dropped open even wider and from within it shot the bloody end of a broken spear shaft, which had been thrust clean through the beast's head from behind.

Walker blinked as stinging wolfen blood splattered down on him. The wolf man stiffened and fell limply to one side. As it did, Walker was able to see the warrior who had killed the beast and saved his life.

It was young Bowstring.

The boy extended his hand, and helped his war chief to his feet. Only then did Walker realize that silence had descended upon the killing ground.

He looked around to see the bodies of the wolf men littering the site; not a one showed any signs of life.

Walker's eyes sought out his brother-in-law. Long Stride stood over the body of his last fallen foe with one shoulder stooped, trails of blood trickling down from the wound inflicted by beastly fangs. But he was still able to smile at Walker.

"It looks like it was a good day for them to die," Long Stride said.

Walker sank down to the ground wearily. He was still attached to the dog rope, still pinned to the ground. He was not allowed to release himself from the rope or the vow it signified, so Long Stride did it for him.

He pulled his knife and cut the rope close to the pin holding it to the earth. Then he lightly tapped his brother-in-law on the back with the flat of his war club, symbolically driving him from the battlefield. Walker rose and gratefully clasped Long Stride's forearm.

"What now?" Bowstring asked expectantly.

"First I thank you for my life," Walker replied, nodding to the boy. "Then we see if any of our brothers still live."

As was expected, though, the three of them were the only soldiers who had survived. One of the wolf men showed the faintest flicker of life, but Walker snuffed it by slitting the beast's throat.

"Make a fire," Walker told Bowstring. "We might as well stay the night."

"I'd rather be shed of this place," Long Stride remarked.

"So would I," Walker agreed. "But you'd probably bleed to death before we got down off this mountain."

"It's not that bad," Long Stride protested, even as his body swayed slightly from the loss of blood still pumping from his wound.

"It's bad enough," Walker asserted. "It needs to be bandaged. And a night's sleep will be good for us all."

"What about the Pawnee?" Bowstring said softly, peering out into the darkness.

"He's probably long gone," Walker said. "Surely, enough Cheyenne blood was spilled to pay for the few ponies you took."

But unseen by him, beyond the base of the mountain in the covering blanket of the forest, Stands Alone was still staring upward. When he saw sparks in the darkness, followed by the glow of the fire started by Bowstring, he knew for sure that some of the Cheyenne had survived.

His red-rimmed eyes narrowed with anger and hate. He was not finished with the hated Cut-Arm People – and especially not with the war chief who called himself Deathwalker. The shaman's mystic senses told him the man who had insulted him before the others was among the survivors. The Dog Soldier still lived.

But not for long, he vowed.

The shaman roughly jerked the bridle of his horse, turning the pony around, and set off for his village.

When the three Cheyenne awoke in the morning, they were amazed to find that all of the slain wolf men had reverted back to their true forms during the night.

"I guess something so unnatural couldn't be allowed to stand," Long Stride remarked. His left arm had stiffened in the night, and hung limply at his side.

"Or maybe magic can only last so long," Walker speculated. He put a hand on Bowstring's shoulder.

"Come on," he said. "We've got work to do."

Without question, Bowstring followed Walker as he set off down the mountain trail. At the base of the peak, as expected, they came upon the body of Crazy Dog.

Gaping wounds marked his body from throat to ankles; his right arm was torn nearly clean off his shoulder. Strangely, there was not a mark to be seen on his face, and his mouth seemed to be frozen into the semblance of a smile. The carcasses of three dead wolves lay around him.

"Poor Crazy Dog," Bowstring said, shaking his head sadly.

"He died as well as any man," Walker declared, "and better than most."

Struggling somewhat under the dead weight, the two warriors nonetheless carried Crazy Dog's corpse back up the side of the mountain.

They then carried him and the other slain Dog Soldiers a short distance off the mountain trail. They laid them out neatly side by side and placed the remnants of their weapons beside them.

Even young Bowstring knew that, as Cheyenne warriors, they would not want their bodies to be buried in the dirt, as was the practice of some peoples. Far better, they believed, to be devoured by the creatures of the wild: wolves, coyotes, eagles, buzzards. To end up in the belly of a beast was no bad thing. Their bodies were, after all, only flesh. Their spirits were already well on the way to Seyan.

Walker and Bowstring stood in reverent silence as Long Stride sang a plaintive death song that heralded the bravery of their brothers and wished them well on the journey all living things must take.

CHAPTER 13

The sun was high on the third day when the three weary warriors topped a rise and found themselves looking down upon their village in its new location.

From the activity and sound rising up to them, they knew their tribesmen had spotted them. Therefore, even before riding down, they dismounted and, using blankets from their horses, signaled the camp. The manner in which they waved the blankets let those below know how many they had lost in battle: seven of the ten.

Because of this, they were greeted by silence rather than cheers as they slowly rode into the camp. Long Stride and Bowstring had taken the time to paint their faces black, as a sign they had slain their enemies, but Walker's face was bare; even his chalky death's head marking had vanished as mysteriously as it had appeared.

The men of the tribe showed no emotion as the returning warriors dismounted in the center of the village. But wives and mothers were already beginning to wail, as they realized which sons and husbands would not be returning. It was a sound with which Walker was all too familiar; some nights, he even heard it in his dreams.

Walker spoke to no one, but set out for the tipi of his father, where he knew Listens To Elks and the three other chiefs would be waiting to hear what happened. As he drew near to that lodge, its door flap flew open and Snow Dancer raced out. She stopped in front of him, her eyes asking the question her lips couldn't form.

"He's all right," Walker said softly.

A choking sound caught in her throat and her eyes welled. She patted her brother on the arm, then ran on to greet her husband, Long Stride.

Not far away, another woman stood in the doorway of her lodge. She too wanted to run to her man. But Crow Woman was wise enough to know such a gesture would not be welcomed at this moment. So she went back inside the lodge alone, to cry and offer thanks.

That night, long after Crow Woman had pretended to drift off to sleep, Walker remained awake, sitting quietly and staring into the dancing flames of his lodge fire.

Normally, a war party returning victorious would be cause for celebration. But so great had been the cost of this victory that no one felt right celebrating, not even the proud father of Bowstring, whose courage in the battle had been recounted briefly by Walker shortly after their return.

No sounds of joy carried through the night air, but nor was it totally silent. The wails of mourning women could not be shut out, even if Walker had tried.

The wives, mothers, grandmothers, even sisters of those who had died on that frightful mountain peak had already expressed their sorrow by cutting their hair and slashing their faces and legs. They would not wash away this blood for days, and some might leave their scarred legs bared for months to come.

With his own eyes, Walker had seen the inconsolable mother of Daydreamer give action to her grief by sawing off the little finger of her left hand.

The male relatives of the fallen heroes expressed their sorrow in a different, quieter fashion, by unbraiding their long hair and letting it hang loose over their shoulders.

Some had speculated that this was why Walker always wore his hair loose, surmising that in a sense he constantly mourned the dead, both his friends and loved ones and even those he himself had killed in the service of Death. Walker never spoke of it.

A soft sound behind him caused Walker to look back over his shoulder. Crow Woman was sitting up, staring at him with sad eyes.

"Go back to sleep," he said.

"I wasn't asleep."

"If you don't rest," he growled, "you won't be of much use in doing your chores tomorrow."

She didn't reply for a long moment, then quietly said, "Why don't you go see your father, or some of your soldiers?"

"Why don't you shut up and do what I told you?" he snapped. "Go to sleep."

He rose to his feet and pushed his way through the door flap of his tipi before she could reply.

He walked alone without destination around the village. No one who saw him thought anything of it. He often walked thus in the night, nor were there many who would dare intrude on his solitude.

Walker paused for a time, watching as men took down a pair of lodges that stood close together. These had been the tipis of Blue Feather and Bear Killer.

Such was the custom of the Cheyenne when a man died. As soon after death as possible, all his belongings – including his tipi – were given away to villagers who were not his relatives. His widow and children were left with little more than a blanket, and they would go to live with the widow's father or brother.

Blue Feather had not been married long, and had no children, but Bear Killer left behind two small sons.

Walker would make sure they knew about their father and the events that led up to his death. He would tell them a great story of their father's life and of his brave death. Walker, for all that he kept within himself, had a reputation among the people for being an exceptional storyteller, in a nation of storytellers.

He was always much in demand as a guest for dinners or other celebrations for that very reason. A good meal was gladly paid in return for one of his good tales.

It was said, probably truly, that he had learned this skill at the feet of a master, an old Arikara named Stands All Night, who had passed on to him the fine points of storytelling.

Doubtless, had the mood of the village been less somber, Walker would now be feasting on buffalo hump and regaling the other villagers with an only slightly exaggerated retelling of their incredible battle with the wolf men.

As Walker turned to head for the outer edge of the camp, he bumped into a small figure in the dark. It was Long Stride's little sister, Two Doves, carrying a bundle of branches to stoke her family's fireplace.

"I'm sorry, little sister," Walker said gently, kneeling to retrieve a piece of wood he had inadvertently knocked from her hands.

"You know, I'm not so little any more, Walker," she said, the slightest hint of a pout causing her lower lip to protrude.

"No. Of course not," he replied in a conciliatory tone. "You're nearly a woman fully grown."

She smiled at this acknowledgement of her maturity, then hurried past him, only to pull up and turn back toward him.

"Walker?"

"Yes?"

"Thanks for bringing my brother back home alive."

"I had to, Two Doves," he said, smiling. "Or else my sister would have killed me."

Two Doves giggled and trotted on her way.

Two others had witnessed this brief exchange. One was Crow Woman, peering around the door flap of her lodge. The other was the Fox soldier, Lame Calf.

Both thought dark thoughts, best kept to themselves.

Walker did not notice either as he walked a short distance outside the camp. He stood and sucked in great gulps of cool, clean air while staring up at the stars twinkling on and off in the night sky.

"This may not be over," that familiar voice said. Walker lowered his gaze to see Buffalo Boy standing beside him, also stargazing.

"What's that, little man?"

"Your war with Stands Alone," the impish spirit boy replied, shifting his eyes to Walker.

"What do you mean?"

"You heaped fresh insults on him up on that mountain," Buffalo Boy responded.

"None he didn't deserve."

"No doubt," the almost-boy agreed. "But even his spirit guides are bad. His heart is black and is turned against you."

"Then let him come against me," Walker said defiantly. "And I'll feed him that black heart."

"Just be careful," Buffalo Boy said, both his voice and his image beginning to fade away, "that it isn't you that gets eaten."

Walker merely shrugged, then turned back to the village. Once in his tipi, he again sat before the fire, and no one could have read his thoughts as he stared into its light.

He heard a soft rustling sound from behind him, but made no move as Crow Woman's soft arms circled his neck. She said not a word as she pressed her face against the hard muscles of his bare back.

As always, the smell of her sweet perfume seemed to sweep over the both of them. Her tiny hands caressed his chest, and he delighted in the soft crush of her full breasts against him.

He reached behind with his right hand, running it up along the outer swell of her thigh under her dress. He felt nothing but supple flesh, and realized she had removed the restrictive chastity rope from around her middle.

Walker turned, reaching across and behind with his left hand and grabbing Crow Woman by the hair. She offered no resistance as he pulled her forward and around into his lap, wrapping his arms around her.

He buried his face in her luxuriant hair, drinking of the earthy aroma. She moaned into his mouth as he then kissed her hard and deep.

She went limp in his arms as he practically flung her atop his sleeping mat. She raised her hips, allowing him to slide her dress up to her waist, then spread her legs in silent invitation.

The woman gasped as he roughly thrust himself inside her, then bit down on her lower lip as she crossed her legs around his waist and began to rock back and forth in rhythm to his movements.

There was a savagery to Walker's lovemaking that Crow Woman found to be more exciting than she dared admit even to herself. For both, the animal within was loosened without thought or remorse. Her nails bit into the flesh of his broad shoulders, nearly to the point of drawing blood, and the pain she inflicted was returned in kind, to her evident pleasure. Their breath grew deep and heavy, racing faster and faster in perfect unison.

Both man and woman cried out with nearly a single voice as they were swept away in climax. Even then, Walker continued to lie atop her, his elbows preventing his full weight from pressing down upon her slight body. His face was again buried in her hair, and he nibbled lightly at that tender point where her neck met her shoulder.

Her hands slid up and down his back, then snaked their way into his own flowing locks. With arms and legs she gripped him as tightly as she was able, neither ready nor willing to let him go.

Then Crow Woman let out the contented sigh a woman reserves for her husband, and the spell was broken. Walker reminded himself that he should never treat her like a real wife, and he roughly pulled away from her arms.

"It's late," he said gruffly. "Get back to your own bed."

As always when he spoke to her thus, Crow Woman hid her hurt and quietly obeyed him. She rolled off his sleeping mat and crawled over to her own.

Once there, she sat on its edge, not looking at him, and nimbly retied the chastity rope around her middle. By the time she had gotten settled under her buffalo robe cover, Walker was breathing heavily in sleep.

At the sound of this, Crow Woman smiled contentedly, hugging the robe around her and sinking into its warm embrace, pretending it was him.

She could at least take comfort in the knowledge that she had helped send Walker into the sleep he had earned and so desperately needed.

CHAPTER 14

Two nights later, not long before the dawn of a new day, the entire village was mostly asleep. The exception was the two young men who stood watch over the tribe's nearby pony herd. Coyote Friend and his companion Spotted Deer were both conscientious about their duty, but both were also beginning to droop a bit near the end of the night.

It was because of this, or perhaps because of magic, that neither of them heard the faint rustling of the grass behind them. Nor did they see the abomination rising up to their backs.

It could only be described as a giant spider, larger in size than a full-grown horse. Deadly venom dripped from its mandibles as it rose up on four of its legs behind the two men.

Faster than a man can blink, it flashed forward, sinking dark fangs into the back of Coyote Friend's neck. The guard didn't even have the chance to cry out, for the venom injected into the site of the wound paralyzed his vocal chords. He twitched violently, then fell dead to the ground.

Spotted Deer had begun to turn toward his friend as he was attacked, but now found himself to be the giant spider's target. It leaped atop his chest, slamming him to the ground and cutting off the air he needed to cry out in pain and warning.

The spider's hideous mandibles scissored open to either side of the man's throat, then snapped shut with the force of a war axe. Spotted Deer's head was cleanly severed from his shoulders and rolled away in the tall grass.

Crouched low over its last victim, the spider emitted a soft whistling sound. It skittered to one side and around in time to see a dozen painted Pawnee warriors rise up from their hiding places in the grass.

They softly walked past the enormous spider, giving it a wide berth.

The Cheyenne pony herd was their target, and they spread out and began to creep toward it.

Leaving them to their task, the spider quickly set out on spindly legs toward the village laid out below. Nearing its outskirts, it pulled up short as a camp dog leaped in front of it with bared teeth.

As the dog opened its jaws to howl out a challenge, it was caught in the gaze of the spider's multi-faceted eyes. The dog's growl turned into less than a whimper, and it skulked away with its head down and its tail tucked between its legs.

The spider raised up, slowly swinging its black head from side to side as it scanned the encampment. Completing its arc, the head snapped back quickly, its gaze drawn to a single specific tipi. Instinctively, it knew this was the one.

The unnatural creature made almost no sound as it pulled aside the entrance flap to Walker's lodge and eased itself inside. Like spilled water sliding across hard rock, so it moved across the earthen floor of the tipi.

Planting its hairy legs on either side of the sleeping war chief, the beast stared down at its victim. Had it been able, it would have smiled at the sight of the large vein wrapping around the man's throat. One nick of inhuman fangs and the man would bleed out within the span of a dozen heartbeats.

A low moan from nearby caused the spider to pull back in surprise and trepidation. Realizing then that the sound did not come from the man, the spider stepped over him and moved to the second figure it now saw laid out on the tipi's sleeping ledge.

Curious, the spider drew closer, just as Crow Woman sighed in her sleep and rolled over below him. Its eyes widened as her voluptuous form swelled beneath her dress, nearly spilling out as her sleeping robe fell partly away from her.

Never had the beast seen such a vision of delight, and it knew in the moment that it wanted this woman for its own, more even than it wanted to see her man lying dead at its feet.

The spider monster shifted its weight back onto its six hind limbs. Its two forelegs slithered silently under the woman's robes like a serpent.

Crow Woman shuddered slightly in her sleep as the hairy tendrils slid up along either side of her waist, but she did not wake. Insinuating themselves between her arms and body at the pits, the tendrils slowly raised her limp body off the ground.

As her body swung free in the air, the woman's eyes at last began to open. Swimming into view was a black face from her darkest nightmares. Its eyes blazed red in the faint light, and viscous streams oozed from its maw.

Crow Woman's eyes widened in fear and she opened her mouth to scream – but the only sound that escaped was a strangled gasp as the spider tightly clutched her to its chest. The short, black bristles covering its body pricked her tongue.

It then eased its grip slightly, so she could pull her head back just enough to look up into the fearsome visage looming over her. To her fascinated horror, the great black head began to twist and flow like mud upon itself, till it metamorphosed into the head of a man.

Crow Woman had no way of knowing, but the face that leered down at her with undisguised lust was that of the Pawnee shaman Stands Alone. His oily black hair framed a face whose ugly features were distorted even further by the sneering smile that twisted his mouth. His dark tongue licked at his lips in unholy anticipation as he began to pull the woman's face closer to his own.

Then, before he could react, her head snapped forward and to one side. She sank her teeth into his left cheek, biting down until she felt warm blood squirt into her mouth.

Stands Alone cried out in pain, and his spidery tendrils momentarily relaxed their grip on Crow Woman. She seized the moment to suck air into her lungs and then expelled it as a piercing shriek.

The pained shaman's outburst alone had been enough to awaken the lightly sleeping Walker. By the time Crow Woman's scream filled the tipi, he had rolled off the far side of his sleeping mat and sprung to his feet.

In the span of a heartbeat he assessed the danger and recognized its source. His legs coiled under him and then released, launching him up and forward.

Walker landed hard atop the monstrosity, causing it to stagger to one side. He whipped his left arm around Stands Alone's throat, grabbed the wrist of that arm with his right hand and pulled back with all his considerable might.

Stands Alone gagged, nearly swallowing his own tongue as Walker applied pressure to the front of his throat, threatening to crush it.

In desperation, the spider shaman reared up and threw all its weight backwards. Unable to release his grip in time, Walker was carried along with the spider as it flipped onto its back. With the full weight of the monster now atop him, Walker was slammed into the hard-packed dirt floor of the lodge.

Crushing pain tore through his back and ribs as the air was driven savagely from his lungs. His arms fell away from the shaman's throat, and he fought fiercely just to draw the least breath of air back into his stunned body.

Through all this, the spider had never fully released its grip on the woman it held captive. Fearing that Walker may have been mortally injured in attempting to rescue her, Crow Woman found herself in no position to stop the monster as it dashed from the tipi with her firmly in its power.

Still barely able to breathe, Walker nonetheless forced himself to roll over and push himself up to his hands and knees. He convulsed in pain, and his back arched as he spewed the contents of his stomach out on the ground.

He gritted his teeth and shook his head, willing his senses to cooperate. Leaping to his feet, he swayed for but a moment. As much by instinct as by sight, he found his war club and, thus armed, raced out of the lodge.

Screams in the night, coming from women and men alike, brought him up short. Villagers were running about all around him, in all directions. Finally, amid the cacophony, he was able to make out specific words: *Pawnee warriors were inside the village.*

To his left, Walker could just make out the image of the giant spider as it scampered up a ridge hundreds of paces away. Even as its hairy bulk topped the ridge and then began to drop from sight behind it, Walker also glimpsed the struggling captive it carried in its embrace.

Walker took two steps in the same direction, then stopped, brought to a halt by his powerful sense of duty. If Pawnees were in the village proper, he knew they must assuredly be among the tribe's precious ponies as well.

Seeing a familiar figure, Walker raced forward and seized his brother-in-law, Long Stride by the arm. Long Stride spun on him, his own war club poised to strike until he recognized who had grabbed him.

"They're everywhere!" Long Stride exclaimed.

"So are we," Walker snapped harshly. "And we are Cheyenne."

Long Stride paused to take in breath, and nodded his agreement.

"Find as many men as you need," Walker ordered, "and get to the pony herd. We can't lose it."

"What about those in the village?" Long Stride asked.

"Leave the village to me," Walker replied.

Long Stride nodded again, smiling now, then loped off to round up the men he needed.

Walker turned and began to resolutely march toward the center of the village. A Pawnee warrior leaped out of the darkness, lunging at him with a lance.

Walker dodged the thrust, grabbing the shaft of the lance and jerking the Pawnee who held it toward him. Walker drove his forehead into the man's nose, breaking cartilage and dropping him to the ground.

In doing so, the Pawnee lost his grip on the lance, which was still held by Walker, who spun it with one hand and drove it point first down into the fallen Pawnee's belly. He didn't wait for the man to die, but simply left him pinned to the earth and moved on.

Nearby, he saw that a group of his Dog Soldiers, along with some Foxes, Elks and Bulls, had banded together to try to stand against the invaders.

"Ho-ka-hey!" Walker shouted at the top of his lungs. "Ho-ka-hey!"

One of the Dog Soldiers, his lieutenant River Hawk, heard the cry, and his eyes had little trouble finding the imposing figure of his war chief. River Hawk spoke quickly to the other soldiers around him, then led them at a run to the spot where Walker waited.

"Form on me," Walker commanded. Obeying without question, the soldiers fanned out on either side of him to form a wedge.

"Stay with me," he said, "and kill anything that isn't a Cheyenne."

Letting out an ear-splitting war cry, Walker raced forward, with his warriors on either side. As they saw their war chief charging toward them, non-combatant villagers leaped out of their way, or fell to the ground to be leaped over.

The Pawnee soldiers were not so lucky.

Many of them had already stopped fighting their way into the village, intent now on stealing women and any other possession they thought had value.

The looters were the first to be taken down by the wedge of Cheyenne soldiers. Walker brought his war club down on the face of one of the Pawnees, breaking through flesh and bone and trampling on his twitching body as he continued on.

Walker had seized a knife from the Pawnee's belt as he fell, and he used it now on another invader. This Pawnee had the presence of mind to swing his war club at the lead Cheyenne, but Walker blocked it with his own club, then stepped in and shoved the blade of the knife into the Pawnee's stomach.

He had time to see the light of life dim in the Pawnee's eyes before he roughly shoved him aside and continued to move onward.

More Pawnees came out of the darkness, descending on both sides of the wedge of Cheyenne soldiers. In the periphery of his vision, Walker saw River Hawk go down. The next man stepped up to fill in the gap, and the wedge was complete again.

The night was rent with screams of the killers and those they killed. Walker felt the hot splash of blood spattering him from every side, though he could not tell how much of it was coming from Pawnee veins.

A scream issuing from several lungs at once sounded ahead of him. Walker grunted with satisfaction as he saw the source – Lame Calf and yet another band of Cheyenne warriors were charging ahead to meet the phalanx of their advancing brothers.

The Pawnees were caught between the wedge and these new attackers, with no place to run. To their credit, they made no attempt to do so, preferring to die with their enemy looking at their faces and not their backs.

The Cheyenne warriors obliged with fearsome intensity. Walker's arm rose and fell with unwavering fury, the blood of his victims filling his eyes till he could barely see.

And then it was over.

There was no one left to kill.

Still gripped in their killing frenzy, the Cheyenne soldiers cast about for any foe who might still stand against them. But there was none.

With the red haze subsiding, Walker turned back to the spot where he had seen his trusted lieutenant River Hawk fall. The light being thrown off by the nearby tipi that had been set ablaze helped him find his friend, lying under the lifeless body of one of the fallen Pawnees.

Walker grabbed the back of the Pawnee's belt and jerked him up and to one side. As he knelt down, he could see a broad stain of blood in River Hawk's side.

Then he heard a groan, and the fallen Cheyenne opened his eyes.

The first words out of the wounded warrior's lips were: "Did we win, brother?"

"Do you even need to ask?" Walker replied tersely.

He grabbed River Hawk by the forearm and helped him rise to a sitting

"Walker's arm... fell with unwavering fury."

position. The movement caused the soldier to gasp in pain and clutch at the gaping wound in his side.

"I hope dying doesn't hurt this much," he grunted.

"Let's hope you never find out," said Walker. He then called out to two of his Dog Soldiers, and instructed them to carry River Hawk to a doctor who could tend his wound.

Walker remained kneeling on the ground, surveying the aftermath of the attack. Young men were whooping victoriously, and counting second and third coup on the fallen Pawnees who littered the center of the village. Some were busy sawing off fingers and hands from their slain enemies.

One other Cheyenne was neither whooping, nor counting coup, nor retrieving grisly souvenirs. Lame Calf simply stood where he had been when the battle ended, staring intently at Walker.

Walker rose to his feet and walked over to the Fox soldier. Reaching out with his right hand, he gripped Lame Calf by the forearm and smiled.

"You did well tonight, brother," he said to the Fox.

"Only half as well as you, I think," came the reply. "Do you know how many Pawnee you killed?"

Walker blinked, then answered the odd question honestly.

"No."

"I didn't think so," Lame Calf said, then turned and walked away.

Walker stared after him in puzzlement, then wheeled around as he heard his name being called. From between two of the lodges he saw Long Stride come running toward him. He skidded to a halt and sucked in a little extra air before speaking.

"There weren't many of them out there," he began. "I think most of them joined the ones who attacked the village."

"Did they give you much trouble?" Walker asked.

"Not much," Long Stride replied. "And they'll never give anyone trouble again."

"What about the ponies?"

"That's the bad news," Long Stride said. "It's like they didn't even come to steal; not a pony was taken, so far as I can tell."

"Oh, they came to steal, all right," Walker grimly asserted, turning his gaze in the direction in which the spider shaman had fled with the captive Crow Woman.

"Well, they didn't steal ponies," Long Stride continued, unaware of what had transpired in Walker's lodge.

"But they did stampede them. They're nowhere in sight. Except for a few of the ponies staked down inside the village, we don't have a mount left."

"They wanted to make sure we couldn't follow them," Walker declared.

"Who's left to follow?" Long Stride snorted, surveying the carnage around them. "It looks like they're all dead."

"Not all," Walker said tightly, staring intently into the surrounding gloom.

"There's still one of them left for me to kill."

CHAPTER 15

A dark cloud seemed to hang over the Cheyenne village even after the sun began to light the early morning sky. Walker stood alone, surveying the scene.

To the east, he saw a group of the tribe's older boys returning from a grim chore; they had been charged with dragging the bodies of the slain Pawnee invaders out of sight and unceremoniously dumping them. Walker had no way of knowing just how many had been in the raiding party, but he did know that at least twenty of them would never count coup again.

By contrast, only six Cheyenne had been killed: four warriors, a woman and a small boy. A second party had respectfully prepared their bodies and carried them away to a nearby canyon, where they had been laid out with all due honor.

In addition to the tipi that had been burned to the ground, several other lodges had sustained varying degrees of damage. Countless weapons and utensils had been shattered.

From the north, a band of warriors could be seen returning from their own mission. The fact that they were all afoot told Walker they had failed, for they had been dispatched to find and return the tribe's stampeded pony herd.

At the head of this party was Long Stride, and Walker could see he was headed toward the lodge of Listens To Elks. Walker moved to join them, trying to block out the fresh cries of those who mourned for their lost loved ones. There had been too many cries of lamentation heard in the village of late, he thought.

Long Stride and his band were already standing with Listens To Elks and the other three chiefs outside the elder's lodge. Long Stride was clearly waiting until his brother-in-law joined them before he spoke.

"Something's wrong," Long Stride began, once Walker was in their midst. "Unless the horses were being driven, they should have calmed down and come to a halt by now. But though they left much sign, we couldn't catch sight of them anywhere."

"Then maybe they are being driven," said the chief called Blue Raven.

"I don't think so," Long Stride replied. "The Pawnees started them running last night, but we fell on them before they had time to follow the herd."

"Besides," added Walker, "why would they drive them in the opposite direction from their village?"

"It doesn't matter how or why," declared Listens To Elks forcefully. "We have to get our horses back, or we'll be open to attack from every scavenger in the land."

"We'll pack some provisions and set out again," said Long Stride. "The few of us who still have horses will bring them, so we can bunch up the herd when we find them." His eyes sought out Walker's.

"You'll lead us, brother?"

Walker, who had lowered his head to look at the ground, now lifted his face to all who looked upon him. From the shadow of his brow, his eyes looked like smoldering embers, and his voice was low and tight.

"No."

Long Stride took a step toward him, mouth opening to protest, but both motion and words were stopped by Walker's raised hand.

"Hear me," Walker said, in a voice that carried even beyond the circle of warriors.

"You'll lead the band, brother," he said to Long Stride, "and you'll do it well. Move as quickly as you can. Divide the soldiers; a third should go with you, and the rest should stay here to guard the village."

"And what will you do?" Listens To Elks asked his son.

"What happened last night was more than just an attack on our village," Walker declared. "It was an attack on me."

Walker stepped closer to his father and the other chiefs.

"This is no longer between Cheyenne and Pawnee. This is between me and Stands Alone." His fists clenched in barely suppressed rage.

"It was my lodge he entered. My woman he took. My honor he destroyed in front of all the people."

"That's not true, son," said the chief Loves Horses. "No one is honored more by us."

"Then I should act to deserve that honor," Walker asserted. "But I'll have no honor, and our people will not rest easy, so long as that man is still alive."

"Then kill him," Listens To Elks said flatly.

"I mean to, father," Walker replied. "The first chance I get."

He then turned on his heels and began to walk away. He stopped, though, as Long Stride jumped into his path.

"As soon as I have the herd back," Long Stride said, "I'll follow after you."

"I know, brother."

As Walker then continued on toward his tipi, several women came rushing toward him. From their shorn locks and the streaks of blood marring their faces, arms and legs, he knew they were mourners who had lost a loved one.

They made no move to impede him, but rather trotted along behind and to either side of him. As they did, they passed their hands over his bare flesh, leaving streaks of their blood, and cried out to him.

"Kill them all!" one woman wailed.

"Avenge our dead!" shrieked another.

"Don't come home until the rivers run red with their blood!" yet another cried out.

Walker showed no sign that he heard their words, but they knew each was now lodged in his heart, and one by one they fell back away from him.

Now some of the older men began to call out words of encouragement and advice, reminding him that only Pawnee deaths would cause the lamentations of the Cheyenne women to cease.

The sight of a slightly bent figure limping toward him, leaning heavily on a stout branch, caused Walker to stop for the moment. He wanted to step forward and lend a supporting hand to old Bull, but he knew the cussed warrior would take offense. So he stood and waited for Bull to reach him on his own.

"Is this how highly you think of yourself?" Bull snapped at him. "Does the mighty Deathwalker think he can take on the whole Pawnee nation alone?"

"I don't need to kill them all," Walker replied with steely resolve.

"Ahhh," Bull said, arching one eyebrow. "So it's the vengeance trail you mean to ride."

"What I mean to do," said Walker, "is right a wrong that was done to me."

"And if anyone gets in your way?"

"Then I'll kill him."

"Good!" the old man cackled. "That sounds like the man I helped to raise." Bull quickly looked about, to make sure no one was watching, then reached out and squeezed Walker's arm.

"But be careful, boy. Even righteous anger can get you killed. Don't let it blind you or make you forget all I've taught you about being a soldier."

"I've never forgotten anything you've taught me, father," Walker assured him, "and I never will."

"Then what are you waiting for?" Bull groused. He lifted his walking stick and whacked Walker on the arm with it, hard enough to sting.

"Go on. Those Pawnees aren't gonna kill themselves!"

Walker continued on to his tipi, and his spirits rose slightly as he saw that his horse Tall Dog was still tethered to the peg beside it. The pony was leisurely nibbling at the grass around his feet, apparently oblivious to all the furor around him.

"Get ready, brother," Walker said, scratching the pony atop its head. "We're going hunting."

Walker entered his lodge, and was nearly finished packing the weapons and provisions he felt would be needed, when he heard the rustle of his door flap being raised. His sister Snow Dancer stepped into the lodge.

"Shouldn't you be seeing your husband off?" Walker said, looking to his packing rather than at her.

"I will," she replied. "But first I needed to talk to you."

"About what?"

"About this," she said, gesturing at the bundle he was packing.

"Are you truly so hungry for vengeance," she continued, "or is this all about the girl?"

"What are you talking about?"

Snow Dancer stepped closer to him.

"Your tribe needs you, Bird," she pressed. "Your flesh and blood needs you." She reached out and grabbed his arm, causing him at last to look up into her hard eyes.

"She's nothing but a worthless slave," Snow Dancer hissed. "Let the Pawnees have her!"

Walker pulled free of her grasp and rose to his feet, forcing her to take a step back to be able to look up at a face she found vaguely frightening and impossible to read.

"This has nothing to do with Crow Woman," he asserted. "That twisted little man shamed me by taking what was mine, and he'll have to pay for that." Walker shook a finger in her face.

"It's no different than if he had stolen my favorite bow or my war pony. To steal from me is to spit in the face of death – and he'll know that before

I'm done with him."

So good was Walker at showing no emotion save indignation and anger that Snow Dancer was unsure whether he was being honest about his feelings for the slave girl. Nor did he give her the chance to study his demeanor any further, brushing past her and exiting the lodge.

"I hate to say this," said a tiny voice in front of him, "but I think your hag of a sister could be right."

Walker pulled up short, his way blocked by the diminutive Buffalo Boy.

"What do you know?" Walker growled.

"More than you might think," the spirit guide replied.

"I doubt it."

"I know a stolen pony wouldn't have enflamed your heart so much."

"It depends on how good the pony is," Walker said. He attempted to step around his personal pest, but the almost boy hopped back in front of him.

"You know, my friend, that there's nothing wrong with caring about her. She certainly cares about you."

"Pfft," Walker exhaled, reaching out with his left hand. With not too much force he shoved the spirit guide to one side.

Buffalo Boy stumbled, turned sideways, flailed his arms wildly, then fell over right on his shaggy butt. When he hit the ground, he vanished in a puff of smoke.

Striding over to Tall Dog, Walker threw his saddle pad over the pony's back, smoothing it out before preparing to cinch it around its middle.

"Don't draw that too tight," yet another familiar voice said. "You've got to leave him plenty of room to breathe."

"I will," Walker said, the corners of his mouth turning upward slightly as he turned to look at his father.

Listens To Elks walked around to the opposite side of the pony, rubbing its head as Walker tied a rope halter around its nose.

"He's a good horse," the chief commented.

"One of the best," Walker agreed. "I suspect that's why you gave him to me."

"I never gave you anything you didn't earn, son. A good man deserves a good horse. That's what I always tried to teach you to be – a good man."

"I hope your lessons weren't wasted, father."

"They weren't." Listens To Elks turned his head, watching the other men of the village going about their own preparations for the jobs assigned to them.

"Leave a clear trail," he said, turning again to look back at his son. "I'll send soldiers to follow you as soon as I can."

"Let's hope you won't need to."

"Whether they come or not, you'll be all right, Walker. Just remember – it's better to die right than to live wrong."

Walker merely nodded in acknowledgment. Nothing further needed to be said, so Listens To Elks merely patted Tall Dog once more, then walked away.

As he did so, he was passed by an approaching Bowstring. The youth had also managed to hold on to one of his ponies, and was sitting astride it. He pulled it to a halt next to Walker and slid off its back.

"Are you staying here or going after the pony herd?" Walker inquired.

"I'm going with you," the boy declared.

"Oh?" Walker squinted slightly. "I don't recall inviting you."

"A brother doesn't need to ask for help to get it."

"Good words," Walker agreed. "True words. But this trail is only wide enough for one."

"Then I'll ride behind you," Bowstring insisted. "Remember, it's still my fault you have to ride that trail at all."

"No," Walker said, shaking his head. "Whatever mistakes you made were honest ones, and you paid for them all up on that mountain pass."

"That's not what the dead are telling me," Bowstring replied, a pained expression clouding the features of his fair face.

"I had no bad intentions," he continued, "but I've caused bad things to happen to the people. I've got to make them right."

Walker smiled and slapped the youth lightly on his upper left arm.

"Then we'll make them right together, brother. You're welcome to join me."

"Wait up, Walker."

The war chief turned to see a small party of women approaching him, led by old Bull's wife, Morning Sky. She stepped forward and pressed a small bundle into his hands.

"Some extra moccasins," she said. "You never know when you might need them."

"Thank you, mother," he said, accepting the gift.

"It's nothing," she said, starting to turn away, but too slowly, so that he saw the mist in her eyes she sought to hide. "Just kill an extra Pawnee or two for me."

"Gladly."

The other women passed similar bundles to both of the men, containing extra arrows, or tobacco, or food. Two of the women had filled skins made from buffalo paunches with water, and presented them to the soldiers. Each offered words of encouragement and promised to pray for their safe return.

The last to approach them was Long Stride's young sister, Two Doves. She reverently placed a small parfleche pouch in Walker's cupped hands, then slid her own hands to either side of his and squeezed them with gentle firmness.

"Plum cakes, Walker," she said breathlessly, staring up with dazzled eyes at his smiling face. "I made them myself."

"Then I'm sure they'll taste extra sweet, little sister," he replied.

She smiled broadly, then reluctantly stepped back away from him.

Walker took a moment to check his weapons. He did not take his shield with him this time, but was otherwise armed to the teeth. Knife and war club were sheathed in his belt. The panther skin quiver carrying both bow and arrows was slung over one shoulder, and his long spear was in hand.

"Let's go, brother," Walker said to Bowstring, then he lightly swung himself astride Tall Dog. The two warriors kept their ponies to a walk until they were clear of the village.

"Which way?" Bowstring asked.

With two fingers, Walker motioned to the south.

"They'll be heading for home now, I expect," he declared with certainty. "Back to where you first found them."

"He won't be alone," Bowstring said. "The shaman."

"I don't care if he puts the whole Pawnee nation between us," Walker asserted. "And if he does, may Maheo have mercy on them…

"Because they'll get none from me."

CHAPTER 16

Well away from Walker and Bowstring, three Pawnee warriors – the sole survivors of the ill-advised raid against the Cheyenne – pulled their struggling ponies to a halt.

Having been driven on mercilessly through the night, the horses welcomed the respite with wheezing whistles of desperately needed air being sucked into aching lungs. Their coats were slathered with sweat that quickly began to dry into salty streaks rippling across their broad chests.

Dismounting, the warriors slowly walked their steeds for a short distance to let them blow, then rubbed them down and allowed them to stand at rest. When the ponies' breathing returned to nearly normal, the Pawnees poured small amounts of water into cupped hands and let the horses sip sparingly, in brief gulps.

"Where are the others?" one of the Pawnee asked, peering back anxiously along their trail. "Why haven't they caught up with us yet?"

"There are no others," the tall warrior beside him snapped. This man was called Akota, which means Half Journey, and was a leader among their people.

"They're all dead by now," he declared. "Or are wishing they were."

"I can't believe we lost so many," the third Pawnee said.

"Believe what you see," said Half Journey.

"I thought Stands Alone's magic would protect us from the Cheyenne's arrows," the first warrior lamented.

"It might have," Half Journey declared with undisguised disgust, "if he'd kept his mind above his breechcloth."

"You think the woman distracted him that much?"

"I'm saying that even an iruska is a man first. You both saw the way he looked at her."

"I don't care about her," the third warrior stated flatly. "It's who he took

87

her from that has my hairs standing on end."

"Who was that?" the first Pawnee asked.

"The one the Cheyenne call Deathwalker."

"What?" said Half Journey, grabbing the speaker by the arm and turning him sideways. "Are you sure?"

"I saw him with my own eyes," the warrior avowed, "coming from the lodge where Stands Alone captured the woman."

"How do you know it was him?" Half Journey demanded.

"I saw him once before," the warrior said, "on another field littered with Pawnee dead. Even in my sleep, some nights I still see him. It's not a face you ever forget."

"Ee-yah!" exclaimed Half Journey. "I wish a curse on every filthy shaman that walks the earth, including our own. He might just as well have called every demon alive down on us as to make us targets of the Deathwalker!"

"Maybe Stands Alone didn't know," the first warrior offered.

"Oh, he knew," Half Journey replied. "I have no doubt he knew. But he's more full of himself than a ram in heat, and probably believes the Cheyenne is no match for him."

"And you think otherwise?" said the first Pawnee.

"I think I don't want to be around to find out," Half Journey grunted. "Let's go."

To the dismay of his winded pony, the Pawnee leaped back astride it and gigged it in the ribs with his heels.

"What about Stands Alone?" the third warrior asked. "Shouldn't we wait for him?"

"What for?" Half Journey sneered. "He keeps falling farther behind all the time, because of his prisoner. And I think he wants it that way."

Giving a yip, Half Journey urged his reluctant mount to a trot. The other two Pawnees looked at each other, shrugged, then rode after him.

Even as the other Pawnees raced away, Stands Alone was drawing his own mount to a halt in the cover of a small stand of trees. The warriors were long since out of sight, and he smiled at the thought.

Sliding off his pony, the shaman strode back to the second horse he had been leading by its bridle rope. Astride it sat Crow Woman, hands securely bound behind her back.

She said nothing, gave no acknowledgement of his presence at all. Her back was straight as a pole and she stared straight ahead, a look of defiance doing nothing to dim her beauty.

Stands Alone stood next to her pony, gazing up at her with undisguised want. Then his hand went to the place on his cheek into which she had buried her teeth the night before. If anything, the throbbing pain it produced had grown even worse since the shaman had reversed his spell of transformation and had changed back from a spider into his fully human form.

At his touch, the wound sent a fresh wave of pain through his jaw and down his spine. With that, the look on his face became one of spiteful hate. Reaching up, he grabbed the front of the captive woman's dress and roughly jerked her from the horse.

Crow Woman yelped with surprise and fear, then let out a cry of pain as her body slammed hard to the ground.

Moaning, she rolled awkwardly onto her back. Stands Alone stood over her, his feet planted on either side of her waist. There was no mistaking the expression of animalistic desire that caused the man's face to twist even more than it was by nature. Crow Woman gasped at the implications and felt a sickness growing deep in the pit of her stomach. Her legs snapped together, and she tried to roll back onto her side.

The shaman bent and grabbed her by the hair, roughly pulling her back and down. He then dropped, driving a knee into her abdomen. The air whooshed out of her lungs so quickly that she couldn't even cry out from the pain, and her legs parted reflexively.

Taking advantage of the moment, Stands Alone threw himself between her legs, attempting to use his own to pry her limbs even farther apart. She bucked and twisted beneath him, she spit into his leering face, but all to no avail. His left hand began to slide up under the hem of her dress.

Then the woman stopped moving.

Stands Alone had buried his face in the lush carpet of her hair, but now he raised his head to look at her, thinking that she had perhaps passed out. The thought pleased and even excited him.

But now, her eyes were wide open, looking directly into his own. Her facial expression had grown calm, showing no sign now of hatred, fear, or loathing. Indeed, she now even smiled slightly, almost seductively.

"What are you doing?" he asked suspiciously.

"Nothing," she replied meekly. Without prompting, she spread her legs even farther apart. The shaman moaned softly as he felt his loins now grind against hers.

"No more fighting?" he asked.

"What's the point?" she purred. "Either way, you'll get what you want, so why fight?"

His eyes narrowed and he stared sharply down at her, still leery of some trick. But when she made no further move, he decided she had indeed decided to accept the inevitable. Consumed with the desire that had been burning at his core all through the night, he reached down to pull his breechcloth out of the way.

"Hold on," she said soothingly. "What's your hurry? We have all the time in the world." She moved one leg and began to rub it up and down the back of the man's legs. "And the more time you take, the better it'll be for both of us."

Stands Alone grinned down at her, made a grunting sort of chuckle. She smiled back.

"Do you know what the best moment of all will be?" she inquired.

"What's that?" he replied, using his hands to spread her thighs still farther apart. He didn't notice that her eyes suddenly turned icy.

"The moment when I see the Deathwalker standing behind you, watching you act like a bull in rut with his woman…just before he slits your throat."

"What?" Stands Alone gasped, not sure if he had heard her correctly.

"There he is now!" she exclaimed.

Stands Alone cried out in fear, throwing himself off the woman and rolling defensively over and to one side. His eyes darted back and forth frantically, but no one was there. Then he heard the woman.

She was laughing.

"Shut up!" he screamed. He threw one leg back across her so he was practically sitting on her chest. His right hand slapped her face sharply, but she continued to laugh.

"Shut up!" he screamed again. He backhanded her across the mouth, causing her head to snap over to one side. Then he slapped her again, and yet again, before pausing. Now the only sound was his own labored breathing.

"Don't stop!" she yelled up at him, again smiling. "Hit me again, as many times as you like. Mount me like the animal you are!"

"Are you insane, woman?" he hissed.

"One of us is," she snapped. "Me? I'm just giving my man all the time he needs to catch up to us."

"Your man?" he sneered. "Don't you mean your master? You are just a slave, aren't you?"

"Yes," she said. "I am just a slave. But I'm Deathwalker's slave. And make no mistake, you sorry little man – he is coming for me."

A cold smile again flitted across her lips.

"And for you."

All desire drained from him, Stands Alone rose unsteadily to his feet, choosing to ignore the slight tremble in his legs. Reaching down, he likewise pulled Crow Woman up, then shoved her toward the horse she had been riding.

"Believe what you want," he told her as he slung her up onto the pony's back. "The truth is, he's probably already found some skinny little Cheyenne girl who'll gladly warm his bed up nicely."

For an instant, an image of Two Dove's sweet face leaped unbidden into Crow Woman's mind, then was gone.

"Tell yourself that, Pawnee," she said. "Maybe it'll help you sleep at night."

Stands Alone made no reply, simply turning his back to the woman and heading for his own pony. Still, before he jumped up to its back, he turned his head and peered back at the trail behind them.

He saw nothing.

CHAPTER 17

Walker drew rein on Tall Dog, gently pulling him to a halt. His eyes slowly and carefully scanned the horizon ahead. Satisfied that no one was near, he slid off Tall Dog's back. Bowstring remained on his mount, leaning forward to rest his crossed arms on its neck.

"Something happened here," Walker said, sinking to one knee. "A struggle of some sort."

He couldn't know that this was the very spot where Stands Alone had attempted unsuccessfully to rape Crow Woman. What he could see was the broken grass stalks and scuffed earth that spoke of the struggle.

"Are the two riders together still well back from the others?" Bowstring asked.

"It seems so," Walker replied. He picked up a ball of horse dung from the ground, crumbled it in his hand, sniffed at it. "But they're also still well ahead of us."

"And you still think they're bound for the Pawnee camp I raided."

"It seems likely," Walker said. "They're still headed south, but are beginning to veer to the east as well."

"Good," said Bowstring. "That means we can cut the distance between us quickly."

"How so?"

Bowstring motioned to a faint trail that headed off to their left, running toward a range of hills.

"Because we were driving a herd of horses before," he explained, "we had to skirt around those hills. But alone, we can cut right through them and maybe head off the Pawnees. We'll at least close the distance."

"No," Walker said, recognizing the hills Bowstring was indicating.

"First coup is mine!" the youth exclaimed, interrupting Walker. "Yaaah!"

Bowstring punched his heels into his pony's ribs, sending it off at a gallop.

"Stop!" Walker called after him. But the boy's exuberant laughter and the pounding of his pony's hooves deadened his ears to the war chief's command.

"I'd just let him go," said Buffalo Boy, popping into sight next to Walker. "Stupid people are meant to die."

"Maybe so," Walker assented. "But we all act stupid sometimes."

"I don't!" the spirit guide insisted.

"Of course not." Walker turned and leaped astride Tall Dog.

"You're going after him, aren't you?" Buffalo Boy huffed.

"I'm going after him."

"I might as well be talking to a rock."

"A rock wouldn't put up with you like I do."

"Ha-ha," Buffalo Boy said sarcastically. "Are you sure you weren't meant to be a clown instead of a soldier?"

This time, Walker's only reply was to urge Tall Dog forward at the run. They raced past Buffalo Boy, who stood with hands on hips watching them, scowling. Then, as the cloud of dust they left behind them slowly disappeared, so did he.

Leaning low over Tall Dog's neck, Walker asked the faithful pony to pour on all the speed he could muster. Bowstring also rode a good horse, though, and the narrowness of the trail leading through the hills would make it difficult to get out ahead of him. Already, Walker felt sure he would not catch up to the impetuous youth in time. Still, he continued on.

When the winding valley trail briefly widened and straightened out ahead of him, Walker slapped Tall Dog across the buttocks with his quirt. Stung and surprised, the pony increased its speed.

Glancing back over his left shoulder and seeing Walker gaining on him, Bowstring laughed and tried to cajole more speed from his own mount. But in a straightaway, few horses were a match for Tall Dog, and the distance between the two soldiers closed quickly.

When they were at last neck and neck, Walker reached out and grabbed the bridle of Bowstring's pony. As soon as his right hand closed around it, his left jerked back on his own reins.

Tall Dog's hooves dug into the hard earth, sending clods flying as he slid to a halt. The head of Bowstring's pony snapped sharply to one side, and it too reluctantly stopped, showing its displeasure at this treatment by bucking and kicking back with its hind legs. Bowstring, still smiling broadly, patted the horse's neck and spoke soothingly to it to settle it down.

"Well rode, brother!" Bowstring said to Walker.

"You idiot!" Walker snapped.

"What?"

"Do you know where you've led us?"

Bowstring, clearly confused by Walker's vehemence, now looked warily about on all sides. Nothing seemed untoward, and his confusion merely mounted.

"I don't understand. It looks like a perfectly good trail to me, and it'll save us some time."

"Save time," Walker muttered, sighing heavily. "We'll be lucky if we save our skins."

"I don't understand."

"That's because you have mush for brains." Walker shook his head. "Here's a question for you, Bowstring; if this is such a good shortcut…why didn't the Pawnees take it?"

"I don't know," the young warrior responded, sounding more uncertain.

"Of course you don't. But you'll find out soon enough."

"What does that mean?" Bowstring demanded. "If there's something wrong with the trail, let's just turn around and go back the other way."

"And fall even farther behind the Pawnees? No. Besides, we've come too far. By now they know we're here; even if we turned back, they wouldn't just let us go in peace."

"Who? Who are you talking about?"

"Like I said, young bull – you'll find out soon enough."

At a light touch of his master's heels, Tall Dog loped forward past the dumbfounded Bowstring, taking the lead. Shamed into silence, the youth followed close behind, continually eyeing the walls of the shallow canyon.

Just as night was beginning to fall, they emerged into a slightly wider strand of the valley floor, and here Walker reined his pony to a halt. Bowstring pulled up alongside him.

"What is it?" Bowstring asked.

"I think this will be the place," Walker replied.

"And what is this place?"

"Use your eyes," Walker said. "Look around you. It's a place of death."

Only then did Bowstring notice that they were not the only men in this canyon. They were merely the only *living* men.

On either side of them, alone and in small clusters, the bodies of dead warriors littered the canyon floor. It was clear they had met their end many summers ago, but hanks of hair and shreds of leathery skin were still attached to the skeletal remains.

A sighing sound arose in young Bowstring's ears, and he was surprised to realize it was that of his own breathing. No other noise could be heard in this vale of decay. Not even the slightest whistle of wind disturbed the site. There was no cawing of birds, no chirping of insects. It was as if all that made the world alive had left this place.

A battle had been fought here; weapons scattered on the ground and broken skulls and limbs attested to that. Corpses were not only strewn about the floor of the valley, but also along its sloping sides. Gaping mouths seemed still to be shouting unheard war cries. The empty sockets that once contained eyes seemed to glare at him from every direction. He shivered slightly as if their bony fingers were playing up and down his spine, and he turned with troubled eyes to his companion.

"Who are they?" he asked, in a voice barely above a whisper.

"They were a war party of Lakotas," Walker replied. He spoke in normal tones, but with a hint of reverence.

"You were barely off the teat when they came to our village, Bowstring. They were led by a warrior named Mountain Snow. I was young myself, but I remember he looked like his name." Walker waved a hand back and forth above his head. "With a streak of white hair that ran from front to back."

"Why had they come?" Bowstring asked.

"They were on the trail of a band of Hohe – Assiniboins. The Hohes had made off with several Lakota ponies and had left Mountain Snow's young brother dead from the waist down."

"They're a bad bunch," Bowstring snarled, hocking up phlegm and spitting it out in a show of disgust.

"Yes," Walker agreed. "Every right thinking Cheyenne and Lakota knows enough to hate them…and to fear them, too."

Bowstring expelled a heavy chuff of air. "I'm not afraid of them."

"Maybe that's because you've never faced their spears," Walker replied testily. "I have." He gazed sternly at the youth. "You've heard the stories of how the Hohe drove us out of our first homes in the long ago time?"

"Tales told to frighten children," Bowstring replied dismissively.

"Tales meant to frighten men," Walker corrected. "Because they're true."

"So you say."

"So I say."

Bowstring shifted uncomfortably. "So, what happened to the Lakotas?"

"Mountain Snow was no fool," Walker continued. "He knew from the story told by their tracks that the Hohe raiding party had more warriors

"Who are they?"

than he did. So he asked some of us to join him."

"Did you?" Bowstring eagerly prompted.

"No."

Bowstring made no attempt to hide the disappointment in his eyes. "Why not?"

"It wasn't because we didn't want to," Walker assured him. "We were as hot for Hohe blood as he was. But the chiefs forbid us to go."

"Why?"

"As luck would have it, we were in the midst of the sacred arrow renewal ceremony, a holy time. To break it off to go to war would have brought all manner of ills upon us."

"Everybody knows that," Bowstring agreed.

"Every Cheyenne knows it," Walker replied. "We had no choice but to turn down the Lakota's request, at least for a few days.

"But Mountain Snow wouldn't wait. He said he thought we were just being cowards."

"No!" Bowstring exclaimed, amazed and appalled that anyone could believe such a thing of the Cheyenne.

"Yes. And because of his words, some of us were ready to fight *him*. But we were stopped by those who knew better. So we did no more than throw insults at the Lakota as they rode from our village.

"I said Mountain Snow was no fool. But because of hate and anger, that day he talked like one, and acted like one. He led his men here, where the Hohes were waiting in ambush."

"Then what happened?"

"Then they died," Walker replied flatly. "I'm sure they took plenty of Hohes with them – their bodies reside here too – but in the end every last one of the Lakota fell.

"There were so many wails of sorrow from the Lakota camp after this that even today you can still hear some of them being carried on the wind." Walker paused, remembering in his mind.

"Later, we sent a party to the Lakota camp. Along with the news of what had happened to their sons and fathers, we brought gifts to the families of the fallen, and explained to their chiefs why we had not ridden with Mountain Snow and his men.

"The Lakota chiefs understood that we had done no wrong in the affair. They accepted our gifts and our grief, and laid no blame on us.

"But from that day to this, the place of the massacre has been haunted, and is taboo to Lakota and Cheyenne alike."

"I didn't know," Bowstring said meekly.

"I know you didn't," Walker replied. "But you'll learn that what we don't know is even more likely to kill us than what we do know."

Walker slid off Tall Dog's back, and Bowstring followed suit.

"Now what?" the youth asked.

"Our horses are bound to be tired from carrying their own weight and ours for so long. We'll walk them for a ways."

For a time, the only sound was that of footfalls, of the horses and of the men. Bowstring kept looking up to either side, staring at the grim human remains.

He therefore didn't notice those lying on the ground directly in front of him, until his foot slid off an exposed leg bone. He staggered off balance before righting himself.

"Be careful," Walker snapped. He knelt down beside the corpse and straightened the bones Bowstring had kicked out of place.

"I don't understand" the youth said.

"What?"

"Why do you show such concern for dead men?" Bowstring asked. "Especially since some of them are our enemies."

"A man should always show respect to the innocent," Walker explained.

"I'd hardly call a damned Hohe innocent," Bowstring snorted.

"All the dead are innocent," Walker said, "because they've left the deeds of their lives – the good and the bad – behind them."

"I suppose," said Bowstring. "But I still think –"

"Shhh!"

Walker stood, motioning for Bowstring to remain silent. He cocked his head, listening.

"I don't hear anything," said Bowstring.

"You might, if you shut up."

Bowstring scowled but did as he was told. He'd begun to learn that it was wise to do so, when the words came from the Deathwalker.

At first, he still heard nothing. Then the sound crept in on his senses. It was like the wind, but not the wind. Like the buzzing of bees, but not alive. Almost like the wails of grieving women, but in a whisper.

Walker tapped his shoulder, then directed his gaze upward. On both sides of them, high on the walls of the valley, bubbling clouds of fog seemed to be rising from every rock crack and crevice.

Like slow water it flowed down the slopes. Bowstring felt a coldness run through him as the first thin tendrils rolled across his feet.

"We should get out of here!" he said hoarsely.

"It's too late to run," Walker replied. "Stand your ground."

So they did, as the thickening fog continued to build around them until they stood knee deep in it.

A new sound, only slightly muffled, came from beneath the cover of the fog. It was a clacking sound that reminded Bowstring of nothing so much as a game of chance that involved the throwing of bones.

Then, directly in front of the two soldiers, a plume of fog shot upward as an object sprang from its cover. It was the body of a man.

Or what had been a man, for it could not be called so now. Rather, it was the corpse of one of the fallen Lakota warriors, its bones barely held together by the thin remnants of his flesh, muscle and tendons.

"Maheo!" Bowstring gasped.

More plumes of fog erupted into the air, on all sides of them. And each plume left in its wake the upright body of a Lakota.

At first they made no move, standing stiffly and staring blankly with their empty eye sockets. Then, one by one, those sockets became filled with a faint red glow.

The first risen corpse slowly moved his head from side to side. The stiff movement caused a sucking sound, as when a fallen log is lifted free from oozing mud. All the non-dead warriors began to twist and turn in place, stretching limbs that should have remained in forever sleep.

One dead man took a halting step forward on legs long grown unaccustomed to walking. He swayed unsteadily, like a newborn colt, and nearly fell before righting himself. With his glowing red eyes boring into the two Cheyenne, he lurched toward them, followed by his brethren.

"This isn't possible!" exclaimed Bowstring.

"Everything under the sky is possible," Walker replied with more calmness than he truly felt.

"What are they?"

"Siyuhks," said Walker. "Dead men whose spirits refuse to leave them. These look angry."

"Why would they be angry?"

"Maybe the dead aren't as forgiving as the living," Walker suggested. "Maybe they still blame us for what happened to them."

Several of the non-dead warriors had bent at the waist, dipping their hands down into the swirling fog that still blanketed the valley floor. When they straightened back up, those hands now held the weapons that had fallen from their lifeless fingers on the day of the ambush.

"It seems you're right, Walker," Bowstring said.

Walker ignored him, taking a step toward the advancing siyuhks and raising his empty left hand to them.

"Hold up, brothers," he called out to them, nodding as they came to a halt.

"We have no need to meet as enemies," Walker continued. "After you were cut down by the Hohes, we Cheyenne made our peace with the brothers you left behind." He tapped his own chest, then motioned toward Bowstring.

"My young brother and I also follow enemies who stole from us. We meant no disrespect to you or to your resting place by coming here. Let us pass in peace, and your honor will be sung about by Cheyenne fires for as long as I live." He swept his steely gaze over all of them.

"You have the word of Deathwalker."

When his speaking stopped, the pall of silence again descended on the valley. The gaunt Lakotas looked back and forth at each other. A few jaws snapped open and shut in wordless communication.

Then, as if of one mind, they raised their weapons high and charged toward the two Cheyenne. No war cries could issue from the dry remnants of their throats, but their intent was clear.

Only Cheyenne deaths would satisfy them.

CHAPTER 18

All color drained from Bowstring's face. Like most Cheyenne, he held great fear of ghosts. He made to jump on his pony's back, meaning to make a run for it, but Walker grabbed his shoulder and pulled him back down.

"Forget that," Walker said. "We've got to fight them."

"Fight them? How can we fight spirits?"

"They look like flesh and blood to me, boy…or at least the remnants of it. And anything of the flesh can be touched. Can be killed."

The words had barely left his tongue when one of the siyuhks slammed into Walker, knocking him off his feet. Even as he fell, Walker grabbed the siyuhk by the throat with his left hand, pushing him back. His right hand, into which his war club had seemed to magically leap, swung across his body.

The stone head of the club smacked into the siyuhk's skull. With a sickening crack it snapped to one side, nearly severed from its spine. Walker maintained his grip on the non-dead creature's throat as he rose back to his feet. He raised the thrashing, skeletal body above his head and threw it at a cluster of other advancing siyuhks, sending them scattering.

"See what I mean, brother?" he said to Bowstring, who was staring at him with bulging eyes, his mouth open slackly. "Now fight them like you would any other man!"

The siyuhk Walker had thrown away awkwardly regained his feet. He was a grotesque sight, with his head still hanging sideways and downward at an angle. He reached up blindly, taking his head in both hands and pushing it back atop his shoulders. As he did, the bones seemed to knit back together. The dead warrior swiveled his head in a circle, with much crunching and crackling, then began to advance once more toward the Cheyenne.

"Just like any other man?" Bowstring said, his voice cracking.

Walker shrugged. "So they may take a little more killing, that's all." He smiled tightly. "Remember…that's what I do best."

Letting out an ear-piercing war cry, Walker leaped forward. This time he struck the dead Lakota so hard that its head was ripped completely free and sent bouncing away into the cover of the rolling fog.

Gripping the long handle of his war club with both hands, he brought it back in a savage backhand swing. The sharpened edge of its head tore through the tatters of flesh to the spine underneath, snapping it in two. The siyuhk instantly dropped where it stood.

Walker's head twisted to one side as he heard the sound of more bone breaking. He saw that Bowstring had just split the skull of yet another Lakota warrior. The youth raised one foot to the siyuhk's abdomen and gave it a great shove that sent it falling back into the path of some of its brethren.

"Keep moving," Walker called out to him. The newly revived dead men were all still walking slowly and awkwardly. That made speed as great a weapon for the Cheyenne as any other.

Using a large rock as a springboard, Walker leaped into the air and came down right in the midst of a cluster of siyuhks. He clubbed the heads off two of them before either could react.

He ducked as one of the non-dead swung a hatchet at him, then drove his shoulder into the off balance siyuhk, lifting him off his feet and slamming him to the ground.

A cry of pain caused him to turn. Bowstring was holding a hand to his left cheek; blood could be seen seeping through his fingers. The siyuhk who had cut him now drew back his knife to strike again, but Bowstring broke his wrist with a blow from his war club. He next grabbed the Lakota by the hanging flesh of his sunken chest and swung him around to slam into yet another siyuhk.

Letting himself be momentarily distracted nearly proved fatal for Walker. Only his quick reflexes enabled him to twist away from the attack of another once living warrior. Even at that, the siyuhk's war club glanced off the side of Walker's skull.

Walker shook off the jolt of pain that ripped through his head. He drove the heel of his right foot into the siyuhk's left knee. Bone snapped and rotted tendons gave way, dropping the warrior to one knee.

For the shortest of moments, Walker stared down into the sallow face of the Lakota, sought to look beyond the red glow that filled its eye sockets, hoping to find some still living trace of the man he had been. But all he saw was the emptiness of death, before bringing down his war club to shatter the siyuhk's skull.

Nearby, Bowstring was locked in hand-to-hand struggle with another reanimated Lakota. The Cheyenne swung both arms wide; as he did so, the dry arm bones of the siyuhk popped loose from their sockets and dropped limply to its sides. Freed up, Bowstring sank the sharp side of his war club's head into the siyuhk's chest, sending it toppling over backwards.

Bowstring turned from side to side, looking for his next foe. Seeing nothing but a circle of fallen Lakotas around him, he relaxed and threw a smile in Walker's direction.

The smile vanished, though, as the spirit-driven Lakota bodies began to rise back up around him, grim reminders of the difficulty in slaying those who are already dead.

Walker stepped to move to Bowstring's aid, but he pulled up when yet another pale ghost warrior lurched in his path. This siyuhk seemed slightly less decayed than his brethren, as if he had clung more stubbornly to life. Like them, he had no eyes save for the glowing fire in his dark sockets, but more flesh and muscle still clung to his bones. And a thin streak of white could clearly be seen amidst the patch of dark hair that rode atop his head.

This was Mountain Snow, leader of the doomed band of Lakotas.

Walker reflexively took a step back away from the siyuhk. When he did, his right foot came down on and crushed through the rib cage of a slain Hohe who lay behind him. His foot became entangled in the bone, causing him to stumble and fall backward.

As he did, the once living Mountain Snow leaped toward him, rode his body as it slammed hard into the ground.

The air whooshed from Walker's lungs, taking some of his strength with it. With no similar need to breathe, the siyuhk had the advantage. He raised high a bony hand clutching a flint knife and brought it down toward the Cheyenne.

Walker was barely able to twist his head to one side, felt hair being pulled from his scalp as the knife blade barely missed flesh and plunged into the ground. Kicking his legs, he was able to pitch the siyuhk off his chest and to one side.

Rolling atop the siyuhk, Walker dropped his war club and used both hands to grab Mountain Snow's right wrist. With a savage twist, he broke the Lakota's arm, then seized his foe's knife as it fell from limp fingers. In one smooth move, Walker brought its blade to rest against the Lakota's exposed throat.

But he did not make the killing slice.

"Stop!" he yelled, as loudly as his still aching lungs would allow.

Though they seemed unable to speak, the undead Lakota could apparently hear well enough. Those who had encircled Bowstring now froze in their tracks. Both they and Bowstring turned to look at Walker.

"Can you understand me?" Walker asked of Mountain Snow in the Lakota tongue, staring intently at the foe who lay beneath him.

The red gleam in the siyuhk's eye sockets seemed to flare even brighter. Slowly, he nodded his head.

"Can you speak?"

Mountain Snow's jaw opened, but the only thing that came from his mouth was a small gray moth that floated out and then flittered away on tiny wings. But then air could be heard expelling from the remnants of the siyuhk's lungs and a sound issued forth, dry as jerked beef.

"Yesss."

"Then can we sit and talk as men?" Walker asked.

Mountain Snow silently studied the Cheyenne's face, looking for signs of either fear or deceit. When he saw neither, he again spoke in his voice of death.

"Talk."

Walker nodded and removed the knife from his foe's throat. He rolled off the siyuhk and helped pull him to a standing position.

Seeing the actions of their once and ever leader, the other Lakotas lost interest in Bowstring. He watched dumbfounded as they shuffled past him to stand behind Mountain Snow. Bowstring joined the group, making sure to keep all the Lakotas in front of him. Walker made a sweeping gesture toward all of them, then began to speak.

"Killing us will do you no good," he said, "for we would die with clean hearts. Our spirits would leave and travel to the Hanging Road, to Seyan and the great beyond.

"But you will still know no peace. Your bodies will turn to dust, and your spirits will stay trapped in this place of shame. That's not a good thing."

"Nooo," Mountain Snow agreed.

Walker went on to explain to the Lakotas why his people had not joined them in their fight with the Hohe. He told them of the compensation the Cheyenne had given to the Lakotas' families to help ease their grief. He told them that the memory of them and the pride of their valiant deaths were still held in the hearts of every Lakota and Cheyenne. He told them all.

"Disturbing your spirits today was a mistake," Walker concluded. "But that's all it was. There was no evil intent in our hearts." He gestured toward Bowstring.

"My little brother and I will do whatever it takes to make this right. Tell us what we can do to put your spirits at rest."

Mountain Snow lowered his head, staring silently down at the ground. When he raised it, the red fires in his eye sockets seemed now to glow with more light than heat. He swallowed dryly, then spoke.

"Your little brother…is kind of stupid."

Walker smiled, nodded his agreement.

"Sometimes. But he's young. I did stupid things when I was young. Maybe you did, too."

Mountain Snow swiveled his head slowly from side to side, gazing over the battlefield where he and all his men had fallen in defeat.

"Sometimes," he said, "even when I was not so young."

Walker nodded again.

"I think your heart is true," Mountain Snow croaked, "and so are your words."

"They are. Now tell me what you want, and I'll do it."

An expression of sadness and great weariness clouded the remnants of Mountain Snow's face before he replied.

"We've been here too long, to no good end. Will you and your young friend smoke a pipe on our behalf?"

"If that's what you want," Walker replied.

"If we let our spirits go," Mountain Snow said, "they'll be able to ride the smoke away from this burial ground. We'll be able to move on to the land beyond."

"Then that's what we'll do."

"One other thing, Cheyenne, if it's not too much to ask."

"If it's in my power, it'll be done."

"When I left for this place, I left behind my brother. And a son."

Walker, knowing that time passes differently for the dead than for the living, did not feel the need to tell the siyuhk that his brother had doubtless long since passed away from his horrible wound.

"In your own time," Mountain Snow continued, "when you've finished your own business…could you find them, and tell them what became of me? Tell them about this day. Tell them I was thinking of them."

"The first chance I get, brother," Walker assented, "I'll seek them out. I'll tell them you died well, and took many of your enemies with you."

"Then, that's all I ask."

Walker nodded and moved over to where Tall Dog still stood. The horse was skittish, fearful of the dead things he sensed all around him, but he calmed down as Walker spoke soothingly to him. He stood still as Walker fished into the provisions pouch slung over his mount's back, removing at last a small red stone pipe.

"You don't really mean to do this, do you?" Bowstring hissed.

"Why not?"

"They tried to kill us, for Maheo's sake! We don't owe them anything!"

"The boy's right," piped in a childlike voice.

Walker looked past Bowstring to see Buffalo Boy squatting atop a nearby boulder, sucking fiercely on a long blade of grass.

Mountain Snow also turned to look that way; apparently, having one foot in the spirit world enabled him to also see and hear the impish spirit guide.

"Besides," Buffalo Boy continued, "it'll take too much time. Time you don't have, time that'll allow the Pawnees to flee ever farther away from you."

"I wouldn't pay too much attention to this little runt," offered Mountain Snow. "He smells like trouble to me."

"Then you have a good nose," Walker replied. "Or what's left of one, anyway." He then stepped close to Bowstring.

"We smoke the pipe."

Bowstring glared at him, teeth clenched. Then the muscles of his jaw relaxed, and he nodded curtly.

"We smoke the pipe."

"Good," said Walker, smiling and slapping Bowstring on the arm.

"What about me?" Buffalo Boy demanded petulantly. "Do my words mean nothing?"

"Less than nothing," said Walker. Bowstring frowned, not sure who the war chief was addressing.

Walker sat down on the ground in front of Mountain Snow, and Bowstring joined him. Among other things, Walker always carried a small amount of tobacco in the medicine pouch at his waist, and he now fished a goodly portion of it out, to fill his pipe. As he did so, Bowstring quickly and efficiently started a small fire before them.

Walker held a thin, dry stick into the fire until the end ignited, used it to light the tobacco. He sucked on the pipe a time or two to ensure it stayed lit. Holding the pipe with both hands, bowl outward, he presented it reverently to the four directions of the wind.

He then took a deeper puff from the pipe, filling his lungs with its smoke. With eyes closed, he held it there, feeling the familiar burn in his chest. He exhaled at last, expelling a light gray cloud out through his mouth and nostrils.

He passed the pipe to Bowstring, who followed his example. The youth kept the smoke inside a little too long, though, which caused him to cough slightly as he exhaled. Walker thought he detected what might have passed for a smile turning up the corners of Mountain Snow's dry and cracked lips.

The two Cheyenne continued to pass the pipe back and forth, until a fair sized cloud of smoke was rising skyward above their heads.

Walker then began to softly sing a song. It was one of many he had learned in his time at the knee of old Bull. Such songs often proved useful in driving away various types of spirits. But this song, its words and its tune, were merely intended to help speed a spirit on its journey to the bosom of Maheo.

The bodies of the reanimated Lakotas began to twitch and jerk. The mouth of one of them dropped open as if it had been broken, and a blue-white wave of smoke seemed to regurgitate from it.

In the midst of the smoke could be seen, dimly, the face of a man, the man who had inhabited this body before it had been killed by the Hohe and ravaged by time. This was his spirit, and it seemed to be drawn to the rising tobacco smoke.

One by one, the spirits of the other siyuhks were expelled from their bodies. As the spirits left, the earthly bodies crumbled into empty piles of flesh upon the earth. One by one, these spirits merged with the smoke and rose with it toward the sky.

As was fit, the last of the Lakotas to give up the ghost was Mountain Snow. He stepped close to Walker and clasped a cold hand on his shoulder.

"My thanks, brother," he said, as the glow faded from his sunken sockets and the life force within began to spill from between his lips.

"Live well again," Walker replied, as Mountain Snow's now empty body fell backwards away from him.

The ghostly image of the Mountain Snow that was began to rise slowly upward. He gazed down one last time, and his wispy voice could be heard softly.

"Beware the Pawnee horsemen," were the last words spoken by the Lakota before he and his voice faded away to nothingness.

"Hmmph," snorted Buffalo Boy. "What kind of great spirit is he? Since you're chasing Pawnees, that warning seems to be pretty obvious!"

"Don't be so sure," Walker retorted. "The words of the dead can have more than one meaning."

CHAPTER 19

Stands Alone sat staring sullenly into the bubbling skin kettle suspended above the fire in his lodge, as if angry that its contents were not reaching a boil quickly enough to suit him.

A soft shuffling sound pulled his attention to one side, where his captive was shifting about in an effort to get more comfortable. Crow Woman sat with her hands tied in front of her, and a rawhide lariat was looped around her neck and tied to one of the lodge poles.

The Pawnee shaman smiled at her, and she froze still. If he noticed the look of revulsion on her face he paid it no mind. He turned his attention back to his stew.

"Stands Alone!" a voice called from outside.

The shaman grunted in annoyance and rose to his feet. Casting another cold look at Crow Woman, he crossed to the entrance of his lodge and pushed through the flap over the doorway.

Outside, six eminent men of the tribe stood in a small cluster. At their head was Half Journey, the warrior who had led the fateful raid on the Cheyenne village.

Not far beyond them, Stands Alone was mildly surprised to see the rest of the villagers had dismantled their tipis and were moving away to the south. The foremost among them was already crossing a shallow loop of the Rope River.

The shaman had been well aware that the time was drawing near when the tribe would make the move from this temporary encampment. The summer hunting period had ended and it was now time to move back to their permanent earthen lodge settlement, where they would harvest the maize they had planted some three moons ago and lay in provisions for the coming winter.

But he had not known that today was the day of the move, nor had anyone seen fit to make mention of it to him.

"What's going on?" he asked of no one in particular.

"We're moving back to the place of the corn," Half Journey stated.

"I can see that," Stands Alone replied contemptuously. "Why has no one come to strike my tipi for me?"

"Because you're not coming with us," Half Journey said flatly.

"Oh? Why not?" The shaman felt sure he knew the answer, but he wanted the words to be spoken.

Half Journey looked at the others, who nodded at him, before he voiced his reply.

"The tribe has decided to disown you," he said.

"And why have they decided to do that?" Stands Alone felt the anger rising within him, yet at the same time he was enjoying watching these mighty warriors as they squirmed beneath his fearful gaze.

"It's been coming for a long time, *iruska*," said Half Journey, uncowed by either the shaman's eyes or his power.

"It is *Tirawa* the sky-dweller who rules the universe and commands the lesser gods. Some of us fear that you've grown so arrogant and sure of your prowess that you've begun to think you're as great as these gods, maybe even as great as Tirawa himself."

"Maybe I am," Stands Alone hissed.

Half Journey's eyes narrowed. Whether the shaman's words showed mere arrogance, thoughtless blasphemy or utter madness, he wasn't sure. But he was now sure he and his brothers had chosen the right course of action.

"Every man makes a journey," the warrior declared, "and has the right to choose his own path. But he doesn't have the right to drag others along with him."

"Just say what you mean," Stands Alone snapped impatiently.

"You didn't bother to tell us that the village you took us to raid was that of the killer of men."

"Would it have mattered? Are our brave warriors so afraid of the Deathwalker?"

"The mountains themselves are afraid of him, and with good reason," Half Journey declared. "Wherever he goes, death follows." He raised a finger to point at the shaman's lodge.

"And by taking his woman, you've guaranteed that here is where he's coming. You had no right to bring his wrath down on all of us, just to satisfy your own pride and desire."

"And so you mean to run," Stands Alone sneered. "And leave me alone to face his tender mercies."

"You've just told us you may be as great as Tirawa himself," Half Journey retorted. "Surely you don't need the rest of us to help you take down one lone Dog Soldier."

"No," the shaman agreed calmly, "I don't." He turned and gestured toward his tipi.

"But I won't hold this against you. Small men have small bellies."

The six warriors bristled at this insult to their courage, but the shaman merely smiled.

"Please," he said, "come into my lodge. I may no longer have a home with you, but you're still my people. Let me give you medicine to take with you, to help keep the tribe safe."

The others again looked to Half Journey for guidance. He stared intently at the shaman's face, then nodded curtly.

When Half Journey entered the lodge, a movement caught his attention, and he saw the captive woman near the back of the tipi, pushing herself up against one wall. He refused to meet her plaintive gaze.

As Stands Alone began to circle around the fire burning in the middle of the floor, there came a snapping sound, followed by a small rock being expelled to roll across the ground.

The edges of the rock glowed redly, but without hesitation the shaman bent and picked it up in his bare hand. He tossed it back into the fireplace, showing no discomfort, no sign that his skin had been singed in the slightest.

Stepping close to the bubbling stew skin that hung over the flames, Stands Alone again smiled at the six warriors, who had clearly been greatly impressed by his little trick.

The awe and fear evident in their eyes grew even plainer when he then plunged his right hand down into the boiling stew. His eyes never left theirs as he plucked a piece of hot meat out of the stew and popped it into his mouth as though it were an acorn.

"Would you care to stay for supper?" he asked brightly.

"You said you had medicine for us," Half Journey replied gruffly. "We need to catch up with the others."

"Of course, of course," Stands Alone said, kneeling down beside a large pouch that lay on the floor near at hand.

He began to hum a wordless tune as he dug around inside the pouch with both hands.

"Ah! Here we are," he said at last. From inside the pouch he extracted six small amulets, each attached to a rawhide strand.

He walked over to where the six warriors stood and personally placed the amulets around each man's neck. Half Journey took his amulet between two fingers, examined it. It was some sort of green stone, roughly carved into the shape of a horse's head.

"Thank you, Stands Alone," he said. "We'll be going now."

"No, no, no," the shaman replied. "They'll do you no good like that. First I have to put the magic in them."

"Will that take long?"

"Not for me it won't."

"All right then. Get on with it."

Stands Alone smiled and nodded. He quickly padded back to the opposite side of the fireplace and picked up a pair of small rattles.

"This magic will change your lives forever," he declared.

Before any of the men could voice a concern, he began to shake the rattles and to sing an incantation. As usual, the words were in no tongue known to them, and the shaman's voice quickly grew nearly as loud as a howling wind.

That's when the amulets began to burn into the warriors' flesh.

With a cry of pain, Half Journey clawed at the amulet, seeking to remove it. But it was as if it had melded to his skin, and claw as he might it would not pull free. He dug at it so fiercely that trickles of blood began to flow down his torso, but the amulet would not release its grip.

He looked to his friends for help, only to see that they too were caught in the burning spell of the amulets. Wisps of smoke rose from their chests, and their skin began to sizzle and pop like buffalo steaks on a hot rock. The smell of their own flesh burning rose sickeningly into their nostrils.

"You!" Half Journey yelled at Stands Alone, who was now giggling and hopping from one foot to the other like a child.

"Yes!" the shaman shouted gleefully. "You didn't really think I'd let you walk away from here with my blessing after you insulted me and threw me to the wolves, did you?"

Half Journey could make no reply, for the searing pain had stolen his tongue. He was able to clutch at the knife hanging from his belt. If he could just hang onto his senses for a few moments longer, he would make sure the scrawny shaman paid for his deceit.

But such was not to be. A spasm of pain pulled the warrior's arms twisting in front of him. Half Journey moaned in agony as the strength fled from his legs and he dropped to his knees before pitching over backwards.

At the back of the lodge, Crow Woman had risen to her feet and now stepped forward. Even though they were her enemies, she would have been moved to help them if she could. But she was helpless to do ought but watch in horrified fascination.

All six men were on the ground now, writhing like great fish flopping on dry land. Foam bubbled from their lips, and their eyes rolled back in their heads.

Stands Alone came to stand over them, smiling broadly, eyes wide and shining with amusement. One of the warriors tried to grab at him, but the shaman kicked his hand away.

"They say it's almost impossible to beat a Pawnee in a foot race," he said to Half Journey. "Running is said to be as much in their blood as it is in any pony." He squatted down near Half Journey, delighting in the convulsions that wracked the warrior's body.

"But now you'll run toward my enemy, instead of away from him!"

Half Journey felt his skin stretching and pulling tight across his bones, as if something inside was attempting to push its way out. Invisible hands seemed to be pulling at his form from all sides, as if he was clay to be molded into some new and alien form. His back arched sharply, and pain raced down his spine.

Crow Woman's hands flew to her mouth and she bit down on her knuckles. Her eyes locked with those of Half Journey, saw the pleading that blazed within them. He jerked violently, and with a sickening rip the flesh of his body began to split apart.

Both he and Crow Woman screamed at the same time.

CHAPTER 20

L istens To Elks stood alone on a small, grass-covered hill, looking down on the village below. To the west, the sun was just beginning to dip below the lip of the horizon.

"Father?"

He turned to see his daughter, Snow Dancer, approaching from behind him. I'm getting old, he thought to himself, or I would have heard her before she spoke.

"What are you doing?" she asked as she drew up beside him.

"Nothing. Just watching the sun go down."

"Any sign of Long Stride?"

"Not yet. But it's early. He'll be back with the ponies soon. I'm sure of it."

Snow Dancer stood next to him in silence as the sun gave its last gasp before vanishing. Listens To Elks smiled slightly; it was hard for his daughter to go so long without speaking.

"Are you worried about Bird?" she said, before she could burst.

"You should call him by his chosen name, daughter."

"I don't like that name," she said, shivering slightly at the mere thought of it.

"Neither does he, I suspect," her father replied. "But his name is like the mark on his chest, burned into his soul as well as his skin. It's a boulder that would crush most men beneath it, but he carries it with pride and without complaint."

"But you are worried about him?"

"A good father worries about all his children, all the time." He gestured in the direction of the tipis laid out below them.

"They're my children, too," he said, "and right now I'm worried about them."

"Why? What's wrong?"

"I'm not sure. But something is. I can feel it in my bones, the same way I feel a change in the weather."

"Are we in danger?"

"Always. But now our best soldiers are gone."

"Maybe they wouldn't be," Snow Dancer said coldly, "if your son hadn't felt the need to go chasing after a slut."

Listens To Elks looked at her sadly, shaking his head.

"What has the woman ever done to you," he asked, "that you should hate her so much?"

"She's no good," came the quick reply. "Not good enough for him."

"Shouldn't that be for him to say?"

"Maybe not. Sometimes, when it comes to women, men think with their coup sticks instead of their brains."

"Mmmm." The chief's face was turned back toward the village, but his eyes gazed sideways at his daughter. "That's what some people said about Long Stride when he asked me if he could marry you."

"What?"

Listens To Elks fought back a smile as he again turned to look at his daughter. Even in the gathering darkness he could see the blush of color flooding her cheeks, the anger blazing in her eyes.

"Who said that?"

"It doesn't matter," he replied calmly. "When he came to me, I already knew how much the two of you wanted to be together."

"How did you know that?"

"Little girl, the whole village knew."

"Oh!" Her hand flew to her mouth in horror and embarrassment. "What did you think of me?"

"I thought that you were a grown woman, one who would probably go her own way no matter how hard I pulled on the reins. I trusted you to do what was right." He couldn't resist the sudden urge to prick her pride a little.

"Besides, at the time I needed the ponies he offered me for you."

Snow Dancer had hung her head as if in shame. Her father took her chin in his hand and pushed her face up to him, that she might see that he was smiling at her.

"I trust your brother, too," he said.

She smiled back at him.

"You should come back down now, papa. Have a bite to eat, maybe get some sleep."

"I trust your brother, too."

"I'm too restless to sleep," he replied, the smile fading from his lips as he turned his head to again peer down at the village. "Something's just not right."

No sooner had the words escaped his lips than a small, pale ball of light suddenly appeared in the sky over the encampment.

It hovered motionless in the air like a weak reflection of the noonday sun. Then a second ball of light popped into sight, not far from the first. This was quickly followed by others, until a dozen such glowing balls floated above the camp. A murmur of voices carried up to Listens To Elks and his daughter as villager spied the strange orbs, pointing and calling out to one another.

"What are they?" Snow Dancer gasped.

"I don't know," her father said. "But I don't think they're anything good."

As the two of them watched, transfixed, the balls of light began to shimmer and wiggle back and forth. Like a woman's womb at the time of birth, they bulged as if something within was seeking to escape.

They collapsed inward momentarily, before billowing outward like blossoming flowers. From within each, what appeared to be a wavering, distorted image of a man. Like the orbs from which they had emerged, they hovered motionless in the air, immune to the downward pull of gravity.

One of the spirits threw his head back, his mouth flew open three times wider than that of a human man, and a blood-chilling howl louder than a pack of wolves on the hunt issued forth.

This spirit being suddenly dived down from the sky, headed straight for a tipi near the center of the camp. His wavering form passed right through the wall of the tipi without hindrance, disappearing within. His fellow spirits followed suit, flashing down to enter random lodges.

Listens To Elks and Snow Dancer had already begun to descend the hill as quickly as the darkness and footing would allow. A new, more harrowing sound rose to greet them, causing them to pull up short.

It was the sound of human screams coming from the first tipi to be invaded by the spirits.

Screams of horror, and screams of pain.

CHAPTER 21

Tall Dog gingerly picked his way around a cluster of sharp stones that littered the floor of the canyon. Walker held the reins loosely, trusting his mount to choose the right path.

The horse's ears perked up, his nostrils flared, and he nickered softly. Walker patted him lightly on the neck.

"Tall Dog smells water," he told Bowstring.

"Yes," the youth replied. "I think there is a stream near here, just past the end of the canyon. In time, it should run into the Rope River, not far from where the Pawnees were camped."

Walker nodded. As he listened more closely now, he could just make out the faint tinkling sound of running water.

"That'll be a good place for us to make a short stop," he said. "All four of us could use a little rest, a little food."

It was not long before they stood on the banks of the stream. Both men saw to it that their mounts were watered first, before slaking their own thirst. Having done so, they poured out the remaining dead water from their skins, filling them back up with fresh, clean, cool water. As he plugged the neck of his water skin, Walker bent low so that his face nearly broke the dark surface of the stream.

"Thank you," he said softly.

"Why do you thank the water?" Bowstring asked in puzzlement.

"Because it gives us life."

"So? Isn't that what it's supposed to do?"

"Maybe. That doesn't mean we shouldn't be grateful."

"I suppose. But do you think water can understand what you say to it?"

"Who can say, Bowstring? But it can never do any harm to give thanks."

The two soldiers sat on the ground, resting their backs against boulders as they dipped into their provisions to have a sparse breakfast. They finished the meal by treating themselves to some of the plum cakes Two Doves had given them.

"That girl really likes you," Bowstring commented.

"She's a good girl. She'd have done the same for anyone else."

"But not with so full a heart," the youth said wryly. Walker merely shrugged.

Bowstring poked a finger at the crumbs of plum cake that had fallen into his lap, pressing hard enough to make them stick to the skin. He sucked them off his fingertip, savoring the last bit of sweet flavor.

"A lot of people like you, Walker," he said.

"I suppose that's a good thing."

"But you're like a pet wolf," Bowstring continued. "A part of them is always afraid you might bite."

"People are free to feel whatever they want. And they might be right."

"And that doesn't bother you?"

"I learned to accept who and what I am a long time ago, Bowstring," Walker replied. He picked up a pebble lying beside him and tossed it into the stream, watching the ripples fan out in all directions.

"I do what I have to do. I do what I think is right. And if I were to look at the surface of this stream...I would not be ashamed of the man I saw looking back at me. That's all a man can ask of himself, and all that anyone else should ask of him."

"If I looked into the water," Bowstring said, "do you think I would feel ashamed?"

"I don't know. Should you?"

"Maybe," the youth replied. "I don't mean to do wrong, but sometimes... just look at all the trouble I've brought down on you and the others. And I'm still doing it."

"It's like I told the siyuhk," Walker explained, "youth is a time for making mistakes. It only becomes a problem if you don't learn from those mistakes."

"What sort of things should I learn?"

"One lesson I think you're starting to learn is that your mistakes don't hurt just yourself alone. Only a *Contrary* places himself apart from the people, and they're a special case, touched by Maheo.

"Everyone else must always try to think of the tribe above themselves. All of us fail at that sometimes, but you have to keep trying."

"I will," Bowstring said earnestly. "I'd like the people to think of me the way they think of you."

"Well, I wouldn't wish that on you," Walker replied. "Just try to be a good man, and the rest'll take care of itself."

"What does it take to be a good man?"

Walker seemed puzzled by this question. "Hasn't your father told you all that?"

"Sure. But it can't hurt to learn from other people too, right?"

"True, true. A plant needs both sun and water to grow." Walker paused a moment to fish a few sunflower seeds from his pouch and place them in his cheek. He offered some to Bowstring, who declined with a shake of his head.

"I would say," Walker began, "that one of the things every boy should learn is that feeding a widow or an orphan is as much the mark of a man as is the counting of a coup or the taking of a pony."

Bowstring hung his head sheepishly, but Walker pretended not to notice. His purpose was to teach, not to shame.

"Most people measure a man by two things: how much he has…and how much he gives. And of the two, the giving is by far the more important. That's why a selfish man is never chosen by the people to be one of their chiefs."

"You're right," Bowstring agreed, nodding. "What else should I know?"

Walker didn't respond, instead holding up a hand to quiet the boy. They both cocked their heads to one side, listening. At first Bowstring heard nothing but the babbling of the spring, but then he detected the distinctive sound of horses' hooves slowly approaching from a nearby gully.

Using hand signs, Walker directed Bowstring to follow his lead. They grabbed the reins of their mounts and took cover behind a nearby cluster of boulders. Leaving the horses, they quietly slithered up the side of one of the boulders, till they could peer over its top.

As they watched, the heads of several Pawnee warriors bobbed into sight beyond a sloping ridge of the gully, weaving from side to side in rhythm with a horse's gait.

Heartbeats later, the band of warriors fully emerged from the cover of the gully and into the clearing near the creek. As they did, both Walker and Bowstring felt their hearts being constricted in their chests.

The Pawnees weren't riding horses…they *were* horses!

Each of them still had the full form and figure of a human being from the waist up, but at that point it was as if their bodies had been conjoined with the torso and legs of a large pony. Each was armed with a massive war club, and their eyes stared blankly ahead as if they were walking in their sleep.

The two Cheyenne could not know this, but this was Half Journey and his men, mystically transformed by the malign magic of Stands Alone and entranced into serving as his arm of combat.

Bowstring gasped in fear and amazement at the sight of these bizarre creatures, and he hoarsely whispered a repeat of the warning given to them the previous day by the undead Lakotas.

"Beware of Pawnee horsemen!"

CHAPTER 22

Crow Woman furiously gnawed at the rawhide strap binding her wrists together, desperately attempting to loosen them. Her jaws ached with the effort, but the knots seemed not to have slipped one bit despite her persistence.

Periodically she would pause, to glance in the direction of Stands Alone. Some time earlier, shortly after he had performed the horrible spell that had transformed his own tribesmen into abominations of nature and dispatched them on their mission, he had smugly informed the captive woman that he was performing magics that would guarantee no rescuers would be coming to her aid.

After planting himself cross-legged before the fire and chanting some long song of evil design, he had sprinkled a strange gray powder into the flames.

Smoke laced with fingers of red and yellow, smelling of death and putrefaction, had swirled around him. His eyelids grew heavy and closed, and he had remained in a deep trance ever since.

Fearing her efforts to free her hands would continue to prove pointless, Crow Woman decided to try a new tactic. She turned and scurried to the post to which was tied the end of the lariat around her neck. If she could untie it, she could make a run for freedom and be able to loosen her wrists at a later time.

This hope faded quickly, though, to be replaced by trepidation as she heard a sharp intake of air from behind her.

Stands Alone's eyes snapped open, and he loudly sucked air into his lungs. He pitched over onto his side, physically drained by his supernatural exertions.

As his breathing slowly returned to normal, a self-satisfied smile further twisted his black lips. Two spells were working at once now, a magical feat not to be underestimated.

First, he had placed the unbending desire in what remained of the minds of his slavish Pawnee horsemen not to rest until they had found Deathwalker and slain both him and all who might be with him.

Beyond this, the shaman had used the full extent of his powers to conjure up spirits of disease and decay and dispatch them to bedevil the village of the Cheyenne.

The working of such magics had siphoned away much of his strength, but would ensure that even if any of his enemies survived, their last thought would be to come searching for either him or the girl.

Pushing himself up to his hands and knees, the shaman crawled to the spot where he had filled a large wooden bowl with the meaty stew he had cooked up previously.

He didn't bother with either ladle or spoon, but lifted the bowl in both hands and brought it up to his lips. The still warm broth slid down his throat while he chewed at bits of meat and vegetables.

His loud gulping and smacking of lips reminded Crow Woman of a scavenger plunging its snout into the belly of some carrion, and it caused her own stomach to heave and turn with revulsion.

The meat and hearty broth seemed to replenish Stands Alone's depleted strength in short order. Setting the nearly empty bowl back down on the ground, he wiped his mouth on the back of one hand. Using his tongue and one long, cracked fingernail, he dislodged a small piece of meat from between his cracked teeth and swallowed it.

Rising to his feet, he slowly turned. Standing as he was between the fire and his captive, Crow Woman saw him mainly as nothing more than the shadow image of a man. Even so, she could see the whites of his eyes, and the less white of his teeth as his mouth cracked into yet another hungry smile.

But now, she knew, he hungered for something other than food.

As he approached, she scuttled back away from him, until the wall of the lodge impeded her. He bent over her, and she could see he now wielded a knife. Grabbing her arm with his left hand, he slid the blade of the knife between her wrists and sawed away the band that bound them together.

Before she could even begin to try to shake the blood back into her hands, the shaman had clumsily fallen atop her, pinning her painfully to the ground. He smelt of lust and dark magic, and both sickened her. She tried to wriggle out from under him, but he was like a dead weight holding her down.

His breathing grew faster, and she could feel his growing arousal. His head lay alongside hers, and she tried vainly to twist enough to enable her to bite off his ear. She cried out in soft desperation as his hand began to slide up under her dress. Her flesh crawled as his fingers slid along the inner swell of her thighs.

It was with unexpected relief that she felt his hand suddenly stop. He lifted himself up enough to glare down at her. One eyebrow arched in puzzlement as his hand again moved slightly beneath her dress, stopped again.

"What's this?" he asked.

The shaman slid down, grabbed the hem of her dress and began to pull it up. Crow Woman tried to kick out at him, to buck him off her, but he merely insinuated himself more firmly between her thighs. He actually giggled then as he roughly pulled the dress up over her hips and stared down at the purity rope secured around her middle.

"Is it the Cheyenne who's slave in your lodge?" he sneered. "Or is he just stupid, to believe you possess anything that needs to be so protected?" It delighted him to see the shame burning in her eyes.

"Or does he have to keep you on the rope so you don't spread your legs for every ram in heat?"

"I *choose* to wear the rope," she replied hotly, "as a sign that none but Walker may touch me." Now it was her turn to sneer.

"But I don't *need* to wear it, because there's not a man alive foolish enough to try to take what's his!"

"You think?" Stands Alone said, grinning wickedly. He reached over to where he had dropped his knife and retrieved it. He held it up to make sure she could see it clearly.

"You're about to see how wrong you are, girl. After all...it's only a rope."

Unfortunately for the shaman, the circulation had returned to Crow Woman's hands. Both flew now to the sides of his face. She dug in her nails as sharply as she could, then raked them downward sharply.

Stands Alone screamed shrilly as he felt and heard furrows of flesh ripping open. The knife dropped from the fingers of his right hand, which he then curled into a tight fist.

He brought that fist slamming down on the woman's face, snapping her head sharply to one side. A second and a third time he pummeled her, till blood spurted from her cracked lips.

He raised his fist for another blow, only to stop. It shook with the effort as he struggled to regain control. He lowered the fist, began to lightly pound it against the center of his forehead, willing himself to remain master of the situation.

He pulled away from between the woman's legs, and she quickly pulled her dress down to again cover them. Stands Alone turned from her only long enough to retrieve another length of rawhide rope to retie her wrists together.

Crow Woman did not resist him, but when he looked up at her after tying the final knot, she spewed a stream of blood-flecked spit into his face.

This time, the shaman showed no reaction. Wiping the spittle from his cheek, he then rubbed his hand dry on her dress, the part covering one breast. Her own expression showed him nothing but scorn.

"Maybe a few days without food will soften your heart, Absaroka," he hissed, "and make my touch more welcome."

She smiled.

"My killer of men will have arrived here and gutted you like a fish, little man, long before I could ever get so hungry."

"How long do you think you can cling to that dream?" the shaman said. "How many meals will you miss before you realize your master isn't coming at all? Right now, he's probably out looking for his tribe's lost ponies rather than for you. After all, they're worth more than you are."

"Which of us is dreaming?" she replied haughtily, drawing herself up straight and staring directly into her captor's eyes. "Walker shows a cold heart to me, and to others, but there's fire beneath it. A fire only your blood will quench."

Stands Alone gave no response, and the two eyed each other silently for several heartbeats. Seeing something even blacker lurking behind his dark orbs, Crow Woman's own eyes widened in recognition.

"He is coming!" she exclaimed. "You know it. You fear it!"

She yelped in pain as Stands Alone grabbed her by the hair and pulled her close to him. Now, all she could see in his eyes was rage and madness.

"There's no man dead or alive I fear," he snarled. "No beast. No god or demon."

He shoved her savagely to the ground and rose to his feet.

"And no woman!"

Turning on his heels, he stomped out of the lodge.

But though her body throbbed with pain and her heart still raced in trepidation, Crow Woman smiled again.

CHAPTER 23

"What do we do?" Bowstring asked softly.

He and Walker were still crouched down atop the crest of the boulder from which they were watching as the strange horsemen picked their way down toward the stream. The beasts walked rather awkwardly, neither exactly like men nor like horses. More like skittish mounts that resist the rein.

"I'm sure they've been sent for us," Walker replied. "Stands Alone likes to twist nature for his own ends. But I'd just as soon avoid them as to have to fight them."

"Why? There's only six of them."

"And only two of us," Walker reminded the impetuous youth. "And none of them is the Pawnee I want." He turned and pointed to a narrow pathway worn in the grass alongside the stream, heading away from where the horsemen had come.

"If we can ford the stream without them seeing us, we can leave them behind and go on our way."

Bowstring looked back almost longingly at the approaching horsemen, then turned to Walker.

"You know best."

Sliding down the boulder to where the horses patiently waited, Walker took Tall Dog by the reins and set off walking down the faint path as quickly and quietly as possible.

Before following his lead, Bowstring decided to take one last note of the pursuing horsemen's progress. As he looked around the side of a rock outcropping, he could see they were still some distance away. Like hounds on a scent, they were circling a patch of open ground for sign of their quarry.

The horseman who appeared to be their leader jerked upright, his head twisting to one side. He let out a cry that sounded almost like the whinny of a horse, and pointed straight toward Bowstring's position.

The Cheyenne jerked back out of sight, cursing himself for being spotted. The sound of pebbles being dislodged and sliding into the water caused his eyes to trace the path Walker was taking. He could clearly see the older warrior and his mount trotting away. He also realized that, given the angle from his own location, it had been Walker the horseman had spied, not him.

Rather than immediately trailing after Walker, the young soldier first risked another look in the direction of the Pawnees. It was certain now that they had indeed caught sight of Walker, for they were all racing toward the place where, unknown to them, Bowstring stood.

The youth took one last look at Walker before the war chief and his horse disappeared around a bend in the rocky terrain. Making up his mind quickly as to his own course of action, Bowstring swung himself up onto his pony's back.

Bowstring kicked both heels sharply into the pony's ribs, and it sprang forward – not in the direction Walker had taken, but straight for the Pawnee horsemen.

The lead Pawnee, Half Journey, was taken completely off guard as Bowstring's pony slammed into his broad chest. The horseman's hooves slipped and slid under him and, still not acclimated to his new form, he pitched over onto his side.

Bowstring didn't slow for a moment, but charged right into the midst of the other horsemen. He let out no war cry, for fear Walker would hear and return to join the fight rather than continue on his journey.

The Pawnees felt no such constraint, and one of them gave a howl of pain as Bowstring's war club cracked open the side of his head. Gray matter flew, and his four legs collapsed beneath him.

Bowstring swung at a second target, but this warrior was able to block the blow with his own war club. Bowstring urged his pony forward, at the same time pulling his knife from its sheath.

Clubs still locked together, Bowstring and the Pawnee were face to face. Thus the horseman never saw Bowstring's knife, though he felt it sharply as its blade slid between two ribs and into his right lung. It quickly filled with blood and the Pawnee fell away, choking and gasping for air.

This had given the other three Pawnees time and opportunity to surround Bowstring's pony, however. Bowstring's right arm went instantly numb as the head of a war club rapped his bicep. His own club fell from nerveless fingers.

A horseman in front of him swung at his head. Bowstring instinctively jerked back, but he couldn't maintain his balance and tumbled over his pony's rump, landing heavily on the ground.

Death was all around him now in the form of stomping hooves, both those of the Pawnee horsemen and of his own mount.

He rolled to the left, eyes growing wide as a flashing hoof landed so close to his head that dust flew up his nose. He had lost grip of his knife when he fell, and his bow and lance were still tied to the riding pad of his pony. He was unarmed and surrounded, so he tried to slither away on hands and knees. One of the horsemen rammed him sideways, lifting him and flipping him through the air.

A whistle like the sound of a hawk diving after prey tore through the clearing. It ended with a hollow thump, and the horseman who had slammed into Bowstring looked down in astonishment to see the bloody, barbed head of an arrow protruding from the middle of his chest.

Shocked almost to insensitivity, still he clawed at the place in his chest where blood was now bubbling forth. A second arrow struck the back of his neck, fully emerging through the front of his throat and snuffing the light from his eyes.

As the horseman collapsed in a heap to the ground, Bowstring was greeted with the sight of Walker, now astride his horse, charging into the clearing.

As if he was in the midst of a buffalo hunt, Walker loosed several arrows in quick succession, even as he continued to guide Tall Dog at full speed using no more than the pressure of his legs.

One of the Pawnee horsemen reared on his hind legs as an arrow sank its head into his equine rump. His doing so caused the next arrow to flash beneath him.

A second horseman was not so lucky, for the arrow continued unabated, slicing into the human flesh of his belly. Screeching in pain, he lunged forward toward the advancing Cheyenne, only to be met by two more arrows that tore through his chest like icy wind.

The knees of his front legs gave out, and he flipped forward head first, sliding along the ground before stopping directly in Walker's path.

Without breaking stride, Tall Dog bounded straight over the body of the fallen horseman. The impact of Tall Dog's front hooves striking the ground on the other side caused Walker to pitch forward and nearly spill from his seat astride the war-horse.

Quickly righting himself, Walker used his knees to turn Tall Dog, then urged him back the way they had come with a tap of his heels. As he did, he took aim at the Pawnee horseman he had wounded in his first pass. The horseman was bucking, still trying to dislodge the arrow protruding from his hindquarters.

Bowstring, just now rising back to his feet, stared in amazement as Walker loosed three shafts in the time it would take an ordinary man to fire but one.

One of the arrows flew just wide of its wildly pitching target, but the other two struck with deadly accuracy. The first flew completely through the Pawnee's left shoulder. The second struck the base of his neck, just above the breastbone, sinking in through half its length.

The human half of the beast died first, at least six heartbeats before his four-legged half collapsed in a heap and lay still. Walker grabbed Tall Dog's reins and pulled him to a sliding halt.

"Walker!" Bowstring cried.

The attempted warning came too late. The last of the Pawnee horsemen, Half Journey, had regained his footing from where he had fallen to Bowstring's initial charge, and now leaped toward Walker from his blind side.

The horseman slammed into Tall Dog's right side. The Cheyenne pony's left legs slid under him even as his right legs were lifted clear of the ground. He pitched over sideways with such force that Walker was thrown from his back and sent flying.

Helpless to stop himself, Walker sailed through the air, limp as a young girl's doll. As he slammed to the ground, the top of his head cracked against a protruding rock.

As he rolled listless onto his back, flashes of light began to dance before his eyes. The lights turned red as streams of blood from his lacerated scalp gushed down his face.

He tried to rise, but a bolt of pain and a wave of nausea knocked him flat. His left hand flew to his face, swiping at the blood stinging his eyes and impeding his vision. He succeeded in regaining partial sight in time to see the Pawnee horseman rearing up over him on its hind legs, preparing to bring his front hooves down on the Cheyenne with skull-crushing force.

In the next breath, young Bowstring came hurtling in from the side, throwing himself atop Walker's body even as the flashing hooves descended.

Walker was looking directly at Bowstring's face as the horseman's hooves fell with the beast's full weight behind them. Bowstring's features contorted in agony, and a sound like river ice breaking free in spring assailed Walker's ears. The boy's body went limp and slid away from Walker.

Walker's right hand fell on the shaft of his fallen bow, and he grasped it firmly as he rose to his feet on trembling legs. He had no more arrows, but he gripped the horn bow like a club as he leaped into the air toward the Pawnee horseman, who had staggered back a step after inflicting the crushing blow to Bowstring's back.

Walker screamed as he swung the stout bow. The Pawnee raised an arm too late, and the bow crashed down atop his skull. The bow shattered in two from the force, the top half spinning wildly away. Half Journey teetered, blood spurting from his fractured skull. His hooves tangled and he pitched over sideways.

Walker followed after, leaping astride the Pawnee's equine chest. He still held half the bow and raised it overhead. He drove it down with all his might, plunging its jagged end into Half Journey's belly.

The Pawnee bucked beneath him as he pushed the bow deeper into the wound and gave it a savage twist. Half Journey grabbed the Cheyenne's arms with blood-slickened fingers, pulling him close.

"Thank you," he gasped, before his eyes closed forever.

Walker stood over the body of this mockery of nature, yet another crime for which he meant to make the shaman Stands Alone pay. He again pushed blood from his eyes, swaying unsteadily until his breathing returned to normal before turning his attention to the fallen Bowstring.

He managed but a single step before the world began to spin madly around him. He sank to his hands and knees, trying to focus past the roaring in his ears. With force of will he again rose to his feet, limping over to where Bowstring lay.

It took but a glance to realize the boy's spine had been hopelessly shattered.

As gently as he could, he turned Bowstring over. Gathering together a small pile of leaves, he pushed them under the youth's head. As Walker dribbled a little water over his lips, Bowstring's eyes fluttered open.

"How bad is it?" he asked weakly.

"I've seen worse," Walker replied, half truthfully.

He could tell by the blood oozing from Bowstring's ears, nostrils and mouth that he had suffered massive internal injuries, from which there would be no recovering.

"I...think you'll have to go on alone," Bowstring said. Tears moistened his eyes. "I'm sorry."

"Don't be," Walker assured him. "It shouldn't take more than one of us to kill a single scrawny Pawnee shaman."

Bowstring smiled, then coughed up a fresh stream of blood.

"What will you tell my father, Walker?"

"Only the truth," Walker said. "That you atoned for all your mistakes. That you saved my life. That you fought like a man. That you died like a man. That I was proud to have you as my brother."

Bowstring convulsed, grabbed at Walker's arm, then succumbed.

Walker knelt over the fallen soldier, head bowed respectfully. He began to weave back and forth, singing a death song in praise of Bowstring, asking Maheo to accept him into Seyan with open arms and to treat him with respect.

He groaned, gripping his head in both hands as a wave of dizziness again swept over him. His own wound was enough to lay out most men, but he would give it no power over him.

Pushing himself to his feet, he scanned the area around him, grunting in approval when he saw a small tree nearby that had managed to wend its way upward through the rocky soil.

Retrieving a deerskin blanket from Bowstring's provisions, he carefully wrapped the boy's body in it. He lifted Bowstring in his arms, swallowing hard to keep down the bile that rose in his throat from the effort.

One painful step at a time, he made his way to the tree. It took three tries, but he finally succeeded in hoisting Bowstring up into the arms of the tree's lowest branches.

He flopped down at the base of the tree, fighting for breath and wiping away blood-tinged sweat from his eyes.

When he had rested sufficiently, he went back to Bowstring's mount, leading the pony to stand under his master's body. Walker tied the pony's reins to the tree, then hobbled its front legs with a small length of rope. He placed one hand over the horse's eyes, and drew his knife with the other.

With one swift motion, he drew the knife's blade across the pony's throat, laying it open from jaw to jaw.

The animal shrieked in pain, but Walker held it in place as it bled out and collapsed to the ground. Bowstring would have a fine mount to carry him in the great beyond.

Walker was further weakened by this exertion but was determined to carry on the mission that had brought him this far, and for which Bowstring had valiantly given his life. He talked softly to his own steed as he approached it.

"It's just you and me now, brother," he clucked.

Tall Dog was nervous, frightened by the smell of equine blood on his master's hands. But he stood still as Walker grabbed his reins and pulled him closer.

Walker tried to leap on the pony's back, but the movement triggered yet another wave of nausea, and he slid back down along Tall Dog's heaving side.

Spooked, Tall Dog bolted forward. Taken off guard, Walker staggered and fell. The rope of the horse's reins looped around his left wrist. Entangled thus, he was dragged along the rocky ground.

He yelled for Tall Dog to stop, but the frightened horse merely quickened his stride. Bouncing painfully along the ground, pummeled and gouged by protruding rock edges, Walker desperately clawed at the rope around his wrist.

He succeeded in loosening the rope just as Tall Dog rounded a curve in the trail. The momentum sent Walker flying over the edge of a slope that overlooked the stream below.

He tumbled wildly down the incline, bouncing and somersaulting madly. Mercifully, consciousness had fled his body by the time it rolled to a halt at the edge of the dark stream. Face down, he was lucky that only one arm was submerged in the water. Above, the terrified Tall Dog continued to run away unabated.

Silence gradually fell around Walker. No wind could be felt, yet the black surface of the stream began to ripple as something moved just beneath it.

The water parted slightly, and a serpentine head nearly as big as that of a man rose partially to the surface. Unblinking red eyes stared intently at the fallen warrior, and the snake began to swim forward.

Using Walker's submerged arm as a ramp, the serpent slowly slithered up out of the water. It was a monstrous creature, bigger around than a man's leg, and three times as long as the span of a man's spread arms.

Light reflected from its scales in small bursts of green and red as it lazily coiled back and forth until it covered Walker's entire torso.

The Dog Soldier was unaware as the snake's body began to twist and ripple. A wet, sucking sound accompanied it as its serpentine body began to transform.

Arms and legs erupted from its sides, growing outward. Scales slowly took on the soft suppleness of human flesh. Dark hair sprouted from atop its head, which itself was altering its shape.

When the transformation was complete, what now appeared to be an unworldly, beautiful *woman* lay atop Walker. She moaned lightly as her naked body drank in the warmth exuded by the warrior's body. A still serpentine tongue flicked out, caressing the lobe of his ear.

"I think I'll keep you, man," she whispered seductively.

CHAPTER 24

"**W**ell, well. You've gotten yourself out of one mess and into another, haven't you?"

Walker's eyes snapped open at the sound of the childlike voice. He blinked several times until his eyes adjusted to the light, then tried to sit up. As he
did, his head began to pound and his vision swam.

He dropped back flat, clutching at his head, feeling and hearing the throbbing pulse in his temples. When the pounding subsided and his breathing
returned to normal, he again attempted to rise, more slowly.

This time he succeeded in doing so without undue stress, thanks in part to
the fact that he was able to prop his back up against a rock wall. He was now
able to take in his surroundings.

He was lying atop a short stone shelf, made soft by a thick covering of furs.
A buffalo robe covered his nakedness. With his fingers he gingerly probed
the egg-shaped bump atop his head.

It was clear that he was in a cave of some sort. Its interior was illuminated
by a fire that crackled inside a fissure that ran up the height of the opposite
wall of rock.

And perched atop yet another rock was the oddest little creature he had
ever seen, at least so far as he knew. It appeared to be a little boy, but one
who strangely had a pair of horns sprouting from his head, and shiny hooves
where his feet should have been.

"Who are you?" Walker asked.

"You're joking, right?" Buffalo Boy replied, hopping down from the rock
and skipping over to stand by Walker's makeshift bed. Walker slowly shook
his head.

"I don't think so."

"Take a closer look."

Buffalo Boy shoved his head forward. Walker recoiled, banging the back
of his already aching head against the wall of the cave and letting out a yelp.

"Who are you?"

"Maybe you just can't see right." The impish spirit held up one hand. "How many fingers do you see?"

"Two."

"Close enough." Using thumb and forefinger, Buffalo Boy pushed the upper and lower lids of Walker's right eye open farther. "Your eyes seem fine. But you don't know who I am?"

"No."

"Hmmm." Buffalo Boy pondered this deeply. "Do you know who *you* are?"

Walker opened his mouth to speak, then closed it. He grimaced in concentration, sighed deeply.

"No."

"Oooh," Buffalo Boy said, smiling brightly. "This could be fun."

A scraping sound caused both to turn their heads to one side. The sound had come from beyond a dark opening that led out of the cave, which Walker had not noticed before. The sound indicated someone was approaching from outside.

Walker turned to look at Buffalo Boy, but the spirit had disappeared, leaving no trace save for the faint echo of a giggle. Unsure if the weird little boy had ever really been there at all, Walker returned his attention to the cave entrance.

The breath caught in his throat at the sight of the woman now standing there. Tall she was, with long and sinuous legs. Magnificent breasts were accentuated rather than concealed by the only article of clothing she wore: a shimmering cloak that seemed almost to have been crafted from the skin of an enormous snake.

She was carrying a small bundle of twigs in the crook of her left arm, which she carried over and deposited on the stone floor near the crackling fire. When she turned back toward him, Walker could see that she was also carrying a small wooden cup in her right hand.

She came and sat beside him on his sick bed, smiling and extending the cup toward him.

"Take a sip," she said, in a voice that sounded both ancient yet vital at the same time. "It'll make your head feel better."

Hesitantly, he accepted the cup, raising it to his lips. The liquid within seemed to slither down his throat like cold fire, spreading outward when it reached the pit of his belly. As promised, it quickly dimmed the pain in his skull.

He took another sip, then more closely examined the woman's face. The pale beauty of her skin stood in stark contrast to her onyx black, diamond-shaped eyes. Her smiling lips were full and sensuous, red as blood on virgin snow.

"Who are you?" he asked.

"Just call me Snake Woman," she replied.

"All right. What happened to me? How did I get here?"

She paused before answering him, tilting her head to one side and studying his expression closely.

"What do you remember?"

"Nothing," he admitted.

"Nothing?"

"No." He was clearly growing agitated. "I don't know who you are, I don't know who I am, I don't know anything!"

"Shhh," she hushed, gently but firmly gripping his shoulders and pushing him back down into his bedding.

"I know who you are," she assured him.

"Tell me," he urged. She smiled again and stroked his cheek softly with one hand.

"You're my husband."

"Huh?" He grabbed her hand tightly, stopping its movement. "Why wouldn't I remember that?"

"You will," she crooned, "in time. You simply fell and hit your head while you were out hunting. It's left you a little confused, that's all. You'll be good as new in no time."

"Are you sure?"

"I'm sure."

"But this all feels so strange to me."

"Maybe this will put you at ease."

Snake Woman lowered her face to his, covering his lips with her own. Her hands undid her robe and she shrugged it off her shoulders before sliding under his bed robe.

Instantly drunk with the taste, the smell and the feel of her, Walker used his hands to explore every curve of her body. Her own hands caressed his chest and her body wriggled sinuously atop his. With a single move he rolled them both, so that it was now he who was on top.

"Yes," she sighed, gladly surrendering to his desire, for it was now even greater than her own.

Even as the man and woman melded together as one, in the branches of a tree outside the cave Buffalo Boy sat and shook his head, making clicking sounds with his tongue.

CHAPTER 25

Crow Woman ravenously shoved another handful of pemmican into her mouth, filling both cheeks before even beginning to chew and swallow. For a second time she grabbed up the water skin on the floor, washing the food down with great liquid gulps. She paused only to catch her breath before she resumed eating.

Stands Alone stood over her, watching with disgust as she sated herself. When he had come to realize, after the better part of four days, that the woman truly would rather starve to death than submit to his advances, it was he who had to concede defeat.

He knelt beside her bowed figure, but she paid him no mind. From another bowl she scooped out portions of some vegetable concoction she did not recognize. Nor did she care overmuch; for now, it was sweet as honey. Scowling, the shaman grabbed her by the hair, twisting her head to face him.

"You might at least thank me, woman," he growled.

"Thank you?" she spat. "For what?"

"For the food, the water. I could have let you die."

"And for that you expect gratitude?" The look of utter contempt on her face did not escape him. "I figure you only did it because even you aren't sick enough to rape a corpse."

"Aaah!" he exclaimed angrily, shoving her head roughly away from him. She merely snatched up another bowl and resumed her eating.

"You don't still believe he's coming, do you?" the Pawnee asked. He knew that one of the few ways he had of wounding her was by planting seeds of doubt within her heart.

"And you still believe he's not?" she replied.

"Think about it, girl. A child on foot could have reached here by now. Yet there's no sign of him."

"A rabbit seldom sees the hawk that kills him."

"Yes, but I think your hawk has flown after other game."

"Or maybe he just had to take the time to kill another Pawnee or two before he got to you."

Stands Alone frowned, thinking of the transformed horsemen with whom he had lost all mystical contact. He jerked from his reverie as Crow Woman suddenly began to giggle.

"What's so funny?" he demanded.

"I just had a thought," she said, using the back of one hand to wipe grease away from her mouth before taking another long drink of water.

"Maybe, when Walker gets here," she continued, "I'll ask him to let you live...for a while."

"How generous," he replied, making a sucking sound with his tongue against the back of his decayed teeth. "And why would you do that?"

"So you can watch the two of us make love," she said wickedly. "And see how a real man satisfies a woman."

With a screech more animal than human, he launched himself at her, riding her to the ground. Straddling her body, he began to slap her, first with his right hand, then with the left.

Grabbing the lariat still tied to the lodge pole, he again looped it around her neck, pulling it so tight it bit into flesh. He similarly restrained her wrists and ankles before staggering toward the entrance of the lodge.

As he pushed his way outside, he could hear her again giggling as she rolled on the ground behind him.

He stood staring up at the stars, his mind racing. The woman must be crazy, he thought, to still believe that the Deathwalker was coming for her.

But what then did that make him, for the fear was growing inside that she was right.

He lowered his gaze to the fire he had started earlier a short distance in front of his lodge. Taking a seat before its licking flames, he determined to once again take matters into his own hands.

The shaman tossed sweet pine needles into the fire. As aromatic smoke arose, he used both hands to sweep it over him, in a rite of purification.

Next he threw leaves of the chickadee plant into the flames. The smoke released by them swirled in lazy spirals around him. His eyes grew heavy as he breathed in their soothing fumes, making it easier for him to enter into the necessary trance state.

"Help me, Tirawa," he murmured sleepily.

A buzzing sound filled his ears as *maiyun* – spirits – in the form of mosquitoes flitted around his head. The sound lulled him even deeper into a dreamlike haze.

His eyes slowly opened, and it almost appeared as if the pupils had disappeared, replaced by a milky film that covered the sockets entirely. A stunning light flashed before him, and he threw his hands up to protect his vision.

When he lowered his hands, the world had changed around him. He was standing in pools of colored lights that swirled around him like currents of water. Tilting his head, he peered up into a night sky where the stars were now spinning in dizzying circles.

And when he lowered his gaze, he saw himself.

The body of Stands Alone was still seated before the fire, still staring blankly ahead.

The Stands Alone that stood watching over him was his spirit form, released from its fleshly shell by magics few others dared to practice or even learn.

This spirit shaman began to float slowly off the ground, till he hovered high enough in the air to take in his bodily form and the lodge behind it with a single glance.

Some force, some lure of the other world began to tug at him, to pull him through the night air. He knew it to be the essence of the Deathwalker, for he had used his spell to cast about for it.

Faster than any pony could run, the shaman's spirit form now flew through the air. He couldn't feel the wind, but he could hear it as it whistled past him.

A hill rose up darkly ahead of him, and his form passed through its stone walls as if they had been made of water. Indeed, the solid rock rippled as he swam through its unyielding surface.

Heartbeats later, he found himself standing within a dimly lit cavern. On silent non-feet he walked to the stony bed set against one wall.

If this spirit form had possessed a heart, it would have quickened at the sight. His enemy lay sleeping heavily beneath a buffalo robe. Beside him lay a woman whose beauty may have surpassed even that of Crow Woman. She lay on her right side, with one hand resting on the man's heart as she slept. But she meant nothing to Stands Alone, and he paid her no mind.

The spirit shaman stretched out a translucent hand toward Walker. As the fingers passed through the skull of the sleeping Cheyenne, Stands Alone could again feel mystical forces tugging at him. He surrendered to them, and almost instantly all that he was stretched out as it was sucked into the very mind of the Dog Soldier.

A plaintive wail like that of a bull elk rose and fell, and the spirit sha-man was now standing on the barren plain that formed the outermost edges of the dream world.

Nor was he alone. The figure of another man stood not far away, with his back to the shaman. As Stands Alone walked toward him, the other turned to face him. It was Walker, or at least the spirit form of him that lived here in the asleep land.

"We meet again, Deathwalker," the shaman said. His own voice sound-ed strangely alien to him. Walker merely stared at him in puzzlement.

"Do I know you?" the Cheyenne asked.

"Don't play the fool with me!" Stands Alone snapped, stepping ever closer to Walker.

"I don't know what you're talking about."

"Then let me be clear. Consider this a warning, the only one you'll get. Go home, and you'll live."

"I am home," Walker replied, confused by the words.

"Don't taunt me, Cheyenne," the shaman hissed, not knowing that even in the dream world Walker's memories were not accessible to him. "And don't ever forget that I can kill you with the snap of my fingers!"

Walker's eyes narrowed menacingly. Bereft of memory or not, he was not one to be threatened.

"You can try," he growled.

Stands Alone's hands flew to Walker's throat, incoherent curses flying from his tongue. In the real world, he would have been no match for the physical form of Walker. But in spirit form he felt sure his skill with magic would give him an edge.

Such seemed to be the case, for the savagery of his attack drove Walker back and to his knees, choking and gagging.

Stands Alone smiled. He had hoped to do no more than frighten the Cheyenne into giving up the hunt for him, to convince him to forget the slave woman and return to his own people. But if the shaman could suc-ceed in killing his spirit form, he knew the Walker in the real world would die as well.

The smile on the shaman's lips twisted slightly, then fled altogether as the spirit Walker grabbed him by both wrists. So strong was the grip that, if the shaman's arm had been flesh and blood, he would have felt bone grind on bone.

As it was, his spirit fingers were pulled loose from the un-flesh of

Walker's throat. Without releasing his hold, the Cheyenne slowly rose
back to his feet, while forcing Stands Alone down to his knees. The shaman's eyes bulged with fear as Walker's face drew so near to his own that
their noses practically touched.

"I'm going to kill you, Pawnee," Walker hissed, "and eat your heart!"

Stands Alone screamed in fear and horror. As he did, the arms of his
spirit form evaporated through Walker's fingers. The shaman was still
screaming as the remnants of his dream self soared away from Walker.

Before the echoes of his scream had faded from the dream world, the
spirit shaman had been expelled from its borders, out of Walker's skull,
out of the cavern and back through the night sky.

On the south side of the Rope River, the physical Stands Alone was
ripped from his trance as his spirit form caromed back into his body. His
fingers clawed at his eyes and he pitched to one side, rolling on the ground.

He groaned in pain, and in the light cast by the fire he could see purple
bruising appearing around his wrists. His heart was racing, and the deep
gulps of air he sucked in burned his lungs.

The greatest pain was that which gripped his belly and twisted it on the
inside.

The pain wrought by fear.

Back in the cavern of the Snake Woman, Walker awakened with a start.
He moaned and grabbed at his head, which now throbbed like the beating of a hundred drums. He fought back against the pain, finally causing
it to retreat.

And as it fled, it left his mind once more free.

The shaman's mystical attack had succeeded in doing nothing but restore Walker's memory. He turned his head as a movement caught his eye.
It was Snake Woman, still sleeping as she rolled over onto her left side.

Walker remembered her, too, remembered how she had used his afflic-
tion to deceive him and seduce him into her arms and into her bed.

What he didn't remember was just how long he had been here. He
pushed such concerns out of his mind, telling himself that Stands Alone
must have gone to ground in order to have the time to cast such a spell as
had just been used against him.

Fearing its failure might prompt the shaman to flee anew, Walker flung
off the bed robe covering his nakedness and sprang from the stony bed.

He quickly pulled on his moccasins, leggings and breechcloth, cinch-
ing its belt snugly around his middle after securing his knife and medicine
pouch to it. He was pleased to see that the Snake Woman had also brought

his remaining weapons when she had transported him from the stream. He slid the handle of his war club into his belt, then took up his spear and headed for the exit from the cave.

"Where are you going, husband?"

Walker turned to see that Snake Woman had slid from their shared bed and was now standing but a few feet in front of him, looking as magnificent in her nakedness as any creature on Maheo's earth. The light cast by the nearby fire seemed almost to reflect from her flawless skin, creating a rainbow-like aura around her. Even though he now knew she had used deception on him, her raw sexuality still caused a stirring in his loins that he controlled with great difficulty.

"I'm not your husband," he said at last.

The hurt and sorrow that clouded her eyes upon hearing these words was genuine. A hopeful smile tugged at the corners of her mouth as she stepped toward him.

"You could be," she said softly in a voice that tinkled like icy boughs plucked by a gentle wind. "I want you to be."

"No," he replied, with more effort required than he would have imagined. "You took me in. You nursed and fed me, and more. You have my gratitude...but that's all."

"You wanted more than food from me before," she said. She now stood less than an arm's length away from him.

"Maybe I did," he acknowledged. "But now I have to go."

In reply, Snake Woman threw her arms around his neck and pulled his face to hers. He didn't resist as her lips sought his, for his hunger needed sating. He was disappointed when she broke off the kiss and pulled her head back away from him.

"Please," she pleaded. Her dark, reptilian eyes were moist with tears, and they mesmerized the man, these twin pools that threatened to drown him.

"Please don't leave me. Don't leave me ever."

She kissed him again, harder and more deeply. Her tongue slid between his lips, causing him to moan. He pulled her more tightly against him, pleased by the warm feel of her breasts as they spread out across his own rock hard chest. Her right hand slid down between their bodies, slithering up under his breechcloth.

The woman cried out as Walker suddenly shoved her away. She stumbled back a few steps, surprise and confusion evident in her face. His own expression was conflicted, and he shook his head sadly.

"I can't do this," he said.

"Why?"

It was a reasonable question, but to answer it truthfully would require the baring of more of his heart than he was willing to show, even to himself. So he chose not to answer it.

"I'm grateful for the kindness you've shown me, Snake Woman. And I will repay you if I can…some day. But now I have to go."

Unable to look further at the misery her face reflected from her heart, he turned without another word and headed for the opening leading out of the cave.

He was violently pulled up short as his ankles suddenly slammed together, and he was thrown forward heavily onto the cold stone floor.

It felt as if he had stepped into a snare whose noose had snapped tight around his legs. But as he rolled over and looked down, he was amazed to see what appeared to be the thick body of a snake coiled around his ankles.

His eyes followed the twisting serpentine body from where it was wrapped around him across the floor. They grew wide with surprise and horror as he witnessed the snake's form rise up off the floor until it met and blended into the upper torso of Snake Woman!

Only now did he realize her true nature. From boyhood, he had heard stories of mysterious creatures that dwelt beneath the water. They normally shied away from the company of people, yet possessed the power to assume human form if they so desired.

"*I* say when you leave!" Snake Woman screamed at him.

As if again being dragged by Tall Dog, Walker felt himself sliding roughly across the cavern floor. Cracking her tail like a whip, Snake Woman caused Walker to bang against the floor and then bounce up slightly. When he did, she looped still more coils around him, up past his waist.

Walker gritted his teeth against the pain as the coils constricted so tightly around his middle that they threatened to crush his ribs. Like a toy, she hoisted him into the air, drawing him close to her.

"Dead or alive," she threatened, "I mean to keep you here with me forever!"

"Then it'll be dead!" he snapped back.

His face twisted in agony as her coils again tightened around him. Her eyes were now more serpentine in appearance, and he could see twin, awl-like fangs growing downward from behind her upper lip.

Mouth stretched wide, she snapped her head forward. Barely in time, his left hand caught and grabbed her by the throat, stopping her fangs from reaching his own throat by a mere hairsbreadth.

It took all the strength he could muster to push her head back slightly, only to see her pushing back toward him.

Focused as she was on this struggle, Snake Woman relaxed the coils looped around the man ever so slightly. His right hand shoved down on the top coil, only to slide off of its slimy curve.

He pushed again, felt the coil slide downward slightly, just enough to uncover the hilt of his knife.

He could now feel her hot breath on his face. Whether her fangs bore venom or not, he knew they were sharp enough to rip out the flesh and veins of his throat. Summoning all his strength, he pushed her back yet again.

This gave him the opening he required, and before she could react he pulled his knife from its sheath and thrust upward blindly. He felt it hit and slide off a rib as it penetrated her body just below her left breast.

Snake Woman screamed in pain and recoiled. Her lower body whipped about wildly even as it lost its grip on Walker. He was thrown across the cavern, slamming into the far wall and sliding to the ground.

He clutched at his stomach with both hands, huffing from the effort to restore air to his lungs. He could do nothing but watch as, across the room, Snake Woman continued to scream and thrash about on the floor.

The snake half of her body seemed to slide up and envelop the half that still resembled a woman, until she was once again all snake. The transformation caused Walker's knife to loosen and fall to the ground.

Leaving behind a smeared, winding trail of blood, Snake Woman quickly slithered through a narrow crack in the back wall of the cave, no doubt crawling off to die alone.

Having regained his breath, Walker used the cavern wall as support to push himself back up to his feet. Retrieving his knife and lance, he raced from the cave into the cool night. He stopped a short distance from the cavern, casting his eyes about right and left.

"If you're looking for your pony," a girlish voice said, "you can forget about it. He's long gone."

Walker looked up. Above him, hanging upside down from a tree limb by his legs, was Buffalo Boy.

"Then I'll just have to get where I'm going on foot," Walker declared.

Buffalo Boy released his grip on the branch, dropping down. He executed a somersault in mid-air, landing lightly on his cloven feet in front of Walker.

"Maybe you should just go on home," the imp suggested. "You used up so much energy servicing the big snake for the last few suns that you might not have enough strength left to kill even a Pawnee."

Walker glared down at him.

"What do I have to do to get a new spirit guide?" he asked.

Buffalo Boy merely smiled.

"So I'm stuck with you forever?"

"Pretty much."

Walker pushed past him. The stars above told him which way he needed to go, and he meant to waste no time.

Buffalo Boy gazed back at the cavern of the Snake Woman, frowning slightly and shaking his head. Then he turned to follow behind Walker.

CHAPTER 26

Stands Alone was still lying face down on the ground, dewy blades of grass tickling his skin. His arms were stretched out in front of him, his hands clenching and unclenching, his fingernails tearing shallow furrows in the ground.

He flopped onto his back and clutched at his chest as a new, sharper pain twisted at his heart.

Pushing himself up to a sitting position, wheezing as sufficient air refused to fill and expand his lungs, he began to rock back and forth. In a low monotone he chanted the words of an incantation that slowly worked to ease the ache in his heart.

Still breathing heavily, he gazed out beyond the running waters of the nearby river, looking to the north and west, knowing this would be the direction from which the Cheyenne war chief would be coming. Time was growing short.

He scrambled to his feet and rushed back into the shelter of his lodge. He paid no heed to Crow Woman, who was pressed up against the dwelling's back wall. The shaman moved to a low ledge, on which sat various gourds. He pulled the stopper from the neck of one, sniffed at its contents, returned the stopper and set the gourd back down. He repeated this process twice more, until he found the gourd he wanted.

Sitting on the dirt floor, he tipped this gourd up and began to drink noisily from it. He gulped desperately, like a man gone three days in the desert, ignoring the small streams of dark liquid that spilled out of his mouth and rolled down either side of his chin.

The brew of which he partook was a concoction he always kept on hand, as a counter to the enervating effects of casting magic spells. It was a tea brewed from the leaves and flowers of the eskowanio plant, and acted as a stimulant.

Draining the gourd dry, he fell back on his elbows, sighing heavily and smiling. Like fire spreading across dry prairie, he felt the energy flowing back into his body. Even his mind seemed strengthened and more clear.

Quickly scuttling across the lodge floor, he began to dig frantically amongst his stash of magical potions and powders. Already, a new plan to deal with the Deathwalker had sprung nearly full-blown from his head. All he needed was the right tools.

Crow Woman, puzzled by his actions, wormed her way across the floor, drawing closer to the shaman. He still paid her no heed.

"What are you doing, Pawnee?" she asked. He ignored her, not even giving her a glance as he continued pillaging through the tools of his dark trade.

"Aaah," she said at last. "He's nearly here now, isn't he?"

With that, she finally got his attention. He turned to look at her with hatred in his eyes. His jaws clenched as she opened her mouth and began to laugh at him.

"Why aren't you singing your death song?" she taunted. "You may not have time later."

The words had barely left her mouth when he viciously backhanded her. Her jaws snapped shut and her teeth bit into her tongue. She spit blood to one side, just as he grabbed her chin and twisted her head so she faced him.

"If you don't keep your mouth shut, witch," he warned, "you'll be dead before your master gets here."

"You won't kill me," she replied, with more confidence than she actually felt. "You still want me."

"I did," he corrected. "But you're more trouble than you're worth. Your only value to me now is as bait!"

"Just be sure you don't get caught in your own trap," she said. "My only fear is that your death will be too quick and easy."

"It won't be me who's going to die," he asserted. "It'll be your precious Walker."

Stands Alone drew back slightly so Crow Woman could see the wicked grin that spread hideously across his ugly face.

"But why should you care?" he said almost sweetly. "After all, it's me he'll be coming after, not you."

"What do you mean?"

"I told you before. He's already moved on to a new slut," the shaman declared, delighting in the hurt expression that darkened the woman's face before she was able to straighten her back and glare at him.

"You're lying."

"Why lie," he replied, "when the truth can serve much better?"

Leaning back, Stands Alone waved one hand in front of Crow Woman's face as he quietly mouthed a simple incantation.

With that, a small, swirling globe of smoke materialized in the air. As Crow Woman stared with unwanted curiosity at the phenomenon, an image began to take shape within it, dimly at first.

The image grew sharper and clearer, and Crow Woman choked as her heart rose up in her throat. What her eyes saw was Walker lying in the arms of the Snake Woman. There could be no mistaking or denying that both were caught deeply in the throes of passion, oblivious to all else.

What Crow Woman couldn't know was that the tableau playing out before her eyes was from an earlier time, and reflected only a memory that Stands Alone had plucked from Walker's mind during that brief time when the shaman had been inside the world of Walker's dreams.

With a strangled cry, Crow Woman slapped at the smoky image with her shackled hands. Like real smoke, the orb and that within it disintegrated and swirled away to nothingness.

Chuckling maniacally, Stands Alone hopped to his feet. Gathering up his potions, powders, feathers and rattles, he scampered out of the lodge to make preparation for the magics yet to come.

While inside, Crow Woman threw herself down flat on the ground, her trembling body wracked by deep sobs of anguish.

CHAPTER 27

At dusk of the following day, the people of Listens To Elks' village were startled to hear whoops and hollers and thundering hoof beats coming from the north.

As they stood and watched, they saw the source of the noise. Their lost pony herd was galloping toward the encampment. To the sides and rear of the herd rode Long Stride and his comrades. They yelped and waved blankets to spur on the ponies.

Nearing the village, several of the Cheyenne horsemen began to turn the racing herd. As the villagers looked on, the ponies made an arc around the camp. Reaching a lush meadow to the west of the circle of tipis, Long Stride's soldiers expertly circled the herd, slowly bunching the ponies together and bringing them to a halt. Upon stopping, several of the horses immediately lowered their heads and began to crop at the luxuriant grass.

Assigning several warriors the task of remaining on guard with the herd, Long Stride turned his own mount toward the village proper.

As soon as he entered its confines, he sensed something was not right. Instead of joyous cheers of congratulations and honor, he was met only by sullen silence. He slowed his pony to a walk, giving him opportunity to stare down at the villagers who slowly moved out of his way. There was a deep weariness evident in their eyes, as if none had slept since he and his band had left in pursuit of the stampeded herd.

His ears detected mournful singing from within one tipi, accompanied by the slow, measured beating of a drum. The keening wail of a woman mourning was clearly audible from inside yet another lodge.

It was then that Long Stride caught sight of Listens To Elks himself, standing alone outside the tipi that belonged to Walker. Concerned, Long Stride urged his pony to a trot, eager to talk with the old chief.

As Long Stride slid off his pony's back, he noted the grim look on

Listens To Elks' face. Still, the chief smiled and gripped his right arm in warm greeting.

"It's good to see you, son."

"And you too, father," Long Stride replied. "I'm sorry it took us so long, but the ponies just wouldn't stop until they were exhausted and ready to collapse. I think maybe the Pawnee shaman had cast a spell on them."

"Yes," Listens To Elks concurred, casting his eyes around the village. "We've learned the hard way that Stands Alone can work some of his magic from a distance."

"Well, we'll soon put a stop to that," Long Stride assured him. His eyes lit up as, for the first time, he noticed Walker's pony Tall Dog picketed next to his lodge.

"Or maybe it's already stopped," Long Stride said, smiling. "I see Walker's returned."

Listens To Elks turned to look at Tall Dog, sadly shaking his head.

"His pony's returned."

"What do you mean?"

"It came back yesterday. Alone."

"Aaah." Long Stride frowned. "I'll need a little time, father – just enough to rest a little, and eat and gather provisions, and then I'll go after him."

"No," Listens To Elks said sternly.

"What?"

"You're needed here, Long Stride. You and all the men."

"I don't understand, father. What could be more important than going after Walker?"

"Walk with me, son," the chief said, placing a hand on his son-in-law's shoulder, "and I'll show you."

The young soldier let the chief guide him in the direction of the lodge Long Stride shared with his wife, Snow Dancer. The thought of her filled him with sudden grave concern.

"Where's Snow Dancer?" he asked. "Why didn't she come out to greet me?"

"She would have if she could."

"What does that mean? Is she all right?"

"See for yourself, son."

Listens To Elks bent to pull aside the entry flap to Long Stride's tipi. When he did, a noxious odor leapt out and assailed Long Stride's senses. He gagged as he was pummeled by the smell of meat left to rot in the sun. Without thinking, he took a step back, but Listens To Elks motioned for him to enter. Unable to read his father-in-law's eyes, and fearing the worst, he nonetheless nodded.

Holding one hand over his nose and mouth, Long Stride stepped into the lodge. He stood just inside the entrance, letting his eyes adjust to the dimmer light.

He finally made out the figure of a woman standing nearby, but it was not that of his wife. He recognized her as being Smoke Woman. She was the wife of Sees Far, a man who was widely regarded as being the best doctor in the village. Several doctors called the camp home, including those such as Eyes Dance Wildly who specialized in specific ailments and diseases. But for general knowledge, and for efficacy in treating even the rarest and deadliest of afflictions, none was better than Sees Far. He, too, was in the tipi, standing just beyond his wife.

"What's going on here?" Long Stride demanded.

By way of response, Sees Far merely stepped to one side. Behind him, Long Stride could now see Snow Dancer lying in bed. She seemed delirious, writhing and moaning in pain. Long Stride rushed toward her, but the doctor stepped between them.

"It's best you not come too close," Sees Far said gently.

Long Stride was close enough to see his wife more clearly now, and he himself grew sick at the sight. Snow Dancer's body was heavily spotted with angry purple boils. Her slightest movement would cause some of the sores to burst and ooze black slime, filling the tipi anew with the smells of putrefaction. Her body convulsed, and she cried out in pain.

"Snow Dancer!" Long Stride called out, trying to push the doctor aside. "I'm here!" He felt a hand fall on his shoulder from behind, and he turned to look into the stern face of Listens To Elks.

"Come away, son," the old chief said. "Leave the doctor to his work."

Long Stride let his father-in-law pull him away from his ailing wife, walking away with him to stand out of the way to one side of the tipi's entrance.

"What happened to her?" he asked the chief, pleading with both eyes and tongue.

"It's not just her," Listens To Elks explained. "Nearly half the village has the stinking sickness. Men, women, children…no one's safe."

"How long will it take her to get well, father?"

Listens To Elks lowered his eyes to stare down at the floor before answering.

"So far," he said at last, "no one has gotten well. The bodies of at least half a dozen villagers, including chief Cut Calf, have been carried away so far."

"Where did the sickness come from?" Long Stride asked, gripping the chief by both arms. "If we know that, maybe we can figure out how to stop it."

"We think the Pawnee caused this as well," Listens To Elks replied.

"The shaman? Stands Alone?"

"It's the only answer," Listens To Elks stated. "Every night for the last three nights, evil spirits can be seen rising up out of the earth. Our priests have told me that they are called *hohotamaitsihyoist* – the spirits who live in the ground." He glanced over at his ailing daughter, then back to Long Stride.

"These spirits are especially active at night. If they have been offended, they've been known to cause sickness, as they've done now."

"But what did we do to offend them?" Long Stride asked. "And how can we make it right?"

"We've done nothing to them," Listens To Elks said firmly. "All the priests agree on that. But still they rise out of the ground after sundown. They float up into the air, then fly into our homes. And when they leave, they leave the stinking sickness behind. All our doctors are doing their best; they've worked night and day, and tried every medicine they can think of. Nothing's worked."

"But if we haven't offended them, why are they here?"

"Like I said, we think the shaman summoned them up, then turned them loose on us."

A fresh cry of pain from Snow Dancer brought both of them closer to the center of the lodge. Sees Far was kneeling beside the fire, rummaging through a large pouch.

"For Maheo's sake," Long Stride begged, "do something for her, doctor."

"I intend to, Long Stride," Sees Far replied. "Just stay back out of the way."

Sees Far tossed a handful of sweet grass into the middle of the fire. He stuck his hands out and began to rub them together, cleansing them in the rising smoke. As he did, he spoke a prayer so low only Maheo's ears could hear it.

He rose and stepped over to his patient. With his purified hands, he gently rubbed Snow Dancer's temples, praying and singing as he did so. No man could practice this type of medicine alone, and Smoke Woman had been thoroughly trained to assist him. As he continued to pray, sing and massage Snow Dancer, his wife knelt on the other side of the pallet, singing her own song and keeping time by shaking a rattle made from buffalo skin and filled with special pebbles.

Sees Far's right hand slid down the side of Snow Dancer's face and around to the front of her throat. Gripping the top of her dress, he tugged it down far enough to expose the place just above her breastbone. There, an especially large and inflamed pustule could be seen. Taking a deep breath, he bent over and placed his mouth over the sore.

"What's he doing?" an incredulous Long Stride whispered.

"I think he's going to try to suck the poison out of her," Listens To Elks replied in an equally hushed tone.

Both men jumped as Sees Far suddenly cried out in pain and jerked away from Snow Dancer. He looked, wide-eyed, first at the two other men, then at his wife. His mouth was torn and bleeding.

A movement caught everyone's eye. At the center of the sore he had been treating, a small, snake-like appendage had sprung from Snow Dancer's chest. The tip of the appendage, waving in the air, was almost perfectly round and lined with small, needle-sharp teeth.

Smoke Woman recoiled in horror and revulsion from the sight of it, but she continued to shake her rattle more fiercely and to sing her healing song. Meanwhile, the snake thing slithered farther out of the sore from which it sprang, sliding up the front of Snow Dancer's neck toward her mouth. She was unaware of this, having mercifully lapsed into a state of near unconsciousness.

Wiping the blood away from his mouth and regaining his professional composure, Sees Far lunged forward, grabbing the wriggling thing and yanking it out of Snow Dancer's chest with a single jerk. Snow Dancer bucked upward, as if the creature's roots had been wrapped around her heart, and let out a hoarse cry of pain.

Sees Far rolled toward the fireplace in the center of the lodge and threw the unholy creature into the flames. It whipped about as it blackened and burned, and it gave off an odor that would make a skunk smell sweet by comparison. Then it died, if even it could truly be said that it had been alive.

Sees Far next pulled a knife from his belt and held it in the flames of the fire while blessing it with a prayer. He then knelt beside Snow Dancer and started lancing the boils that dotted the exposed skin of her arms and legs. The odor of burning flesh now blended with the stink rising up from the lanced sores.

"He gently rubbed Snow Dancer's temples..."

Smoke Woman's nostrils filled with the smell and she jerked aside, her belly heaving and emptying out in a spray of vomit. Sees Far tossed her a small water skin. The first gulp she swished around in her mouth, then spit out. A second, longer pull on the skin helped to settle her stomach, and she resumed shaking her rattle and singing her medicine songs.

Sees Far set aside his knife and picked up a large gourd. Inside it was a thick liquid made from the roots and stems of a type of wild onion called *potsewots*, which had been ground fine and boiled in water. Muttering prayers in a singsong rhythm, he proceeded to pour the potion into the sores he had freshly opened.

Snow Dancer screamed as if the medicinal concoction burned more than had the knife blade. Her arms and legs thrashed about uncontrollably, and both the doctor and his wife had to throw themselves atop her to hold her down.

Her eyes bulged and she appeared to be choking. Sees Far grabbed a short, stout stick and jammed it between her teeth, so she could neither bite off her tongue nor swallow it.

"Ohohyaa!" Long Stride wailed pitifully.

Long Stride turned away, closing his eyes tightly and covering his ears so he could neither see nor hear the suffering of his beloved wife. Though equally anguished by the agony of his daughter, Listens To Elks let Long Stride lean on him but did not himself turn away.

Finally, Snow Dancer's writhing subsided, and she seemed to drift off to sleep, her breathing returning to normal. Listens To Elks stepped closer, followed by Long Stride.

"Will she be all right now, Sees Far?" he asked.

The sadness in the doctor's eyes as he looked up at the chief spoke more loudly than words. He turned to look down at the woman, as did Listens To Elks and Long Stride. Before their very eyes, fresh sores were already beginning to form just under her skin. Soon, they would swell up full blown and burst.

Sees Far stood up and motioned for the other two men to walk with him to the tipi's entrance. Once there, he looked back to see that his wife had placed a cool, wet rag on Snow Dancer's forehead and was softly singing to her what could have been the lullaby a mother croons to her baby.

"It's what we feared," Sees Far said softly. "This isn't a natural illness. If it were, she'd be better. But I also have to fight spirits and evil magic that have seized her insides."

"Can you do it?" Listens To Elks asked.

"Honestly? I don't know. Our own priests and shamans have tried to counter this spell, with no more luck than we doctors have had."

"Would the spell be broken," Long Stride asked grimly, "if the one who cast it was to die?"

Sees Far shrugged. "Probably. But I'm not sure. I deal in medicine, not magic. But I won't give up. I'll keep trying to cure Snow Dancer, and all the others under my care. That's all I can do."

Long Stride nodded curtly, then turned and walked out of the lodge. Listens To Elks followed, and found his son-in-law squatting outside the tipi, angrily tearing at blades of grass. The chief looked off to the west; the sun had completed its slide below the lip of the horizon, and full darkness was quickly descending. He went down on one knee beside Long Stride.

"What are you thinking?" he asked.

"I'm thinking that it's even more important for some of us to go after Walker. Stands Alone has to be eliminated."

"You don't think Walker can do that alone?"

"I don't even know if Walker is still alive, father," Long Stride replied bluntly. "And even if he is...well, you've seen the kind of power that shaman has. I left seven brothers up in the mountains because of it. I don't know if any man alone can kill him. After what I've seen the past few days, I'm not sure he can die at all."

"He's a man," Listens To Elks asserted, "and any man can die."

"Are you sure?"

"Sure enough. And sure that Walker can bring him down."

Long Stride rose to his feet. "He won't have to do it alone."

Listens To Elks reached up and grabbed him by the arm. "I told you I need you here."

"To do what?" Long Stride demanded. "I'm not a shaman or a doctor."

"No, but we've already got plenty of them. What we need is soldiers."

"To fight what?"

"Look and learn," the chief replied. He used his grip on Long Stride's arm to help himself rise, before pointing to a spot on the ground just a few feet in front of them.

Long Stride squinted as he saw a tiny point of light appear on the bare ground. The circle of light grew until it was two hands wide. Then, like a ball bobbing up from below the surface of the water, so too did this light pop up out of the ground, a glowing orb that stopped and floated a few feet in the air.

Listens To Elks pulled Long Stride's war club from his belt and slapped its handle into the palm of the soldier's right hand.

"They look like nothing but little balls of fire, and they dart about quicker than a rabbit," he explained, "but they have some substance to them. We've discovered that sometimes we can hurt them and send them running for the hills. So far, it seems to be the only thing that works against them."

Long Stride nodded and leaped forward. As he neared the ball of light, he swung his war club up and then down. The ball of light zipped to one side, causing the intended blow to miss and making Long Stride lose his balance and nearly fall.

Back and forth he chased the mystic light, sweat beginning to bead on his forehead as he missed his target again and again. Finally, as if tiring of this game, the light ball began to rise straight up in the air. From what Listens To Elks had told him, Long Stride knew its next move would be to attack and infect its chosen target.

The Dog Soldier took a running start, then leaped as high off the ground as his legs would propel him. Holding his war club with both hands, he brought it back over his head before swinging forward with all his might.

This time he was rewarded by seeing the head of the club connect with its target. Sparks flew in all directions, like those from a roaring fire when a fresh log is tossed in.

The light ball was propelled forward by the blow, then wobbled back and forth before fully righting itself. Like a wounded beast, though, its first thought was for escape.

With a fading whistle it shot eastward through the night sky until it grew too small to see. Long Stride heard more such whistles, and spotted two other balls of light seemingly pursuing after their fleeing brother.

Looking around him, Long Stride now saw every able-bodied soldier in the village chasing after more of the mystic lights. As he watched, a Bull Soldier named Spotted Leg struck one of the balls with his own war club. But it was only a glancing blow, and instead of fleeing the light ball flew straight at the warrior.

It struck Spotted Leg full in the face, and when it did it seemed to fly apart like the head of a dandelion in a high wind, splintering into a hundred points of light that quickly faded away to nothing.

By the time the last spark had disappeared, Spotted Leg was on the ground, rolling in pain as the stinking sickness raced through his body and began to erupt in angry sores from his head to his feet.

Long Stride knew there was nothing he could do to help the soldier, so he instead turned to seek out another target. He managed to chase away two more of the spirits, while barely escaping the lethal touch of a third.

Then they were gone, at least for this night. The only lights remaining in the village were those that could be seen dimly within some of the tipis. Listens To Elks came walking toward him, cautiously gazing right and left up into the sky.

"Good work, son," the chief said, slapping his son-in-law on the back. "We should be safe for now."

"But how long can we keep this up?" Long Stride asked. He could now hear fresh cries of pain, and knew that for all their efforts more than just Spotted Leg had been newly infected with this illness that seemed to have no cure.

"Until we manage to make peace with these angry spirits," Listens To Elks replied. "Or until we kill them all."

"Or they kill all of us," Long Stride finished the thought.

"We just have to make sure that doesn't happen, don't we?"

"As you say." Long Stride slipped the handle of his war club back into his belt. "For now, I think I'll go home and see if there's anything I can do to help Sees Far."

"That's good," the chief agreed. "But you should also try to get some rest. Eat something. Renew your strength for what lies ahead."

"I will. And you should do the same, father." Long Stride smiled weakly and turned away.

Listens To Elks stood alone in the center of the village. He hung his head as screams of pain and screams of sorrow assailed his ears as they did every night.

How can I rest, he thought…when my people are dying?

CHAPTER 28

The tiny sliver that was all that showed of the moon was high in the heavens when Walker reached the north shore of the Rope River. The directions young Bowstring had given him proved to be dead on, for across the expanse of water he could see the lone Pawnee lodge still standing. He correctly surmised that the rest of the tribe had abandoned their shaman.

"Looks like it's just you and me now," he whispered aloud.

"And me," said an impish voice.

Walker rolled his eyes as Buffalo Boy popped into sight. The spirit guide plucked a long blade of grass and began to suck on it industriously as he stared across the river.

"That's him, all right. Just cross the river and he's yours."

"Not just yet," Walker replied. Bending over low, he set out walking eastward along the bank of the river.

"What are you doing?" Buffalo Boy asked. "Stands Alone was straight ahead of you!"

"And no doubt expecting me," Walker said. "I'll find a place to ford upstream, and maybe I'll have a chance to take him by surprise."

Walker found a suitable spot a mile upstream. He knelt down on the damp ground, close enough to the river that its light waves lapped at his knees. Removing his medicine pouch from his belt, he began to examine its contents.

"Now what are you doing?" Buffalo Boy asked impatiently.

"I'm looking for a suitable offering."

"What?"

"You know, for a Cheyenne spirit, sometimes you seem mighty ignorant of Cheyenne customs."

"Hey!" the imp yelped defensively. "I *am* a Cheyenne custom!"

"Then you should know that before a Cheyenne crosses a river or a lake, he's first expected to present a gift to the creatures who might live under the water."

"What creatures? I don't see any creatures."

"Sometimes you're invisible too."

"Yeah? So why don't you ever give me any gifts?"

"I put up with you – that's gift enough."

"There isn't time for this!" Buffalo Boy insisted.

"There's always time to do the right thing," Walker said, trying to remain patient. "My father has often told me that doing what's right is the greatest power a man can have."

"Did he also tell you that Pawnee shaman across the river is preparing spells to use against you even as we speak?" Buffalo Boy hissed. "He's almost finished with them. You don't have time to waste!"

"Ho-bapa!" Walker barked at him. "Shut up!"

Buffalo Boy's face twisted in a petulant frown, and he vanished.

Promptly forgetting him, Walker laid a small square of deerskin down on the ground. Atop the square, he sprinkled the rest of his tobacco. Next, he poured half of his remaining precious sunflower seeds onto the tobacco. Finally, he plucked one of the spare arrowheads from his hair and set it in with the mixture.

He pulled up the corners of the deerskin to form a makeshift pouch, tying it closed at the top with a strand ripped from the fringe of his leggings. Cupping the pouch in both hands, he reverently held it out over the rolling waters of the river.

"I ask your permission to pass through your domain," he said, "and I make you this offering to show my respect and gratitude. It isn't a lot, I know, but right now I don't have a lot to give. I hope it's enough, and that it pleases you."

So saying, he dropped the pouch, watching it sink beneath the surface even as it was being carried downstream.

Walker then stepped into the chill waters of the river. At the point he had chosen for his ford, the water was no deeper than his waist. Still, to lessen the risk of being seen, he dived under the waves, holding his breath as he half swam and half crawled swiftly along the riverbed to the opposite shore.

Had there been anyone to see him when he emerged on the far bank, they would have felt fear clutch at their hearts at the sight of his face. Once again, the upper half of it appeared to have been painted a ghostly white, in the form of a human skull.

Not even his fellow Dog Soldiers or his own father knew that he did not need ritual or prayer or special herbs to manifest this fearful aspect. All he need do was think of it to make it so.

He tried not to think of it overmuch, or what it may represent. Was it a gift – or curse – laid upon him by the lifeless personage in his long ago vision? Or worse, merely a reflection of the deadness he sometimes felt within him? A mask that brought fear to his enemies…or his true face?

Regardless, it was his, to use as he saw fit. Given the particular enemy awaiting him, he felt it fitting to go into the expected battle in all his dreaded power.

His hair plastered wetly against the sides of his head, and water streamed from his body as he rose up beside the river. His eyes were drawn to a point where the bank rose up and away from the shore, and his breath caught in his throat.

Standing atop the ridge, little more than a silhouette in the faint night light, was the largest and most magnificent looking stag he had ever beheld. It seemed almost frozen in place, unmoving save for a slight turning of its head in his direction.

A trace of a smile tugged at the man's lips. Had this been another time and place, he would have taken great delight in trying to snag the buck's hide. But it was neither, and he turned away from it and set off quietly along the shore, moving in the direction of Stands Alone's lodge.

He pulled back in surprise as a hulking black shape suddenly flew down from above, blocking his path.

It was the stag.

Walker tightened his grip on his lance as he eyed the animal. It was bigger than the biggest pony he had ever seen, and its pelt was red with flecks of gold. The two stood in silence, each sizing up the other.

Turning so it was head-on to the Cheyenne, the stag reared up so it was standing on its hind legs. To Walker's growing amazement, the animal's form began to rapidly change.

A harsh cracking sound could be heard, as if Maheo himself was breaking every bone in the stag's body and re-setting them in a new and different shape. Skin stretched and morphed into a totally foreign form.

When the transformation was complete, the stag's body now resembled that of a naked man, one whose body was still covered with downy fur. It stood at least four hands taller than a normal man did, though, and its head was still that of a stag, complete with a rack that sprouted at least a dozen prongs. Walker had not doubt that once again Stands Alone had perverted nature itself for his own ends, his own protection.

Not wanting to see harm come to yet another innocent victim, Walker slowly approached the solitary sentry. He extended his right hand out, palm forward, and kept his lance at his side to show his peaceful intent.

"You have nothing to fear from me," he said softly.

And with that the stag lowered his head and charged.

So quickly did he leap forward that Walker was caught off-balance, in mid-stride. Still, so animal fast were his own reflexes that he managed to avoid being impaled on the stag's antlers.

He was, however, lifted from his feet by the impact of the top of the stag man's head plowing into his midsection. He flew back through the air before slamming back down to the ground flat on his back. The impact loosened his grip on his spear, and it rolled away out of his reach.

Walker was not fully risen back up to his feet when the stag man charged yet again. Barely bracing himself, he managed to grab the beast's rack and lock his arms to keep the deadly prongs at bay. The force of the stag man's attack pushed him backwards, the soles of his feet skidding and digging into the soft wet soil.

One heel caught, and he felt himself beginning to topple over. He did not release his grip on the stag's horns as he fell, but rather used them to pull his attacker over with him. As he hit the ground and began to roll, he got one foot up under the stag man's belly, using the momentum to flip the beast over and slam him down on his back.

Knowing how fast his opponent was and how quickly he would doubt-less recover, Walker leaped to his feet. Pulling his war club from his belt even as he spun around, he crouched in a defensive posture.

The stag man had rolled over and risen to a similar position, but stooped even lower, his fingertips touching the ground so that in stance at least he resembled his more natural four-legged form.

Pawing at the ground with his right hand, the stag man snorted loudly through flared nostrils. With a grunt, he launched himself forward. This time, Walker chose to go on the offensive and charged also, war club raised.

Like two mountain sheep they slammed together. Walker struck down with his war club, hearing stone impact on antler. He cried out as, the next instant, he felt a tearing pain in his left leg.

The stag man tossed his head and Walker was sent spinning off to one side. Rolling to a stop, his left hand flashed down to his inner thigh. It came away wet with blood.

He rolled again as the stag man followed up his attack. The prongs of his antlers barely missed the Cheyenne, merely digging up divots of dirt.

Walker rose to one knee, war club raised. The stag man had not yet fully elevated his head, giving Walker what might be his only opening.

He brought the head of the war club smashing down on top of the stag man's head with such blunt force that the club's handle splintered and shattered in half, sending the head flying off into the darkness.

The stag man staggered back on unsteady legs. Even in the darkness Walker could see blood fountain up from the top of the beast's head and begin streaming down either side of his face.

Ignoring the lancing pain in his leg, Walker sprang forward. He was still clutching the end of the war club's handle, and he brought it across in a stunning blow to the stag man's left jaw. The animal's head snapped to the side, and his body followed.

He stumbled as if about to fall, and Walker facilitated this by leaping astride his back. The stag man fell to earth with the Cheyenne riding atop him, both hands firmly gripping the base of its rack, where it sprouted from the beast's skull.

With his right knee planted firmly in the small of the stag man's back, Walker pulled at the creature's rack with all his strength, drawing the beast's head back toward him. The stag man bucked and flailed his limbs, but to no avail. The Cheyenne had the greater leverage and continued to pull the stag's head back farther and farther, though his own arms quivered and shook from the exertion.

A loud snap pierced the night air, and the stag man's thrashings ended instantly. Maintaining his grip on the beast's horns, Walker tugged them back and forth, satisfied by the way the head flopped loosely from side to side that the neck had indeed broken and that life had fled.

He stood over his slain foe, watching grimly as in death the beast reverted to its true form. He knelt down and ran his hand along the soft fur of the stag's neck, patting it gently.

"Forgive me," he whispered.

This was followed by a moan of pain, and Walker dropped back on his rump. With the battle won, he now took the time to more closely examine his own wound.

Using his knife, he cut the tear in his legging even farther open. Luck had been on his side, insofar as the stag man's prong had missed slicing the femoral artery, which would have bled him out in heartbeats. Still, the gash was long and deep, and blood still flowed freely.

Again making use of his knife, he cut a long strip from his breechcloth. He grunted from the pain as he wrapped the buckskin tightly enough around his thigh to staunch, at least temporarily, the flow of blood.

Crawling in the darkness and feeling about with his hands, he was able to retrieve his fallen lance, which was now the only weapon he possessed besides his knife.

The spear also now served him well as a crutch on which to lean and relieve some of the weight from his torn leg, which was already beginning to stiffen somewhat. Limping along, ignoring the jolting pain each step brought, he made for the lodge of Stands Alone.

A light shining brightly in the night made it even easier to find his way. It came from a roaring fire that had been freshly lit at a distance halfway between the shaman's lodge and the nearest shore of the river.

Walker approached cautiously, stopping and dropping to the ground when he was still a good arrow's flight distant from his target. He could clearly make out the figure of a person seated beside the fire, its back to him. What appeared to be a deerskin robe, ornately decorated, covered the figure's head, flowing all the way to the ground and preventing Walker from positively identifying it as being Stands Alone.

With the patience of a wolf, Walker lay on his belly and watched the figure for a long time. It made no gestures, did not move at all that he could discern. Fearing at last that it was perhaps nothing more than a tree stump Stands Alone had dressed to serve as a decoy, Walker rose to his feet.

Lance held out in front of him with both hands, prepared to thrust or throw as needed, the Dog Soldier slowly advanced toward the crackling fire. Every few steps, he would stop and look to either side in expectation of a trap. Finally, no more than twenty paces separated him from his target.

He froze in his tracks as the figure beside the fire rose up in one silent, fluid movement. Clearly, he knew now, it was a human being he had been stalking. His hands tightened on the shaft of his spear. But the robed figure made no move against him, made no move at all. It did not even turn to face him, though he felt sure his presence was known.

"I've been waiting for you, High Bird," a musical voice said to him.

Walker drew back slightly, puzzled and cautious. The voice that had just spoken to him, the voice coming from the robed figure, the voice that had addressed him by his boyhood name, had almost surely been than of a *woman.*

He was equally sure this was not Crow Woman; the voice sounded older, more weary. Yet there was a familiarity to it that eluded him and kept him from identifying its owner, like a memory too far behind.

In a slow but fluid movement, the robed woman turned to face him. Against the swirling light of the fire behind her and the robe that lay draped over the top of her head, her face was too shadowed for him to see clearly. She extended a slender hand out toward him.

"Come on, Bird," she said sweetly. "There's nothing to be afraid of."

Despite the soothing tone of her words, Walker kept up his guard. Each step forward he took carefully and deliberately, half expecting a pit to open up in the ground below and swallow him. When he had closed the distance between him and the woman by half, he again stopped. He still held the lance out in front of him, its head pointed straight at her midsection.

"Let me see your face, woman," he commanded sternly.

At the harshness of his words, the woman lowered the hand she had extended to him. After what seemed to Walker like a long time, she then raised both hands up to where the robe was draped over her head, tugging it back to reveal her face.

It was a pretty face, belonging to a woman of perhaps forty summers. A few strands of white hair slithered through the long black tresses cascading down either side of her head. Her eyes were dark and sparkling, and she smiled benignly. There was something about her, Walker thought, something about the sculpted bones of her cheeks that reminded him slightly of his sister, Snow Dancer.

Only slightly less cautiously, he advanced a few steps closer to take a better look. The woman said nothing, merely tilting her head slightly to one side while continuing to smile at him. Even this faint gesture plucked at something deep in his mind.

And then the pieces fell into place. He sucked in his breath at the very thought. His eyes widened, and his heart seemed to stop beating in his chest.

"Mother?" he choked.

CHAPTER 29

"**I**t's good to see you again, son," the woman said in that soothing voice.

Walker took a step back, his guard up. Certain this was a trick of some sort, he cast his eyes about in all directions, swinging his spear to ward off any attack. None came.

He spun back to face the woman. She had not moved, but there was now a hint of sadness in her smile and she was shaking her head slightly. Walker again stepped forward, studying her face intently. He had been barely five summers old when an illness of the lungs had taken his mother, Three Willows, away from him.

But he still had vivid memories of her. He remembered the way she would sing while gathering firewood or digging for roots. He remembered her cool hand on his fevered brow when he was sick. He remembered that she liked to dance.

And he remembered every detail of her face, as clearly as if it had only been yesterday when he had last seen it, as he, Snow Dancer and their father left her so-tiny body behind them on the prairie. Every line and crease on her face. The shape of her mouth and eyes. All were just as he remembered, slightly different only in the way that all faces are changed by the passage of time.

Now, slowly and hesitantly, she took a step toward him. He recoiled slightly.

"You're dead," he stated flatly.

"But I'm not, son."

"Don't call me son."

"What else would a mother call her child?" She took another step forward. "You've grown tall and strong, Bird. Just like I told your father you would. How is Listens To Elks?"

167

"He's well."

"And Snow Dancer? Does she have a husband? Children?"

"A husband, yes. No children yet." Walker's eyes continued to dart from side to side even as he carried on this bizarre conversation. Still there was no sign of danger.

"And how have you been, mother?" he asked, hoping to catch her in a misspoken word that would betray her. "Since you've been dead, I mean."

She who looked like Three Willows laughed lightly at this, and the knife in Walker's heart twisted. It was truly the laughter of his mother; he'd heard it too many times to forget it.

"I saw you die," he said. "Even though I held your hand and begged you not to."

"I'm sorry," she replied, in a hushed voice. He could clearly see tears rising up in her eyes. "So, so sorry."

"If you are who you say, where have you been all this time?"

She opened her mouth to speak, then stopped. Her gaze dropped slightly, a querulous expression on her face. Then she looked back at him.

"I'm not sure."

"How did you come to be here, in this place, now?"

Another pause.

"I'm not sure of that, either."

"I was only a boy the last time you saw me. How did you know who I was?"

This time there was no hesitation.

"That was easy. You have the look of your father, and of his father. But I didn't need my eyes. My heart told me who you were."

He realized just how deeply the boy called High Bird wanted to believe her, to believe she was whom she said. But the man called Deathwalker had left such boyish dreams far away, long ago. No matter what the small voice in his heart was saying, the voice in his head still cried out in warning.

"You could be a spirit," he said to her, "a ghost sent to haunt and betray me."

A single tear rolled down her right cheek, and she stretched both hands out toward him.

"Prove it," she said. "Can a ghost be touched? Touch me, so we'll both know!"

The woman slowly walked forward, seemingly unmindful that Walker's lance was still pointed at her. He stood his ground as she closed the gap between them.

"Stop," he said, in a voice lacking the authority it should.

"Touch me," she said again, continuing to advance. Walker took a step back, but still she came on.

At the last possible moment, he pulled the lance aside. He kept it gripped in his left hand, but lowered it to his side. She stepped within arm's length of him, her hands still reaching out to him.

"Please," she implored.

His eyes narrowed, his steely gaze hoping to see into the woman's heart. If there was deceit in it, it was not reflected in her face or eyes. He slowly raised his right hand, stretching it out until his fingertips reached hers.

He felt warm flesh beneath them.

With a sobbing cry, Three Willows clutched his hand and pulled him forward. As their bodies came together, her arms flew around his waist. She trembled, and he could hear her muffled weeping as she pressed her face against his heaving chest.

His own arms remained at his sides, and his eyes and ears continued to seek out trouble. None seemed imminent, and his gaze lowered to the little woman clinging to him as if he was life itself. Unbidden, his left hand dropped his lance.

His arms circled her, pulled her tighter against him. His face dropped down to lay against the thick hair atop her head.

Then he screamed in pain, and his knees nearly buckled under him.

The nails at the end of the woman's fingers had turned into curved talons that she sank deeply into the flesh and sinew of his back. Jerking down, she raked deep furrows in his skin that quickly filled with blood.

Walker tried in vain to pull free from her grasp even as she drew her head away from his chest. Her face now looked like a grotesque caricature of Three Willow.

Her lower jaw unhinged, and her mouth opened wide enough to swallow a rabbit whole. Fangs the size of a panther's blossomed above and below, and her eyes seemed to fill with blood.

The robe covering her fell away, revealing a naked, skeletal body that appeared as one that had been stripped of all flesh, exposing raw, red cords of muscle underneath.

Walker knew now that she had spoken truly when she said that she was not a ghost. This was no intangible spirit, but rather a cursed demon that had been summoned into this world with murderous intent – summoned by Stands Alone.

The demon's mouth gaped open even farther, saliva dripping from its fangs, and she lunged for Walker's exposed throat. He clutched at her hair and tightened his arms. She shrieked as she was pulled up just short of the seductively throbbing artery at the side of his neck.

He could feel her breath on his skin, and the mucus that oozed over her lips sizzled and burned as it fell to his chest. It took all his strength to pull her head back away from him.

But as he did, she sank her taloned fingers deeper into his back. A fresh wave of pain shot down the back of both legs, robbing them of their ability to support him.

As they gave way beneath him, he managed to kick out at the she-demon's ankles. Her legs flew out from under her, and she fell along with him. As they did, he twisted his body so as to fall heavily atop her. Her head banged against the ground, and her claws relaxed their grip just enough for the man to break free of her and roll to one side.

With a screech like that of a wild animal, she launched herself at him again as he rose, her clawed hands extended and aimed at his eyes.

Bracing himself, Walker caught her by the wrists. He jerked his arms wide, pulling her toward him. Lowering his head at the same time, he butted her face with brutal force. Her nose flattened and spurted black, brackish fluid that passed for blood.

She sagged as if about to collapse, then sprang back up. Her right foot swung up between his legs, kicking him in the groin.

Now it was he who dropped to his knees. While so doing, he lost his hold on her right wrist. She pulled it free and swung her hand at him. Demon's talons ripped the skin of his left forehead, barely missing his eye.

He still gripped her left wrist, and pulled down hard on it. As her upper body was drawn downward, he brought up his knee. It connected just under the demon's chin, with such force that several of her teeth flew out of her mouth in a bloody spray of foam.

Walker lunged at her, grabbing her by the throat and riding her to the ground as she toppled over.

Seizing her ears, he raised her head, then slammed it as hard as he could back against the unyielding earth. Again and again he banged her head, until he saw her eyes begin to roll to the top of their blood red sockets.

Rising to his feet, he twisted the fingers of both hands into the curling tresses of her head, then roughly dragged her, kicking and screaming, across the hard ground.

His own breathing had grown harsh and ragged by the time he pulled her into the circle of light cast by the enormous campfire. Still holding her hair, he half lifted the demon off the ground – and thrust her headfirst into the roaring flames.

Her screams were as unhuman as was she herself. Even as her hair began to smoke and burn, she clawed frantically at Walker's arms in hope of escaping.

The dark talons scored his flesh nearly to the bone, but Walker was for the moment beyond feeling even the flames that were likewise licking at his arms.

The skin on the demon's face was starting to melt and run like tallow. Walker had smelled burning flesh before, but that of a demon was far more noxious. This too he ignored.

With a last, gurgling whimper, the demon went limp. In the same instant, Walker flung his scorched arms and hands free of the fire. Slithering down to the demon's feet, he gripped her by the ankles and flipped her body so that it fell in its entirety into the fire.

He sank to his knees, watching with hate-filled eyes as the demonic corpse was consumed. But he was being equally consumed, by hatred. Hatred not directed at the demon, who had been but a weapon used against him, but hatred for Stands Alone.

It was Stands Alone who had done this horrible thing, who had so cold-bloodedly desecrated the blessed memory of Walker's mother, who had twisted the sacred into a profanity that would have caused Maheo himself to avert his eyes in shame.

And it was Stands Alone who would pay.

On his first attempt to rise back to his feet, Walker's wounded leg failed to sustain him, and he fell back heavily to the ground. Refusing to let weakness or pain betray him, he pushed back up. He swayed unsteadily for a moment before limping over to where his spear had fallen.

The feel of the lance's shaft in his hand seemed to strengthen him. Still, he leaned heavily on it as he limped across the open space leading to the entrance of the shaman's lodge, conserving his strength for what was to come.

Inhaling deeply, he lunged through the door flap of the lodge, spear thrust out ahead of him. He crouched slightly as he cleared the entranceway, anticipating attack from either side.

At no sign of movement to left or right, he stared straight ahead. It was nearly dark inside the lodge, the only light being that cast faintly by a small fire that was close to dying out in the center of the floor.

A growl rattled in the Dog Soldier's throat as he at last spotted someone seated beyond the fire, near the rear of the dwelling. Eyes quickly adjusting to the dim light soon discerned that it was Stands Alone. Of Crow Woman, he could see no sign.

The Pawnee shaman sat unmoving, simply staring straight ahead. Suspecting yet another trap, Walker advanced slowly into the lodge. As he drew nearer to the fire, he was better able to make out the features of the shaman's unmistakably ugly face. Still Stands Alone sat motionless, his eyes staring into the fire rather than at Walker, as if he did not deign to even acknowledge his presence. This seeming indifference caused the anger in Walker to surge.

At last, the shaman's eyes rose up from the fire, they and his head turning slightly in Walker's direction. As those eyes met with the Cheyenne's, Stands Alone's lips peeled back from his jagged black teeth…and he smiled.

With a roar of killing rage, Walker launched himself through the air over the flickering fireplace. His eyes were still locked on those of his foe – but the point of his spear was aimed squarely at the Pawnee's chest.

CHAPTER 30

Time seemed to slow down to that of a snail's pace as Walker hurtled across the gap between him and Stands Alone. With rage powering his arms, Walker began to thrust the lance down toward his motionless enemy. His eyes never left those of the shaman, even as those eyes grew large in terror.

At the last possible instant, though, Walker suddenly twisted his grip on the shaft of his lance. The head of the spear turned and barely nicked the shaman's right shoulder, sailing past him. Still gripping its shaft, Walker followed along behind the lance, vaulting over Stands Alone as the spear point took a downward trajectory and buried itself in the hard dirt floor of the lodge.

With Walker's weight behind it, the shaft of the spear curved like a bow drawn to full tautness, groaning beneath the pressure bearing down on it. A loud crack rent the air as the lance shaft snapped in two.

Walker was unable to stop his momentum, and he fell atop the sharply jagged piece of the shaft protruding up from the ground. He bit back a cry of pain as the shaft penetrated his right side and tore a ragged hole out his back.

He rolled to the side, and the remnant of the spear popped free from the ground and went with him. Fighting to breathe, he arched his back and grabbed at the length of wood projecting out from his front.

Walker pulled on the shaft, but it didn't move. Gritting his teeth, he pulled harder, this time feeling a slight movement. He slid his hands farther down the shaft, felt his fingers growing sticky with his own blood, then pulled again.

His strangled cry of pain mixed with the tearing sound of flesh and muscle releasing their grip on the broken spear shaft. He fell back onto the floor and flung the lance fragment away. A wave of nausea kept him on his

"Walker thrust the lance toward his...enemy."

back for the span of several sharp intakes of air.

Rolling to his left side, he propped himself partly upright on his elbow. Spying a small deerskin cloth lying on the floor, he grabbed it up and pressed it against the ragged wound in his abdomen.

Only then did he swing his gaze to seek out Stands Alone. The shaman was still seated on the ground, his legs up under him, staring with bulging eyes at the fallen Cheyenne soldier.

Eyes from which tears were now streaming.

As Walker watched, the very air around Stands Alone began to shimmer like the waves rising up from a dry lakebed in summer's heat. The shaman's face and figure folded inward, quivering from top to bottom. Features began to shift and remold themselves into a new and softer form. Walker closed his eyes tightly, rubbing them with the back of his hand.

When he reopened them, they gazed not at the gaunt image of the evil Pawnee, but at the soft and rounded body of Crow Woman. A band of cloth gagged her mouth; her arms and legs were bound together behind her with rope.

Crawling over to the woman, Walker tugged at the gag with fingers stiff with blood. She desperately sucked fresh wind into her lungs as tears began to flow even more freely down her face.

"You knew it was me!" she gasped at last. "But how?"

"It was your eyes," he replied. He reached up and brushed tears away from her left cheek, then pulled his hand away quickly as he saw he had left a smear of blood on her face.

"He changed everything else about you, but he couldn't change your eyes."

Walker pulled his knife and reached around to cut the rawhide strands binding her limbs. As soon as her arms were free, she threw them around him. He groaned in pain and fell away from her. Only then was she able to see clearly his wounds. His arms were scorched and blackened to the elbows, and laced with rivulets of blood, as was one side of his face. More blood could be seen seeping from under the edge of the cloth he held to his abdomen.

"Gods," she moaned. "What has he done to you?"

"Not so much as he'd hoped," Walker replied, attempting a smile for her.

The smile faded as he saw a thin trickle of blood rolling down her right arm, coming from under the sleeve of her dress where it had been torn by the head of his lance.

"I hurt you," he said.

"It's only a scratch," she assured him.

"But you have so many wounds, Walker – we've got to take care of those."

"There isn't time," he insisted. Then he felt fresh blood spurt from his side. "Well, maybe if you could find something to stuff in this hole…?"

Crow Woman scampered over to the ledge where Stands Alone kept his various potions and other concoctions. She frantically searched through pouches and inside bowls, until she found a bag filled with a feathery moss she recognized.

Hurrying back to Walker's side, she pulled his hand away from the wound in his side. She gulped, horrified at the ugliness of the gaping hole. Trying to hide her fear, she smiled at him. Gently, and yet as firmly as she dared, she packed the moss into the wound, watching it begin to absorb and slow the flow of blood.

"Hold it in place," she instructed him, pulling his hand to the wound.

She grabbed his knife and ran over to the bed where Stands Alone had slept. Finding a thin deerskin blanket, she proceeded to cut and tear it into long strips before returning to Walker's side.

"Roll over a bit," she told him, "so I can reach your back."

As he did so, she grimaced. Not only could she now see that the wound in his side went all the way through, but he also saw the bloody furrows left by the demon's claws. Determinedly setting to work, she packed more of the healing moss into his exit wound. She then used the long strips of deerskin to wrap around his middle and hold the moss in place. When she had finished, she slowly pulled Walker back down on the ground.

"It feels better already," he said.

"We've barely begun," she replied insistently. "Those other wounds – "

"Will have to wait." He raised his head, looked around.

"Where'd the Pawnee go?"

"I don't know. He grabbed a torch from the fire and a rolled skin with his damnable potions inside, and was barely out the door when you came in."

"Then he can't be far away," Walker said, painfully sitting up, and silently cursing himself for not having seen the shaman make his escape. "I've got to catch him."

"And do what?" she replied, horrified. "You're so badly hurt right now that a sparrow could beat you in a fair fight – and that fatherless snake won't fight fair!"

"Do you have so little faith in me, woman?"

"I just don't want you to die!" she cried, placing a small hand to his chest and trying in vain to push him back down. "You've beaten him. Why not just let him go?"

"Because he won't stay beaten," Walker replied grimly, pulling her hand away and holding it in his own. "He's already proven that. He's like a dog with the foaming sickness; he has to be put down for good."

"If you're gonna do somethin', you'd better do it soon."

Hearing the familiar voice, Walker looked over to see Buffalo Boy had returned. He was sitting on the floor, holding a large bowl of cold stew between his legs. Sticking a finger into the gooey blend, he popped it into his mouth and made a face of disgust.

"That crazy Pawnee still has one trick left up his sleeve," he said, "and he's getting ready to use it."

Ignoring the spirit, Walker spoke to Crow Woman.

"Take a look around, see if you can find any weapons."

She made a quick but thorough circle around the lodge, looking into and under anything large enough to hold so much as a small knife, but found nothing.

"It doesn't matter," Walker said. "No bigger than he is, I could beat him to death with a willow switch." He reached toward her. "Just give me a hand up."

Throwing an arm around Crow Woman, Walker leaned on her as he rose to his feet. She put an arm around his waist and started to walk with him toward the lodge's doorway, but he stopped and disentangled himself from her.

"You need to go," he told her.

"What? Go where?"

"Home, back to my village. At the very least I can buy you the time you'll need to get a good start away from him."

"No," she said fiercely. "I'm not leaving without you."

"Yes," he replied firmly, "you are." He softly laid a hand over one of the many bruises Stands Alone had inflicted upon her face.

"You've done enough, Crow Woman, suffered enough at his hands. And don't worry...I mean to catch up with you in just a little while, just as soon as I finish wringing the little Pawnee's neck." He removed his hand.

"But if I don't...if I fall...I want you to tell my father that I died trying to do the right thing."

Tears welled in her eyes, but she said nothing further. He turned and limped toward the doorway. When he reached it, he paused and turned back to face her. The slight smile on his lips seemed out of place beneath the fearsome skeletal markings that still covered the upper half of his face.

"And tell my father too that it was my last wish that you be set free and returned to your people."

He turned away, stooping and pushing his way out of the lodge. Thus he didn't hear Crow Woman as she softly replied, "You're my people."

Walker stumbled as he staggered out of the lodge. His legs gave way and he fell forward onto his hands and knees. He lifted his head and saw that Buffalo Boy was squatting in front of him, sadly shaking his head from side to side.

"This doesn't look good, brother," the imp declared. "You're growing weaker by the heartbeat, and the only weapon you have left is your knife."

"I don't need a spirit guide to tell me the obvious," Walker growled. He reached out and pushed Buffalo Boy over onto his rump. "Now leave me alone."

Buffalo Boy had vanished by the time Walker was back on his feet. Fortunately for him, it was not hard to determine which direction Stands Alone had taken. Walker could see the light of his torch bobbing back and forth in the darkness some distance to the west.

Ignoring the pulsing pain in his leg, Walker began to run after the shaman as fast as he could. Even in his current state, his strength of body and will was prodigious, and he slowly began to close the gap.

As he drew nearer, Walker saw the shaman take a quick turn to his right, racing toward the river. Barely slowing, Stands Alone leaped from the bank into the river's running currents. The water here was even shallower than the spot where Walker had forded the Rope earlier, and Stands Alone splashed through it quickly, scrambling up the opposite bank.

Once there, the Pawnee turned back toward the river and dropped to his knees. Shoving one end of his torch into the soft, damp earth, he quickly unrolled the medicine bundle he had been carrying under his arm.

Chanting loudly, he lifted a small gourd and sprinkled its powdery contents on the ground. He repeated this ritual three more times; each gourd he used held a powder of a different color, and when he was finished mystic emblems of various hues and shapes were spread out before him.

Walker tried to increase his speed, but a stitch in his right side exacerbated the pain from his wound. He slapped his hand against it and could tell that blood was seeping through the moss and wrappings. His back was on fire, and the leg that had been gored by the stag man was beginning to feel dead as wood.

"You've got to do better than this."

Walker glanced sideways, scowling as he saw Buffalo Boy effortlessly trotting alongside him.

"You're prancing along like a little girl, while he's almost finished his spell," the spirit warned, before disappearing anew.

Grimacing, Walker attempted to increase his speed. The ground ahead of him dipped slightly, and he was thrown off balance. He stumbled forward, arms flailing as he tried to maintain his equilibrium.

The effort was fruitless, and he fell heavily headfirst to the ground. Every animal on earth seemed to be screeching in his ears, and he wanted nothing more at that instant than simply to remain where he was.

Instead, he used his arms to push himself up, got his legs once more beneath him. Rising to his feet, weaving slightly, he pulled in several breaths of clean air before starting to run again.

He didn't make it twenty paces before he fell again.

He cried out in anger at his own body for failing him, but this time there was no thought to staying down. To do so would be to admit defeat, something he refused to do.

As he struggled to rise anew, he felt hands grab him to help. He thought perhaps Buffalo Boy was actually doing something useful for a change, until he looked over one shoulder and saw it was Crow Woman.

"I told you to go," he growled.

"And I refused," she said defiantly.

"Women, you know that when we get out of this, I'm going to beat you."

"That's your right," she said simply, with no dread in her voice. She draped his left arm over her shoulder, and together they continued on toward the river.

Before they could even reach its bank, though, Walker knew it was too late. On the far side of the river, Stands Alone had again snatched up his torch, waving it over his head. The magical incantation he was singing rose to a crescendo, then ended as the shaman lowered the torch and touched it to the arcane sigils he had drawn on the ground.

Bursting into multi-colored flames, the symbols seemed to leap up into the air. The night became almost as bright as noon as the flaming symbols floated out over the river. They began to spin in midair, casting out tongues of fire.

This wheel of fire then dropped, plunging into the waters below in a billowing cloud of moldy-smelling steam.

Darkness again descended, and for a moment, as he gazed at the softly running water, Walker dared to hope that the spell had failed. Such was not to be.

The change in the river was subtle at first, but he then noticed a slight increase in the speed of the current as it raced by.

Then it was as if a dam had burst upstream, for great rolling waves suddenly gushed forward. This flash flood of raging water caused the level of the river to rise dramatically, threatening to spill over its banks and out onto the prairie.

As Walker squinted into the darkness, he saw the current in the middle of the stream rise up as if it was bounding over a submerged boulder. But the "boulder" itself grew larger and began to rise also.

With a great upward spray of water, an enormous monster burst from below the waves. It stood four times taller than a man and resembled a great horned lizard. But unlike any lizard, it stood erect like a man, and stiff bristles of green hair sprang from its head and flowed down its back like a mane.

"What is it?" Crow Woman gasped.

"It has to be one of the *Mih'n*," Walker answered. "Underwater monsters who have a taste for human flesh."

The Mih'n roared, revealing rows of massive fangs, and the ground trembled beneath their feet. A voice called out to it, and it turned to see Stands Alone. The shaman drew more mystic emblems in the air, chanting in a voice that sounded no more human than did the monster. Then he extended one bony finger, pointing to the opposite shore where Walker and Crow Woman stood.

Still standing in the middle of the river, the great lizard swiveled its hips and glared silently at the pair of them. It then spun back to look again at Stands Alone.

"Kill them!" the Pawnee screeched.

The Mih'n turned again. Its cold reptilian eyes fixed on Walker as it began to stride toward the riverbank. Walker pushed Crow Woman behind him and pulled his knife, determined to sell his life dearly.

When the monster lizard had nearly reached shore, it stopped and turned yet again to look back at Stands Alone. The shaman's eyes blazed with madness, and spittle dripped from his lips as he laughed in anticipation of what was to come.

The Mih'n roared again, and its huge head whipped around and down toward the Cheyenne Dog Soldier and his woman.

CHAPTER 31

The celebration in the Cheyenne village of Listens To Elks had already gone well into the night, with no sign that it would end anytime soon.

A large fire lit the center of the encampment. Young girls continuously brought platters heaped with food for the revelers who circled the fire. Laughter, which had been sorely missed in the camp for many days, now filled the night air. From time to time, a celebrant would briefly burst into song.

So happy was the occasion that the tribe had decided to go all out, to feast as if there was no tomorrow, to gorge until their bellies were near to bursting.

There was buffalo aplenty, with many eager hands reaching for such choice bits as tongues and noses, and livers seasoned with gall.

There was venison and bear steaks, fish and turtles. Chokecherries, plums, bullberries, corn, squash and beans. Fingers were dipped into wild honey. All was washed down by cups of rich mint tea.

At the east end of the ring of celebrants, in a place of honor, sat Walker. Among the many dishes being served, he had been presented with a special delicacy, in the form of a plump puppy his sister Snow Dancer had personally strangled and prepared for him.

Walker's face and body were now painted entirely in black, to symbolize that he had killed an enemy in combat. Even crotchety old Bull had limped out to join in the festivities, and as he walked behind Walker he bent and gave him a congratulatory slap on the back, causing Walker to flinch slightly; it would be some time yet before his many wounds were completely healed.

One of the serving girls approached Walker, and he looked up to see the smiling face of Long Stride's sister Two Doves. She knelt before him and extended a platter teeming with various cuts of buffalo meat. Returning her smile, he reached out and scooped some of the meat into his own wooden bowl.

The girl leaned over and placed her lips close to his left ear so she could be heard over the joyful din.

"You're the greatest man I know," she said earnestly.

He turned his head and smiled back at her as she drew away and began to rise to her feet.

"And you're the prettiest girl!" he told her.

Two Doves giggled self-consciously and threw one hand over her eyes before turning and hurrying away.

Walker began to chuckle, but stopped as his eyes fell on the visage of Lame Calf, who was staring intently at him. The Fox Soldier frowned, then stood and left the circle of celebrants.

Walker merely shrugged, then leaned forward to seek out another tribesman. A few paces to his right sat his lieutenant, River Hawk. Though still weakened by the wound he received when the Pawnees had attacked the village, the soldier was now on the mend and refused to let his convalescence stop him from joining in the honoring of his war chief.

Straightening back up, Walker licked fat from his fingers and belched contentedly, smiling at those around him.

Next to him, Long Stride rose to his feet and motioned for the rest of the partygoers to quiet down.

"Listen," he said loudly. "We still haven't heard the end of the story!"

The other villagers quickly grew still, leaning forward eagerly to listen. A baby started to whimper, but her mother promptly hushed her by thrusting a teat in her mouth.

Walker took another bite of pup before setting his bowl down on the ground. Knowing that a crucial ingredient of good storytelling was to build anticipation in your audience, he took his time, running his fingers through his loose hair, then looking about from side to side to assure that all eyes and ears were on him.

All would agree that the story he had told them thus far was the best they'd ever heard from him; quite possibly, it was the best story anyone in the village had ever heard.

He had already told them in bold and only slightly exaggerated detail of the encounter with the non-dead Lakotas, of the battle with the Pawnee horsemen and the tragic death of young Bowstring.

There had been many "oohs" and "aahs" from the women when he painted in vivid words the story of his time with Snake Woman (and envious glances from a few of the men). Shouts of approval met his recounting of the battle with the stag man.

There had been sighs of sympathy at the story of the demon disguised as his mother, and gasps of relief (from all save Snow Dancer) when he told how he had barely avoided killing Crow Woman.

All had marveled at the strength and stamina he displayed as he pressed forward despite his many wounds. Truly, they thought, this was a man to be reckoned with – and he was theirs.

Now, with the story dangling at the moment when the monster lizard was charging at him, when death seemed imminent and inescapable, he knew he had kept his audience waiting in suspense long enough.

So he told them the rest of the story.

CHAPTER 32

Walker stood his ground unflinchingly as the Mih'n lizard lunged downward. With nothing but his knife to employ, his only hope was that he could manage to leap aside in time to evade the beast's initial charge. If he could, he might be able to go on the attack himself; if he could perhaps jam his blade into one of the Mih'n's eyes and puncture it, there was at least the slight chance the pain would drive the creature away.

He never got the chance to try this desperate scheme.

The chin of the Mih'n's enormous head slammed down to the ground a few paces in front of Walker, causing a shock wave powerful enough to make both Walker and Crow Woman stagger back a pace. It lay still as dust swirled around it before settling to the ground. For longer than it takes to tell it, man and Mih'n simply stared at each other in silent challenge, neither showing the slightest sign of fear. Crow Woman pressed herself tightly against Walker's broad back.

Finally, the monster's mouth opened. Streams of brackish water spilled out from between its flint sharp teeth, two rows of which lined both upper and lower jaw, one spaced right behind the other. The creature made a huffing sound, and fine warm mist sprayed over Walker.

Finally, its massive blue-gray tongue, which had been curled back toward its throat, rolled forward and out onto the ground, carrying with it the faint odor of dead fish. And there was something else. Walker's eyes widened slightly at the sight.

There, on the tip of the Mih'n's tongue, could plainly be seen the tobacco, sunflower seeds and arrowhead that Walker had earlier offered to the spirits of the river before he made his crossing.

The giant tongue rolled back into place and the Mih'n closed its maw. Walker stared more intently into its eyes. As he gazed into the intense blackness of its pupils, they seemed to spark with pinpoints of light, and it was as if he had risen from the earth to stand in the midst of the stars. He nodded, as if acknowledging words the creature was speaking only to him. Stepping forward away from Crow Woman and motioning with one hand for her to remain where she was, he walked toward the Mih'n.

It remained motionless as Walker strode to one side of its head. He reached out and lightly ran his left hand along the cool, slick scales of the beast, which seemed almost to purr in response. At the base of its skull, he grabbed two handfuls of its hair and mounted it by throwing one leg up and over its neck as though it were a pony. Its strangely green hair, softer than the fur of a bear cub, tickled the inside of his thighs.

As he settled behind the head, he leaned forward and grabbed hold of the bases of its twin horns. In response to a tap of the man's heels on the sides of its throat, the Mih'n reared back up to stand fully erect. Walker smiled slightly as he looked down to see Crow Woman staring up at him in stunned amazement, her mouth hanging open in awe.

Walker tugged at the beast's left horn, and it obediently turned away from the south shore. With sure steps, it proceeded to carry him across the swollen and raging river.

Seeing this most unexpected turn of events, Stands Alone at first found himself frozen in place. Then the heat of fear sent his blood bubbling to his heart. Panicking, having expended the last and greatest weapon in his mystical arsenal, he turned to run.

At Walker's urging, the Mih'n increased its speed, its churning legs sending up great sprays of water with each step. Upon reaching the far shore, the Mih'n stopped abruptly, thrusting its head forward sharply. Walker released his grip on the river monster and was sent flying forward like an arrow launched from a bow.

Like that arrow, his flight was true, and he slammed heavily into the back of the fleeing shaman. Both men were thrown to the ground and rolled. Ripping pain swept Walker from head to toe, and blood began to spew anew from several wounds.

Refusing to be stopped when he had come so far, he cried out and willed himself to his feet. He needn't have hurried, for Stands Alone was still rolling back and forth on the ground, just a few paces away, clutching at his back and whimpering in pain.

Walker staggered to where the shaman lay and dropped down astraddle his mid-section, causing Stands Alone even more pain. Through all this the Cheyenne had maintained his grip on his knife and he raised it now and held it up for the Pawnee to see.

"No!" Stands Alone wailed pitifully, tears bubbling in his eyes. "I beg you – don't kill me!"

He saw no pity in Walker's eyes, no sign of mercy in his demeanor. With a slow, deliberate motion, the Cheyenne raised his knife up and over his head.

"No!" the shaman pleaded again.

Walker brought the knife flashing down, and the shaman screamed as the blade bit into the ground beside his head. Short, frantic sobs whistled from his nose and mouth. He cried out in fear as Walker grabbed him by the throat and pulled him upright.

"No," the Cheyenne snarled. "I won't kill you."

Stands Alone relaxed slightly, until he looked more closely at the fire in Walker's eyes, and his heart sank. He knew no reprieve was forthcoming.

"Never," said Walker, "not once, have you faced me like a man. Never tried to kill me by your own hand. Always, you sent someone, some*thing* else to do the dirty work for you."

Walker stood, dragging the shaman up with him and shaking him like a rat.

"Now I intend to do the same."

Pulling the shaman along by the nape of his neck, Walker set out for the river, where the giant lizard still stood, avidly watching all that transpired.

"This is for the death and sorrow you brought to my people and to your people," Walker told Stands Alone. "For the death of Bowstring, who deserved a long life. For thinking you could take what was mine and pay no price."

Reaching the bank of the river, Walker stopped and pulled Stands Alone close to his face. The shaman's lips were quivering, and wetness ran down both his cheeks and the inside of his thighs. Walker's contempt for him was as great as his hatred.

"And this is for soiling the memory of my mother."

Keeping his right hand on Stands Alone's neck and placing his left hand between the Pawnee's legs, Walker lifted the squalling shaman up over his head. His own weakened arms and legs trembled from the effort, but he did not falter. Running forward a few paces, he flung the shaman out beyond the riverbank.

The Mih'n's head lunged forward, and his powerful jaws clamped down on Stands Alone's right leg. The shaman's scream of fear and agony was like the sound of a hundred wailing ghosts. He twisted and jerked as he dangled head down from the maw of the monster.

The Mih'n flipped its head upward, releasing its hold on the shaman. Stands Alone flew up, then tumbled downward end over end before disappearing down the gaping throat of the river monster. The sounds of the twisted little man's final death rattles were cut off as the Mih'n's jagged teeth snapped shut.

The great beast lowered its head and roared – and its body in the instant was transformed into a towering column of water that pointed skyward for a moment, then fell back into the river, becoming one with its rushing current. As quickly as it had risen, the level of the river now dropped back to its normal flow. Of either Mih'n or Stands Alone there was no sight.

And with that, Walker stopped his narrative again.

The audience that had been hanging on his every word erupted into cheers and shouts of joy.

Walker smiled and lifted his eyes as a familiar sight caught his attention. Perched atop the lodge poles of a nearby tipi, little Buffalo Boy was smiling down at him and chewing contentedly on a big turnip.

What Walker didn't see, hidden in the shadows of the same tipi, was Crow Woman. Being a slave, she had naturally not been invited to the celebration, but at the moment she didn't mind overmuch. She was content to watch and listen, beaming with pride as Walker and his deeds received their just praise.

As she sat and listened, she clasped to her bosom a new hairbrush Walker had given her when they had returned to their village. It had been made by stretching a porcupine tail over a stick, sewn tight and dried before the quills were neatly trimmed down. The seam where it had been sewn was ornately decorated with quills of many colors.

She sighed as she ran it through her hair. Giving her this gift had been the closest Walker had come to thanking her for standing by him in the face of death, the nearest he might ever come to expressing soft feelings for her.

But to a woman, this simple brush spoke volumes. After all, she told herself, Walker had to have made arrangements for it to be crafted even *before* she had been abducted. That had to mean *something*.

To a woman such as herself, this was enough.

Having stopped on a high note, Walker had chosen not to detail the events immediately following the death of Stands Alone, at least not on this occasion.

He didn't tell how, when the giant lizard had disappeared and the river waters had returned to normal, he had slowly and painfully made his way back across to where Crow Woman still waited for him.

By the time he reached the south shore, his strength was about to desert him. He found it necessary to take Crow Woman's hand to help him climb up the slippery slope of the bank. He had barely done so when the world went black around him, his eyes rolled up in his head and he passed out in the woman's arms.

It was some time the following day before he awoke to find himself lying atop a bed of leaves under the canopy of a small tree. The smell of something burning stung his nostrils and brought him fully alert.

The first sight to greet his eyes when he sat up was that of Stands Alone's lodge in flames. It had already been burning for some time, for its charred poles were now collapsing down, and the fire that had consumed it was beginning to die for lack of fuel.

The second thing he noticed was that all of his wounds had been carefully wrapped while he was unconscious. The sound of a woman softly singing brought his head around. A cheerful Crow Woman was walking from the direction of the river, carrying a skin pail of fresh water.

She told him how, slowly and with much effort, she had managed to drag him to this spot the night before. She could not bear the thought of taking shelter in Stands Alone's lodge, for it carried too strong a stench of pain and evil, nor did she want Walker to have to lie within its confines.

Being a practical woman, though, she had set aside her disgust long enough to ransack the place for anything that would be useful to her and Walker – food, medicines, bedding, utensils – before putting it to the torch.

It took much yelling and finger wagging, but she was at last able to convince Walker to stay there the rest of that day and all of the next, to allow for at least a small amount of rest and healing.

It was well that he listened to her, for that first night had brought with it a fever that threatened to burn his insides as surely as the flames had devoured the lodge of Stands Alone.

He was drenched in his own sweat, and the visions he saw smacked of madness. He twisted and moaned as he lay nestled in the arms of Crow Woman. She had held him thus the whole night long, save when she periodically ran to fetch fresh water with which to quench the fires raging within him.

Walker jerked and mouthed words that mostly had no meaning, but Crow Woman spoke back to him anyway, in soothing tones that cooled as much as did the water. At last he fell into a deep and dreamless sleep.

The first thing he saw upon opening his eyes the following morning was Crow Woman's smiling face. The next thing he saw was Buffalo Boy, standing behind her. The spirit stuck out his tongue and called Walker a baby. Walker merely smiled weakly and drifted back to sleep. Crow Woman brushed his sweat-slickened hair away from a brow that was now cool to the touch, thanking all the gods of the universe.

On the third day, however, Walker had insisted they be on their way. He still had his knife, and he used it to make a crude spear from a tree limb. Packing as much food and water as they could carry, the two had set out for home.

Being afoot, and with Walker weaker than he would ever admit to Crow Woman, their progress was slow. More than once the two of them fought when an impatient Walker would suggest that the woman go on ahead without him; unlike most battles, these were ones he always lost. Happily for the both of them, fortune smiled on them early on the second day out, in the form of a rescue party of ten Dog Soldiers led by an anxious Long Stride.

Listens To Elks had decided it was finally safe to let them go from the village because, at the very moment that the evil Stands Alone was sliding to oblivion down the gullet of the monster lizard, the spirits of sickness plaguing the camp had also disappeared.

When they did, the effects of their malevolence vanished as well. All those still among the living who were afflicted with the stinking sickness, including Long Stride's wife, Snow Dancer, quickly saw their sores dry up and their health return.

Though the war against Stands Alone and his Pawnees had taken a heavy toll on the people, Listens To Elks and the other surviving chiefs had decided that joy needed to replace the sorrow in the village as quickly as possible. Even those still mourning lost loved ones agreed that now it was time for life to return to their camp and to their hearts.

They were happy, too, in the knowledge that before long word would spread in all four directions of how the Cheyenne had done what no others could, by sending Stands Alone to meet his maker. The details of the story would doubtless grow larger with each retelling, and they would be admired and feared by all who heard it.

They had passed through the darkest of shadows into the light, and it seemed only right to celebrate their victory. They did so with as much vigor as they displayed when going into combat or to the hunt.

"All in all," Long Stride now said, breaking in on Walker's reverie of those days just past, "I'd say you were pretty lucky."

"Luck had its place, brother," Walker agreed, "but it was more than luck that saw us through."

"Oh?" Long Stride smiled, looking about at the other villagers. "It sounds to me like the mighty Deathwalker's story hasn't completely ended. Tell us more, brother!"

The other revelers hooted and shouted out encouragement for Walker to continue, quieting when he finally raised his hand.

"You may ask yourself one question," he began, "and that question is this: why didn't the monstrous Mih'n do as he was commanded and kill me? Huh?"

He looked from side to side as if expecting a response, though he knew full well that none would dare interrupt his riveting narrative.

"I think the answer is simple and clear," he stated. "I think it was because Stands Alone did not respect the spirits of the water. Where I took the time to make the proper offerings, the Pawnee just tramped through their home – and then expected them to obey his wishes.

"He was done in by his arrogance. He thought he was above the world and not merely a part of it. Every step of the way in this encounter, I tried my best to do what was right, while he only tried to do what was right for himself."

Walker paused and leaned forward, assuring himself that all eyes were upon him.

"And how did I know what was right? Because I have always listened and learned from my father, as every good son should do, so that his wisdom became my own." He chopped a hand through the air for emphasis.

"And *that's* how I was able to beat Stands Alone!"

The partygoers erupted into cheers and yelps again. Across the fire from Walker, his father Listens To Elks smiled in pride. The other chiefs and elders seated beside him were all smiling and nodding in agreement with Walker's statements.

Among those elders was a man called White Horse, who was the father of the slain Bowstring. One of the first things Walker had done upon his return to the village was to sit down with White Horse and tell him the circumstances of his son's death.

He had assured the elder that Bowstring had been of great aid to him in his journey to confront Stands Alone, and that he owed his life to the boy. He told the father of his son's bravery and how he had died fighting like a man.

White Horse took pride in knowing this, and in appreciation for the special care Walker had taken with Bowstring's body after death, he offered the war chief his daughter Four Moons Gone in marriage, as was a common practice among the Cheyenne.

Walker had thanked White Horse sincerely for such a generous offer, and assured him he would give it all the respectful consideration it deserved. First, though, once he had rested and fully recovered from his many wounds, he meant to travel to the land of the Lakotas; there, he would deliver the message he had promised he would take from the undead warrior Mountain Snow to his son.

As Walker thought on these things, he noticed that all eyes were still on him, waiting to see if he had yet more to say. He was glad to oblige.

"I won the battles of the past few days just by being a man who tried to do the right thing: showing respect for other men, for Maheo, and for the spirits who share the world with us. This should serve as a lesson to all those who are listening to what I've said.

"That's where this tale of mine ends," he concluded. "And let the next teller tie a tail to this story...."

The End

ABOUT THE CREATORS

AUTHOR – R.A. JONES – A native of Oklahoma (originally Indian Territory), where he still resides, R.A. Jones has been a freelance writer and editor for the past thirty years. His credits include newspaper and magazine columns, articles and short stories. He has been a movie reviewer and commentator in newspapers and on radio. He assisted actor Gary Lockwood (*Star Trek*; *2001: A Space Odyssey*) in the writing of Lockwood's autobiography, *2001 Memories: An Actor's Odyssey*. With Michael Vance, R.A. co-wrote the syndicated comic book and comic strip review column *Suspended Animation*. The readers of Comic Buyer's Guide magazine voted him "Favorite Writer About Comics" in 1985, and in 2006 he was inducted into the Oklahoma Cartoonists Collection Hall of Fame. He has scripted more than 100 different issues of various comic book titles in his career. Among the more noteworthy are *Wolverine* and *Captain America* for Marvel Comics; *Harlan Ellison's Dream Corridor* for Dark Horse Comics; and *Star Trek: Deep Space Nine* for Malibu Comics. He also co-wrote, for Image Comics, *Bulletproof Monk,* which served as the basis for the 2003 movie of the same title.

His comic book story, "Cold Hard Facts," which originally appeared in the magazine *Metal Hurlant*, was recently shot as a short film in France.

INTERIOR ILLUSTRATOR – **Michael Neno** – Neno as been writing, drawing and publishing comic books for over twenty-five years. A recipient of the Governor's Award of Excellence for his art from Ohio Governor James A. Rhodes, he has also pursued web design, painting, freelance coloring, lettering and inking for comic books as well as book and album cover design and book illustration. After self-publishing mini-comics in the late '80s (which he still publishes from time to time), he began freelance lettering for Paul (Batman: Year 100) Pope's Horse Press and Dark Horse Comics and began having stories published by Caliber Press, Cracked Magazine and Amazing Montage, the latter's profit proceeds going to the Comic Book Legal Defense Fund. In 2001, he received a Xeric Grant to publish *Reactionary Tales*, the debut of his continuing Signifiers Universe. In addition to a heavy schedule of online freelance graphic design work, he's started two online comic strips, *The Mesh* and *Freak Cave*, at www.nenoworld.com. He recently contributed art to the first three issues of the rock'n'roll/horror anthology comic book, *Nix Comics Quarterly* and also curated four exhibits of 20th century graphic design for the Columbus, Ohio, arts organization *Wild Goose Creative*, the last of which was an exhibition of his own work, *Simplexity*.

COVER PAINTER – **Laura Givens** – Givens is a Denver Based author and artist. Her art has graced the covers of numerous publishers' books and may be viewed at www.lauragivens-artist.com. In 2010 she naively decided she could write stories as well as many she had illustrated. She has sold ten to date. She was co-editor and contributor to *Six-Guns Straight From Hell*, a weird western anthology recently released. She performed improv comedy on stage for a decade, then produced, wrote, directed and filmed her no-budget masterpiece, *The Jerusalem Tango*, which you will never see for good cause – trust me.

IF YOU LIKED THIS BOOK WE THINK YOU'LL ALSO ENJOY:

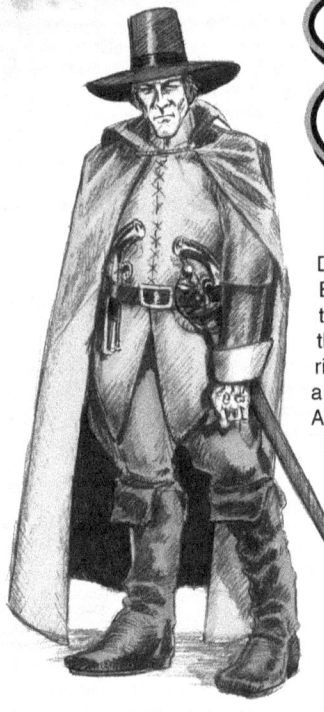

GIDEON CAIN

THE DEMON HUNTER

During the famous Salem Witch Trials (1692-93) British born Puritan soldier, Gideon Cain aided the inquisitions, believing them to be just. Soon thereafter, God revealed to Cain that he and the righteous citizens of Salem had been duped by a cunning, ageless demon from Hell known as Azazel. The guilt of his actions weighs heavily on his conscience and rather than be driven mad by it, Gideon chooses to make atonement. Taking up his sword, the blade inscribed with holy runes, he bids farewell to his wife and children and departs on his sacred mission. Now he wanders the earth doing God's work and destroying evil in whatever shape or guise it appears; his one consuming goal, to find and destroy Azazel.

Airship 27 Productions is thrilled to be bringing pulp fans this great new hero written in the tradition of Robert E. Howard's Solomon Kane. Here are six exciting, action-packed tales of *Gideon Cain the Demon Hunter* by Scott Harris, Brian Zavitz, Ian Watson, James Palmer, David Wright, K. G. McAbee and Van Allen Plexico.

With a special introduction by co-creator, Kurt Busiek.
(Marvels – Astro City)

CORNERSTONE BOOK PUBLISHERS

PULP FICTION FOR A NEW GENERATION!
WWW.GOPULP.INFO

www.ingramcontent.com/pod-product-compliance
Lightning Source LLC
Chambersburg PA
CBHW071238250626
47163CB00001B/227